Woyzeck's Head

a novel by

EKBERT FAAS

Cormorant Books

Published with the assistance of the Canada Council
and the Ontario Arts Council.

Cover from a coloured pencil on matt board,
Perishable Item, (1986) by Tom Lovatt, courtesy of the
artist and the Canada Council Art Bank.

Published by Cormorant Books, RR 1, Dunvegan,
Ontario, Canada K0C 1J0.

Printed and bound in Canada.

Canadian Cataloguing in Publication Data

Faas, Ekbert, 1938-

  Woyzeck's head

ISBN 0-920953-58-1

  I. Title.

PS8561.A315W69 1991   C813' .54   C91-090398-0
PR9199.3.F33W69 1991

To
Maria Antonietta

who can
read
upside down

TABLE OF CONTENTS

I. C. WOYCECK

geboren in Leipzig Aᵐᵒ 1780.

HANS MARTENS' STORY
Border Incident

"He's got a Jew's face, hasn't he, Franz," one border guard said to the other. They joined heads in scrutinizing my passport.

"You're right Josef," answered Franz. "Intellectual's face. Something fishy about him. You go through his suitcase! But properly, Josef. I'll look him over myself."

Then turning to me, he barked, "This way," pointing down a long corridor of wooden planks which reached a room built in raw brick, soundproof and windowless, with three chairs, a bedstead and a table. The room was freezing.

"Clothes off!" he ordered. When I hesitated, he added, lowering his voice. "Better not make a fuss about it. I'm just doing a routine body check on you at this point."

So I took off my clothes, neatly folding them over one of the chairs, trying as best I could to gain time.

"Hurry up!" Franz commanded, then ripped the clothes off the chair, left the room, and locked the door from the outside. He'd let me keep my underpants and socks. All I could think of as I stood there in the vibrating spiderweb light from the single, shadeless bulb, was the Woyzeck Papers hidden in my suitcase. And not just out of fear. I knew they'd arrest me if they found them, and

I'd prepared myself for it. I knew that'd be the end. But there was something about these papers that I hadn't realized before; or at least not as clearly. It suddenly dawned on me that they contained a prefiguration of some of Hitler's most cherished ideas—particularly Schopenhauer's letters, but other parts as well, such as what Goethe was quoted as saying in one of Dr. Adam Bergk's letters.

Perhaps all that had escaped me because of the turmoil I'd been involved in since my friend Klaus had asked me to smuggle abroad this literary treasure he had recently found in his family's Leipzig home. That was as a favour in exchange for the fake Swiss passport he had arranged for me. Our anguish over two visits by the Gestapo; my subsequent, nocturnal flight from Klaus's Kattowitz villa on New Year's Day of 1940; the rush back to Berlin; the hurried meeting with several members of our spy ring in Peter Kindler's Kreuzberg flat; the renewed fears of being shadowed by Gestapo agents; my elaborate manoeuvres to shake them off by travelling zig-zag to the German-Swiss border near Schaffhausen where I'd try to escape into freedom: none of it had allowed me to reflect on what I'd managed to copy of the Woyzeck documents. For the better part of my flight I had, in fact, forgotten altogether about the transcripts which Klaus's wife Gerda had carefully sewn into my suitcase.

I'd even forgotten about that strangely unaccountable malaise which had occasionally seized me in the process of transcription. But now it was back with a vengeance. As I was waiting to have my shivering, denuded body subjected to some degrading and ingeniously sadistic torture, the sense of something deeply unsettling about the Woyzeck Papers re-emerged, until it suddenly revealed its full, ugly grimace: what I was carrying in my suitcase, I realized, and what—ultimate of fate's ironies—I was trying to smuggle across the border, was a part of the original Nazi bible.

Then they were back, both of them, although without either suitcase or manuscript. For a while they just stood there, as if unsure what to do next, side by side, like two jovial clowns.

"He's a fine sight, isn't he," said Josef, in his heavy Bavarian accent, elbowing Franz.

"He sure is," said Franz , laughing. Then after suddenly turning serious again, he screamed: "Take off your socks and underpants!"

Frozen with fear I obeyed. It will start in a second, I thought.

"Now turn round, bend over and display your precious behind!" Franz shouted. "And cough! Cough, I said. Once again, cough. All good things come in threes!" Both were roaring with laughter. That's when I first saw a glimmer of hope.

"He's a crafty fox, our Herr Bährmann," Josef said.

"He sure is," echoed Franz. "Carries nothing incriminating on him at all."

"A lucky dog," added Josef. "We'll have to let him go, says our chief, though we'd rather keep him here."

"So what's he waiting for, standing there?" Franz screamed. "Get out of here. He'll find his rags in the room 'cross the hall."

That's how I found out about my horror of the hidden manuscript. Of course, the anguish caused by Hitler's henchmen may have made me exaggerate the resemblance between certain of its statements and others made by the Führer. But there was another, simpler reason why these parallels should have suddenly struck me with such vehemence: my knowledge of Schopenhauer before I read his letters to Klaus's great grandfather Dr. Adam Bergk had been practically nil; whereas my familiarity with Hitler's diverse publicized pronouncements was particularly acute from my being involved in actively trying to sabotage his regime. I did not just own a copy of *Mein Kampf*, but had actually read the book, had read it carefully, and had listened to Hitler speak on diverse occasions. For good reason, I had anticipated some of the horrors Hitler was to unleash on the world at a time when they were still being hatched in his snake-pit brain. Unlike most people, I took Hitler seriously in whatever he said. Almost everyone, for instance, brushed aside his harangues against the Jews: that kind of thing would wear off as soon as he'd assume power and responsibility. But it didn't.

The one time I actually met him was in '32. My father had taken me along. There were about twenty guests, some sympathizers, others—like my father, persons whom the sympathizers tried to convert to Hitler— were contemptuous or at least sceptical of his so-called genius. One thing that struck me about him right away was his complete indifference to how people might judge him. It's true that everything he did was calculated to create some impression: the almost submissive way in which he greeted the hostess revealed nervous shyness, but of a studied kind, as if he had learnt to enact it in order to outmanoeuvre himself. There was his impeccably polite charm towards women, especially elegant, beautiful women. Other mannerisms were designed to impress the men: after depositing his riding crop, trenchcoat and hat in the lobby, he carefully hung his revolver and attached belt on a clothes hook. Here was a man wearing many masks, each of them fitting him to perfection. Yet as much as he tried to impress us, he seemed totally unconcerned as to whether we'd love or hate him.

The former was clearly the case when the hostess's son, attracted by Hitler's blue eyes, went over to shake the famous man's hand. And to have seen, radiating from those same bright blue eyes, wholly genuine tenderness and affection, as Hitler lifted the boy on his knees and started talking to him as if all the others had suddenly dropped out of sight!

But then, with the boy still on his knees, he suddenly picked up on some flying remark, and, sizing us up with an inexorable stare, began holding forth on the "Jewish problem." There were several Jews or half-Jews like my father in the room, so people fell silent, coughing and fidgeting, or attempting, unsuccessfully, to engage in separate conversations. The one person totally unabashed by all this was Herr Hitler as he went on in his barking, machine-gun-like voice, spinning out arguments with ever more frightening matter-of-factness. That's when I realized that this man meant exactly what he said and that terrible deeds would follow his words.

To put an end to his harangue, my father asked him: "How will you proceed against the church once you're in power, Herr Hitler?"

Without bothering to turn to us, he went on uninterrupted with his monologue:

"When I was young I took the view that dynamite was the appropriate answer to most problems facing us. But then I realized that you cannot just break everything over your knee. The church has to fall by the wayside like a gangrenous limb. The whole era from about 300-1700 A.D. was an appalling regression when you think of the beautiful clarity of Greek and Roman culture. Christ was an Aryan, yet Paulus misused his doctrine so as to mobilize underground elements and to organize a pre-Bolshevik mass movement."

Then, as if sensing that he ought to change his tune, he added: "Take one simple example. Our loving Lord determines that mankind should fall. After he's finally managed that with some help from the Devil, he employs a virgin to give birth to a man who by his death redeems man from this fall."

Seeking relief from their earlier embarrassment,

some of us broke into nervous laughter which increased as Hitler continued: "Christian doctrine's the craziest thing ever invented by the human brain. A real insult to the divine. A good Mohammedan might still get me excited over his paradise. But then imagine that dreary Christian heaven! We've had Wagner on earth, and beyond you'll hear nothing but hallelujahs bawled by babies and octogenarians. Savages are superior to Christians. At least they worship the natural forces. A Negro with his fetish in hand is head and shoulders above the man who believes in the transubstantiation."

So this man did not have just have one personality, but half a dozen perhaps, or even more, all of them separate, though ruled by one iron will. Morally speaking, each of these seemed to lead its independent existence— the brave soldier, the lover of children, the ladies' man, the bohemian, the brilliant conversationalist, ruthless self-disciplinarian, scheming Machiavellian, raging fanatic, and ferocious killer. Later I read of rare somnambulist cases involving multiple selves who are all aware of each other. That's Hitler, I thought, but with a difference: in him the emotional and moral ties still connecting these multiple selves in somnambulists had been severed.

I knew all this and told my friends, several of whom fell out with me over it; some for good, others, just temporarily. These later had good reason to finally come to agree with me. For everything, after Hitler assumed power, bore out my guesses: the enabling act, the laws against the Jews, the sterilization and euthanasia programs, the concentration camps, the annexation of Austria and Czechoslovakia, and finally the invasion of Poland—although, as I said, I could hardly foresee the extent of the horrors to come.

The other thing I hadn't realized until the Schaffhausen border was that Hitler's theorizing had a core with roots in a major tradition of German thought, part of which I carried in my suitcase. One possible reason why that had escaped me, as I said, was my ignorance regarding that tradition. As for Goethe, I'd read his main works, and especially *Faust*, while at school, like every good German; but his nihilistic side, which he kept secret himself, was not revealed to me until I read Dr. Bergk's letter about him. As for Schopenhauer, I'd hardly read him at all; and what I'd heard about him only served to confirm his traditional image as the embittered pessimist, crank, and misogynist.

All I'd sensed while transcribing the papers during that long ago Christmas with Klaus was an eerie sense of *déjà vu:* as if I'd heard it all before, yet without being able to draw the connection. Not until that crucial moment in the windowless interrogation room, while I was waiting for Josef and Franz in the anguish of my terrified body and heart, did I find that link. Then, as I walked with my suitcase in hand along the short stretch of brightly lit no-man's-land between the two check points, a voice rang through my mind, a voice I had heard on several occasions, a voice spouting nihilistic phrases—the bellowing, barking, machine-gun-voice of Adolf Hitler:

"*It's useless to shrink in horror from the fact that in Nature one creature devours the other. The fly is killed by the dragon-fly, the dragon-fly by the bird, the bird by a bigger animal. The strongest creature, when growing old, is consumed by infectious germs. Finally, even these do in some fashion reap their deadly fate. You can't change it, that much is sure. It's better to just stay with it. Even when someone kills himself, he but reimmerses himself in Nature's cycles so as to come back in different form.*"

Hadn't I read it all before, in the identical terms, in Schopenhauer's letters to Bergk hidden in my suitcase?

"*What else is this world but a playground of tortured and anguished beings, who can only survive in that one devours the other; what else but a place in which every beast of prey is the living tomb of thousands of other creatures and its self-preservation a chain of painful deaths."*

Was it Schopenhauer's voice I was hearing or Hitler's?

"It's equally out of place to overestimate individual life. If its existence were truly required, the individual wouldn't perish. A fly lays millions of eggs which perish, but the flies survive. What has to be cherished is not the individual's life, but the blood substance of the species."

"Do you hear, Herr Bährmann? I asked you to open your suitcase," the Swiss borderguard said.

Lost as I was in my thoughts, I'd ignored his command, but now frantically unbuckled my suitcase.

"Slowly, slowly," he said, quizzically staring me in the face as, once again, my heart froze with terror. What would they do if they found it? Send me back to the Germans? Amidst all this anguish, the voice still kept droning away in my mind:

"What seems cruel to man is wise in the eyes of Nature." No doubt this was Hitler's familiar voice. But was what it said his as well? Or was it what I remembered from one of Schopenhauer's letters?

"A people which can't hold its own, has to cede its place to another. Nature destroys without remorse what's not strong enough to survive. But in this seeming lack of compassion lies her greatest wisdom."

The last thing I heard before fainting was something about my suitcase. They had noticed that its top cover was unusually heavy. I woke up again on what felt like a bedstead. No, I would not open my eyes, even though the borderguard and another person were busy around me.

Then I heard one man say: "They must have given him the full treatment," while the other grumbled assent.

"Let's just get him out of here, or he might die on us."

Thus I made my escape from the land of Goethe,

Schopenhauer, and Büchner. And of Adolf Hitler. And how much I wanted to get away from it! Find new roots, perhaps in America, and make it new! Support the forces that would have to topple this monster or submit to its world rule—humiliated, dehumanized and enslaved, to serve the needs of the "superior" German race.

* * * * *

Nearly half a century has passed since this incident. Winter has settled on my youthful devotions; horror and dismay have supplanted the tribulations caused me by the Woyzeck Papers—horror of the atrocities which diverse ideologies have wreaked on humanity during this century, and dismay at my endeavours to combat one such ideology with another. Klaus, at a crucial moment, called them "retrogressive barbarizations of the human mind." How right he was! And how unreal seem to me now the ideational concerns which for so long thwarted my endeavours to carry out the task he entrusted me with, of bringing out these papers. That story of doubt and procrastination will be told in due time—but not before I let the documents speak for themselves. Included in them is a novella, *Woyzeck's Head*, which Klaus completed in 1935, just shortly before our little Woyzeck Circle at school began to enmesh us in a series of interconnected calamities. Let it stand as a memorial to my deceased friend at the beginning of what follows.

WOYZECK'S HEAD
The Sentencing

The town of Leipzig, site of Woyzeck's birth, execution and burial, preserved most of its Renaissance splendour throughout our hero's lifetime. The first railway was not to steam into the city until 1837. Except for one spinning-mill in the suburbs, factories were as yet non-existent. Most of the medieval town walls had recently been replaced by circular promenades; the city's core, however, had hardly changed since Goethe studied there or Bach was *Kantor* at the *Thomas Kirche*. Now, as then, there were the town gates, towers, steeples, and turrets, the steep gabled roofs, narrow cobblestone alleyways, pillared colonnades, intricate passageways, and above all the spacious market place with its massive clocktower townhall.

Only once, during the famous campaign of October 1813, were Leipzigers temporarily jolted out of their bourgeois comfort. It could have been worse. Only Napoleon's retreat on October 19th saved Leipzig from severe destruction under the cannonades of the allied forces. Especially ominous were the reports of engagements at Paunsdorf, a village just a few miles to the East. Here the French were routed by a new species of weapon, recently introduced from England. This Congreve rocket completely confounded their habitual modes of warfare. Trained to march in straight columns right into the mouths of the enemy's cannons, the French at first tried to close ranks each time one of these rockets struck down dozens of them. But when they saw the extent of the destruction and how the victims were literally scorched alive, there was no holding them. Whole columns ran away whenever they saw a rocket coming. The impact was as of something supernatural, and even the victors were stunned when they inspected the field of their triumph after battle. Though prepared to find numerous corpses, they were surprised that several of them were completely burnt.

When compared with the soldiers fighting around their city, the Leipzigers were indeed fortunate. Of course, they experienced food shortages, ever more numerous cases of typhus, an increasing influx of wounded, and even stray cannon balls or shells that came hurtling into the town—slightly damaging houses in the *Fleischergasse, Nicolaistraße* and on the *Brühl*. But what meant death and destruction to hundreds of thousands outside their gates was essentially a spectacle to them. Herr Hänsel, later Woyzeck's attorney for the defence, was one of the witnesses as he kept watch on a city tower. With his telescope he could follow the nearby cavalry and infantry engagements while listening to the patter of gunshots and the muted roar of the cannons. The scene was particularly awesome at night. Thousands of watch-fires gleamed in all directions, and, Bosch-like, here and there raged larger fires in the surrounding villages and farmsteads.

Friedrich Rochlitz, a long-term friend of Goethe, watched what happened just outside the city. As far as his eyes could see, bivouacking soldiers were camped in groups around blazing watch-fires, cooking, eating, and drinking. Their faces turned towards the flames, the soldiers' backs stood out in sharp black silhouettes. Then a sudden breeze hid everything in smoke. The fires just opposite his windows were throwing a dark red glow on the walls of his room. Yet for all his aesthetic detachment, Rochlitz was not blind to the horrors lurking behind this absorbing scene.

As early as October 16th, he had noted an unprecedented urge to do evil taking hold of people under the pressures of war. They took things and destroyed them for no other reason than to give vent to some general, inward anger without understandable motivation. What else was this battle other than an enactment of the same gratuitous malignity. About twenty thousand wounded had streamed into Leipzig during the rainy, wind-swept and chilly days since the battle had started. With the hospitals, churches and other public places already filled beyond capacity and the private houses barred against them, they were largely left to their own devices. They were still wearing their bloodstained, torn uniforms. Not one of them had received a clean shirt, blanket, sheet or bedstead.

Most afflicted were the French. Postmaster Ulricí saw them devour dead horses and fight over garbage. When they ran out of such fare, they even fell upon their dead comrades, cut slices out of their calves, thighs and buttocks, roasted them on small fires lit with the wood of dug-up coffins, and then devoured the flesh. Graves, despoilt of their civilian dead, became the refuge of the living, wounded and dying. Stumbling into St. John's Churchyard, a soldier of the Königsberg people's army was aghast to hear groans and whimperings coming from the subterranean vaults. He hurried inside, finding that wounded men, friends and foes alike, had crawled into these tombs in search of shelter from the nocturnal rain and frost. Two civilian corpses in their burial shifts had been thrown out of a family vault, their coffins now housing the wounded. Similar practises were widely adopted in graveyards all over the city.

Even worse was what Johann Christian Reil, pioneer of German psychiatry, observed in the official shelters for the wounded. Trying to enter the cloth-workers' hall, he found the steps flooded with urine and faeces, overflowing from huge troughs. Stifled by the stench, he entered the hall through the back. There, in a long dark corridor, were some two thousand wounded Frenchmen. The air was filled with their groans, as well as the odours of excrement and gangrenous wounds. Repulsed by what he saw, he rushed to the schoolyard only to find heaps of rubbish and naked corpses being devoured by dogs and ravens. Their fate had obviously been no different from that of thousands of casualties on the battlefields where gangs of looters and marauders instantly stripped the dead and dying of all their clothes and belongings.

To those who had lived through these dire events, the trial of Woyzeck, veteran of the Napoleonic wars, was like the return to a past, more comprehensible order of life. Not in a long while had Leipzigers witnessed a similar spectacle. The last time someone had been sentenced for murder was in 1798; and since then, or indeed since the time when Leipzig during the Renaissance had become famous for the pomp of its murder trials, little had changed in the proceedings. Only torture, declared illegal in 1770, had finally been abolished. Woyzeck's predecessor, the notorious Philipp Jonas Göring, had still been given a head douche of *aqua fortis* so that the arrest warrant, issued upon his escape from prison, could specify his complete baldness. Woyzeck, by contrast, was never tortured, and throughout the judicial proceedings had occupied an airy cell at the *Grimmaische* prison complete with bedstead, chair, and table, instead of one of the cramped, windowless stone dungeons several yards under the banqueting hall of the *Rathaus*.

Woyzeck's sentence was pronounced on October 11th, 1821. After the clock tower bells had rung thrice, the town judge met his five magistrates on a specially erected dais in the assembly hall. Facing them was a table with a crucifix, bible, and judge's staff. Slightly to their left sat defence attorney Hänsel. Next to him stood the prosecutor as well as the bailiff who, white staff in hand, announced in a loud voice that the penal court was now in session. The judge then asked the first two magistrates, addressing each of them in turn, if and how he should conduct this decapitation trial. *"Zwier und eins,"** was the answer. Hence the judge proclaimed for the first, second, and third time, that he was to hold this trial by championing law and defending justice. Had he done rightly thus *zwier und eins*? Yes, he had, replied the third magistrate, again repeating the same formulas.

These were reiterated by the bailiff who then asked the prosecutor to step forward.

"Most venerable judge," the latter began. "Johann Christian Woyzeck has offended against the sixth commandment by assassinating the widow Woostin with a broken sword blade on June 21, 1821. I therefore charge him with capital murder, requesting your honour's permission to do so."

Turning to magistrate number four, the judge then asked how the prosecutor should proceed with his charge.

"Zwier und eins" was the answer—"with drawn, sharpened sword while loudly crying 'murder' as it is law and custom."

The bailiff now drew the sword and handed it to the towncrier. Thrice this man screamed "blood and murder," first on the town hall's outside stone stairway, then in the assembly hall, and finally, near the judge's chamber:

"I cry murder over Johann Christian Woyzeck for breaking the sixth commandment and for murdering the widow Woostin."

At this point the bailiff led Woyzeck through the densely crowded assembly hall to a platform just one

---

* German, "Twice and once."

step beneath the judge's dais. Woyzeck had been afraid that he might start to shake all over even before the judge read his sentence. Instead, a drowsiness overcame him as he watched the proceedings with rapt attention. It was a warm autumn day, and he could hear the laughter and shouting from the market below; he also noticed how the sunlight streaming through the half-open stained glass windows painted the assembly hall floor with dozens of bizarrely distorted figures. When asked to confess his crime, he was surprised to hear his voice, after a short silence, answer clearly and firmly. All his life he'd been afraid of appearing either a fool or a coward. But being stared at by this audience, jostling behind the barriers in the assembly hall, brought out none of these fears.

* * * * *

The whole trial had given Woyzeck an unprecedented sense of himself. When first arrested after the murder he had expected to be maltreated and spat upon. And that was, in a way, what he'd wanted.

"God give she's dead, that's what she deserved!" he had screamed when they took him away, and for several weeks he kept up this defiance. But how could he defy people who, rather than glare at him hatefully, seemed to caress him with eyes of pity. He'd heard that at Jonas's execution tender, elegant women had strewn flowers as they walked to the scaffold. One of them even stuck a note saying "Rest in peace, good Jonas" to the wheel on which they had broken the criminal's body. And Jonas had been a common murderer who had never aroused the sympathy he did.

It all started when Dr. Bergk made it known through the *Nürnberger Correspondenten* that Woyzeck might be insane and hence not responsible for the murder. How had the doctor found out? Bergk had come to his cell the day after his arrest and offered to help him.

But Woyzeck refused. For once in his life, he'd done what he wanted to do and he'd stick to it, telling every one who wished to hear that he was glad he'd killed her, that he knew he'd have to die for his deed, that he'd confessed his crime, and that they should leave him alone, because, anyway, that's what he wanted: to die. But the Herr Doktor insisted. He was a strange man. He must be a priest, Woyzeck thought. What strange questions Bergk asked him! About his dreams, his parents, his childhood. What did he, Woyzeck, think would happen after his death? Or about his sex life: how he had treated his women? And not just the Woostin, no, all of them, going right back to his early girlfriends.

What did the man want? Someone in jail told him Bergk was no priest, but the editor of a magazine, called *Museum of the Occult,* full of strange stories about such matters as Siamese twins, exotic monsters, and talking animals. Maybe that explains it, thought Woyzeck. It turned out that the person who'd told Bergk about his ghosts was newspaper carrier Haase, whose lodger he'd been for several weeks before the murder. Bergk wanted Woyzeck to confirm Haase's story. It might save his life, the Herr Doktor told him. No, he'd never do that, Woyzeck said. He'd rather die than have everyone call him a *Narr** and make fun of him and perhaps lock him up at *St. Georgen.* He even asked Dr. Bergk not to spread Haase's story, and, to his surprise, Bergk agreed. Perhaps the Herr Doktor was really trying to help him! But that bit of trust was lost again when the court, following Bergk's notice in the *Nürnberger Correspondenten,* sent town physician, Hofrath Dr. Clarus, to examine him. Woyzeck vowed not to let Clarus know anything about his ghosts or his madness. But there were certain things he just couldn't hide.

The second time Clarus came to his cell, Woyzeck started shaking all over, because now he knew what the

---

* German, "Madman or fool."

Herr Hofrath was looking for. Trembling like that was nothing new to Woyzeck. He had had fits ever since he was thirty, and usually for the same reasons. It was not because he was easily frightened—in fact, he'd always been quite a courageous man when it mattered. On the contrary, it seemed to occur because he was afraid that people, seeing him shake like that, would *think* he was scared.

Once it had started, he'd never been able to get rid of that strange fear of appearing afraid. The occasion might be quite silly, such as having to sign his name, and knowing that people would watch him, he'd get so worked up just the moment before that he'd hardly be able to hold his pen, his hands would be shaking so much. Was he afraid they might think that he was faking a signature, or that he was mad, in fact, and have him locked up? All people did though was crack jokes about it, like he had been drinking too hard.

But the Herr Hofrath did ask him why he shook so. Was Woyzeck afraid of him, Clarus wondered. No, answered Woyzeck. And he wasn't.

"Can you explain to me *why*, then, if you are not afraid of me," Clarus insisted, feeling his wrist. "Your pulse, too, is much faster than normal."

Woyzeck couldn't explain it and remained silent.

"Then would you tell me at least what you're thinking right now, " Clarus continued.

"I am not thinking anything, " Woyzeck replied, which again was the truth, although Clarus, of course, didn't believe him.

How might he explain it? Should he have said: "I am shaking because when you came in I was afraid that you might think I'm afraid of you, which I'm not?" All the Herr Hofrath would have thought was that Woyzeck was making fun of him.

"Do you think you're a *Narr*?" asked the doctor.

No, he didn't, Woyzeck replied, staring at Clarus's

right shoe, which the doctor whipped up and down.

"What are you staring at?" asked the doctor, uncrossing his legs while Woyzeck refocussed his eyes on the window. Now that his trembling had subsided, he felt as if he were in a trance.

"Could you please answer my question!" Clarus insisted.

So Woyzeck explained that since he was about thirty his thoughts sometimes used to abandon him completely. He'd be in a state in which he would not even notice that people were talking to him.

Clarus scribbled some notes and then said: "Have others—your parents, employers or friends—ever called you a madman?"

Clarus obviously hadn't heard Haase's story about his ghosts, or he would have asked him about that first thing, Woyzeck concluded.

"Once merchant Schwabe, a Jew, told me: 'You're mad, and you don't even know it,'" he told Clarus. He'd been drunk at the time and Schwabe, a good-natured man, had said so in jest, which he'd no doubt confirm, Woyzeck thought. And indeed Dr. Clarus right away asked where he might find the said Schwabe.

But other than trying to hide what might make him appear a *Narr*, Woyzeck did not mince his words. He had always liked to tell stories, and he did so with Clarus. In fact, he enjoyed painting himself rather worse than he was. He soon found out how much Clarus detested him—in spite of the doctor's often jovial manner. But that was exactly why Woyzeck felt safe with him, whereas he didn't with Bergk. He'd never minded people who disliked him. At least you knew where you were at, and could talk openly to them. It was obvious what they thought of you, and they liked it when you told them things which proved to them that they'd been right about you. Clearly, Clarus was out to have him convicted, not proven a *Narr*, which is what he himself wanted. The only thing that had stopped him from killing himself while crossing the *Roßplatz* after the murder was the crowd that would stare at him.

Woyzeck talked and talked, more intensely and openly than ever before. For the most part, Clarus just sat facing him silently, smiling grimly from time to time or snorting disapprovingly. After a while, Woyzeck noticed what kind of stories prompted that smile and that snort, so that's what he'd talk about. As much as he might despise him, Clarus still liked his stories, and the more gruesome they were, the better. War anecdotes clearly were the Herr Hofrath's favourites. Only once, when Dr. Bergk was there too, did he ask him to stop. Woyzeck was talking about the time just after he had joined Bonaparte's army.

So he'd been part of the forces that looted Lübeck, Bergk wanted to know. Yes, he had, Woyzeck replied, and then told them straight out what he did during that looting, when Clarus shouted: "That's enough!"

He was visibly horrified, and so was Bergk, who, however, Woyzeck could tell, would liked to have heard more.

* * * * *

It was only when he heard the shouts in the hall, and here and there an exclamation of protest, that Woyzeck noticed that the judge was reading his sentence. To be beheaded by the sword! Of course, that was what he'd expected. But now it was certain he was nonetheless stunned. Had he nourished some secret hope that Bergk's manoeuvres might save his life after all? In his confusion, he searched for the doctor's eyes in the crowd, but Bergk's face was turned downward, shaking to and fro, signalling disbelief and surprise. The rest, until he heard the locks turn on him in his cell, was lost in a haze of oblivion. Not in a long time had he suffered a similar black-out.

The night after the sentencing Woyzeck had a bad dream. Ever since childhood he'd had fears of being buried alive. Before he'd fall asleep, he would lie in bed thinking of how he'd wake up in his coffin and slowly suffocate, uttering unheard screams in the dark, and beating impotent hands against the coffin-lid six feet under the earth. His father, hearing him sob, would come to ask him what was amiss, but Johann was too ashamed to tell him. There was a second memory in his nightmare, of a pyramid and a mummy as depicted in a book about Freemasons which a guild brother had once shown him in Breslau. Woyzeck dreamt that he was a mummy come alive again in a pyramid's inner chamber with acres of stone-blocks around him, shutting him off forever from the sunlight outside.

Woyzeck woke screaming, just as the grey morning light cast its first faint shadows on the walls of his cell. It took him some time to realize where he was. It was strange. Why should he have a nightmare like that when all possibility of being buried alive was ruled out by his imminent decapitation? He would tell Dr. Bergk, who had often asked him about his dreams.

The doctor came to his cell the same day. No, he could not interpret dreams, he told Woyzeck. But one way to find out was to publish the dream in his *Museum des Wundervollen* and to ask readers who thought they knew what it meant to write to him. Woyzeck agreed.

"Just this last Tuesday, I had a long talk with your former mistress, the Schindelin," Dr. Bergk said suddenly, peering at him with his narrow, bespectacled eyes.

"What did she talk about?" Woyzeck burst out.

"Just about everything. We talked for nearly three hours," Bergk replied.

"She's a cheat and a liar."

"We shall find out soon enough. Everything you have told Dr. Clarus agrees with what she told me."

"I should have killed her like the Woostin, when

she cheated on me. I told her 'Bitch, you must die!' and hit her on the head."

"Was it a brick with which you hit her?" Dr. Bergk asked him.

"She's lying. All I had in my hand was a key. But I damn well did want to give her one that would last her forever."

"I understand," said Dr. Bergk, then, to Woyzeck's surprise, took his leave with a smile.

Meanwhile, there was change all around. People in gaol treated Woyzeck with awe, or perhaps fear, as if he'd not just been sentenced but already to and from the land of the dead. They all, in his presence, seemed to lower their voices, and whisper about him. Once he heard Staffmaster Richter call him "a poet" in talking to jailor Gelbfuß. When Bergk showed Woyzeck Clarus's report about him, he was strangely elated to find himself spoken of as a hardened degenerate wholly indifferent to past, present, and future. After all, that's how he'd acted with Clarus. But Dr. Bergk wouldn't let him play roles. Instead, he was trying to prove him a *Narr*, which Woyzeck tried to resist as best he could. Yet as he kept talking even that resolution began to waver. Perhaps there was hope after all! Also, what was so shameful about suffering from madness? As Bergk explained, some of the greatest men, like Julius Caesar, had been its victims. If only he'd change his mind about Haase's story, he might still save his life, Bergk kept insisting.

Woyzeck had to admit that this denial became increasingly pointless. Bergk had indeed kept his word about not telling Clarus, yet he obviously talked about Woyzeck's ghosts to his friends, some of whom even came to his cell. One of them was Bamberg physician Dr. Marc who had made the whole journey to Leipzig just to see him. With such friends Bergk discussed Woyzeck's "case" right in front of him. How could he have stopped them while talking about it himself? What's more, none of them treated him with Clarus's condescension. They talked to him almost as if he were one of them, while, for instance, treating his hallucinations as a distinction rather than a disorder.

"Did you enjoy killing the woman?" Dr. Marc wanted to know, grinning at Woyzeck who thought he was being mocked. Not even Bergk had ever addressed him this abruptly. But Dr. Marc was in deadly earnest.

Woyzeck pulled down his cap and, after a moment of silence, replied: "I was glad when they told me she was really dead. I stabbed her again and again, for I was afraid she might still be alive and come back to haunt me."

"And then you wanted to kill yourself."

"Yes, as I was running across the *Roßplatz*, but then I got scared of the people who would watch me perhaps wound but not kill myself."

"Is that all you were afraid of?"

"I am also afraid that if I kill myself I'll be damned."

"Don't worry about damnation," Dr. Marc said, turning to Bergk. "We are all damned already, aren't we, Adam? Hell's where we are."

Woyzeck was sorry that Dr. Marc cut short their conversation. For the first time, he felt himself about to say things that seemed close to the truth.

Over subsequent weeks and months, Woyzeck began to suffer unexpected attacks of anguish in thinking about his imminent death. He still wanted to die, but was seized by visions of horror when he thought of the execution. What would happen to him on the scaffold with thousands of eyes staring at him? Would he break down in tears, embrace the executioner's knees, and beg for his life? Woyzeck was stunned when the King turned down his plea for mercy, though he'd bragged about his wanting the King to do just that. After making his second appeal he even revealed part of his secret. Yes, once in his life, back in Graudenz while with the Prussians, he'd seen apparitions and heard strange voices, he told a visiting chaplain.

The chaplain told Woyzeck's defence attorney, who demanded that Woyzeck be re-examined by Professor Dr. Heinroth, author of a well-known study, *Disturbances of the Life of the Soul*. But the court overruled the matter, and, after the King turned down Woyzeck's second appeal, set the date of the execution for November 13th. It was one of those blustering rainy days in mid-autumn when Staffmaster Richter came to tell him. He'd be dead in under two weeks, so suddenly after the months of hearings and examinations! Was this the end?

Things took another turn for the worse when he was transferred to the town hall. Here, by himself, he would spend his remaining days, watching the workmen build his scaffold down in the market below. Even when turning away from the window, he heard the hammer blows reverberate from the high gabled houses. For the first time since his arrest, Woyzeck realized that he had secretly yearned for life even while protesting that he wished to die. Where was Dr. Bergk? He waited for several days but the doctor did not come.

Instead, the prison chaplain came to save Woyzeck's soul. The Reverend warned him of hell. Woyzeck replied that hell was where they were, quoting Bergk's friend. The Reverend was aghast, saying:

"Have you then lost your faith?"

"I still pray each morning and night, as I've done since my childhood," Woyzeck replied.

"So there is hope, but only if you repent yourself of your evil thoughts. Kneel down and we'll pray for your salvation."

But Woyzeck refused. He said he'd rather pray alone.

"God soon change your mind or you'll be lost to the Devil forever," replied the Reverend, making the cross over Woyzeck and getting ready to leave. "All Christian citizens will pray for your soul in Leipzig's churches next Sunday, and not even Satan will stop us."

For a moment Woyzeck thought of the time when, as a young boy, he used to do things precisely because he knew they were evil.

Then he heard himself say: "I went to church on Ascension Day, just before I murdered the Woostin. What good did it do me?"

The Reverend, who had already started to walk to the door, turned around sharply on hearing Woyzeck's remark. "Would you look me straight in the eye," he thundered, staring at Woyzeck who, frightened, had jumped to his feet, but flinched when trying to look into the pastor's furious, twitching face. "See how afraid you are even of me. What your terror will be when you shall have to face the wrath of the Almighty!" he bellowed, then slammed the door shut on Woyzeck.

What if the Reverend were right and Dr. Bergk wrong? Should he call the chaplain back and ask his pardon? But just as he was ready to do so, Bergk arrived. The date was November the sixth, just one week before the execution.

He'd come to tell him, Bergk said without further preambles, that in a letter delivered by hand he'd informed defence attorney Hänsel that he, Woyzeck, had in the weeks before the murder, performed actions proving his madness; also that he'd named newspaper carrier Haase as his main witness.

Why hadn't Bergk at least warned him about this before-hand?

"On the strength of this evidence," Bergk continued, "I have requested that your trial be reopened, and yourself re-examined."

The doctor did not even plead with him, as in the past, to confirm Haase's story. Instead he fell silent, quietly looking at him. Then he said: "Of course, you are free to deny Haase's testimony. But that would simply destroy your last chance to escape execution."

Driven, whether by sudden anger or anguish, Woyzeck jumped to his feet, turned to the window and screamed: "It's all too late anyhow! Look down there! The workmen are almost done. They'll cut off my head before they take down that scaffold."

But Bergk stayed where he was, smiled at Woyzeck and said: "Who knows? But I think you are wrong. There's a good chance that you'll still be alive when that scaffold is gone. But that's not the main thing. They might sentence you once again. If you want to live, you'll have to tell the whole truth, not just part of it as you have done so far."

As it turned out, the workmen below continued their labours and nobody asked him to confirm Haase's story. But then, on November 10th, Staffmaster Richter appeared with two guards to tell him that the execution had been suspended, pending further investigations. Meanwhile, Woyzeck was to return to the *Grimmaische* prison. He was stunned by the speed with which he was taken back there. Yes, someone else would bring his belongings! A coach with drawn blinds was waiting for him on the town square. When they arrived at the jail, there was not a face to be seen of either inmates or guardians. No doubt, all the prisoners had been locked up in their cells. But as he collapsed on his chair he heard the drumming of dozens of spoons reverberating throughout the prison. They knew, and gave him a hero's welcome.

Johann Christian August Clarus (1774-1854) ca. 1830.
Oil portrait by Johann Friedrich Matthai.

WOYZECK'S HEAD
The Retrial

The next day Bergk was back in Woyzeck's cell. Yes, he would tell the whole truth, Woyzeck promised, regardless of whether they'd call him a madman and lock him up at *St. Georgen*. Anyway, that was by no means the only way out, Bergk explained to him. His madness might be a thing of the past. Hadn't he said that not once since the murder had he either had visions or felt suicidal? And what if they did put him into a madhouse! The way he was going, he'd quickly convince them that he had fully recovered, and force them to let him go free, so he could start life afresh.

But how should he go about telling the truth, Woyzeck wondered.

"Tell me those things which are most painful to remember," Bergk replied. That wasn't easy, Woyzeck found. There were things he had never talked of before. Had he been often beaten by his parents, teachers, or officers in the army? Did he masturbate, and how often? Why did he run away from people to roam days on end through the countryside by himself? Precisely the things one felt too ashamed to tell anyone. When did he first see ghosts, feel persecuted by Freemasons, or try to kill himself? Since when had he had black-outs and fits of trembling? At what point did he take to beating his women? The whole litany of his most despicable memories. But where his life was at stake, Woyzeck got over his shame. Before long, he even felt a strange pleasure in retrieving never before remembered events and in describing them in minute detail.

So once more, Woyzeck found himself talking incessantly, but in ways that were new and surprising. Bergk interrupted him just to make sure that he wouldn't "tell stories." As it turned out, Woyzeck felt less and less like wanting to do that. Instead, he seemed to be talking as if in his sleep. Sometimes the words made him cry, sometimes laugh, sometimes they terrified him like his nightmares. But even when he felt hurt, the pain was numbed by a drowsiness through which he heard himself speak in an alien voice—a voice like some stranger's, buried deep within himself. Even when crying, the tears seemed not his but that stranger's.

Only once in a while an invisible hand seemed to suddenly pull him out of this torpor and, as it were, hold him dangling over a void as vast and absolute as eternal damnation. If there is madness, he thought, it's this horror of horrors, not his occasional black-outs and hallucinations. He told Bergk, but the doctor dismissed his fears. If anything, talking about it all would cure him, not make it worse. What's more it might save his life. So Woyzeck continued to talk, for that was all he wanted, now, to escape execution and live!

* * * * *

Hofrath Clarus was amazed when, on January 12, 1823, he started to re-examine Woyzeck. From the sullen ruffian who, whether taciturn or loquacious, had seemed bent on his destruction, Woyzeck had turned into an affable, lively person, eager to please and to talk about all those things he'd previously kept secret. Though suspicious at first, Clarus had to admit that the changes, however implausible, were sincere ones. His second report, which sealed the defendant's fate, observes how Woyzeck had lost the "impassive, cold, coarse and degenerate demeanour" which the doctor had noted earlier. It also notes the delinquent's new urge to want to talk about psychological matters.

But in spite of all the new stories about ghosts and voices, Woyzeck, Clarus insisted, was essentially normal. At least he was sane enough to be held responsible for the murder. Everyone knew that people could see apparitions and yet be quite rational. Had not the bookseller Nicolai given lectures on his spectral visions to the Berlin Academy of Science, dwelling on every detail in the ghosts' behaviour and appearance? Several years ago, a well-known writer from outside Saxony's borders had come to consult Clarus on a similar matter. Day and night, this person felt haunted by sometimes distant, sometimes nearby voices. Nonetheless, he pursued his double career as writer and civil servant in complete command of his reason. Eventually a trip to Carlsbad, recommended by Clarus, rid him completely of his visitations.

Clarus was an outspoken enemy of such newfangled concepts as Pinel's *manie sans delire* or Platner's *amentia occulta*. If anything, these signalled dangerous trends by which all crime would finally be excused in psychological terms. What made things worse in this case was that Bergk, who tried to get Woyzeck's sentence reversed, used such psychological arguments in order to further his anti-death-penalty crusade. Or so at least it appeared to Clarus. Other than having cast the occasional look into his *Museum of the Occult*, he had only read parts of Bergk's *Philosophy of Penal Law* and of his *Psychology of How to Prolong Life*; even that, he decided, was more than enough to dissuade him from wasting more time with Bergk's other, suspiciously numerous publications. All that he'd seen struck him as either ill-conceived or subversive. And after meeting the author on diverse public occasions, this abhorrence for Bergk's ideas was only deepened by his instant contempt for the person. How did anyone dare speak of guilt in terms of its harmful effect on one's health? Or argue that governments, if causing mental harm to their subjects, should be prosecuted and punished like ordinary delinquents. And this man frequented people like Hofrath Rochlitz, or judge Dr. Deutrich; and worse, had free access to Woyzeck's cell and was given permission to sit in on his examinations of the delinquent.

In hindsight, Clarus had to congratulate himself on having kept a safe distance from Bergk. To imagine this charlatan forcing the Court to have Woyzeck re-examined by someone who might reverse Clarus's earlier verdict! These fears had reached their peak when the Court overruled Hänsel's request that Woyzeck be re-examined by Dr. Heinroth. An incorruptible man, Hänsel had simply done what was compatible with both his professional ethics and his friendship with Clarus—the two men had known each other since doing joint observation duty during the battle of Leipzig. Heinroth, who taught that insanity stemmed from sin, would never try to save Woyzeck even if he should find that Woyzeck had shown signs of madness.

What Hänsel suspected was a known fact to Clarus, who had made Heinroth join one of his examinations of Woyzeck. Heinroth, even more than himself, was appalled by what he called Woyzeck's "wilful, obstinate, and self-advertising degeneracy." Even the little he heard him say made Woyzeck appear to him as one of the direst cases of criminal erotomania he'd ever met. If only he'd learnt about Woyzeck earlier! Now that the crime had been committed, there was no point in trying to cure him. One might still have managed that if Woyzeck had been brought to his attention when, early in 1821, he'd been given eight days' arrest for maltreating the Woostin. Some branding and cauterizing (perhaps of Woyzeck's scrotum and penis—a method which a colleague at the Bamberg asylum was currently practising with great success) might have worked wonders. But all requests that he be notified of such cases had been ignored by Leipzig's town council.

Clarus had no doubt as to what was to happen next when the judge, after receiving Bergk's testimony, ordered the execution suspended. Dr. Deutrich would bring in one of Bergk's alienist friends from abroad, have him re-examine Woyzeck and expose his psychiatric report as biased, uninformed, old-fashioned, and careless. Then all of this would be publicized in a scum sheet like Bergk's *Museum* and perhaps in the respectable journals as well. What disgrace and scandal! And the damage to his career! There was no end to the insults that Clarus anticipated as a result of Bergk's manoeuvre. Probably Deutrich and he had been in collusion all along.

But suddenly Dr. Clarus received orders from Deutrich to reinvestigate Woyzeck's dossier. The Herr Hofrath felt elated, but also ashamed. To have suspected the judge of corruption just because he liked to hobnob with charlatans like Dr. Bergk! The mysterious Herr Deutrich! What stories were told about him! People said he used to receive private visits from Bonaparte, or that he was keeping a black, female servant at a country estate outside Leipzig. But what of such rumours! The man had his heart in the right place when it mattered!

Clarus could not remember ever having felt such warmth towards anyone as he did that day towards Deutrich. What he'd thought would be his lasting disgrace might well bring him the nation-wide fame that had so far eluded him! He instantly set about his new task, drew up careful lists of the evidence that had accumulated since his first report, then requested permission to re-examine the delinquent. The permission was granted on the instant. What he'd feared would be carried out by a person seeking to revile him, was to be done by none other than himself! And so, God help him, he would complete his examination with a thoroughness to be a model for generations to come.

* * * * *

Clarus instantly set about his task. He studied all recent publications in medical jurisprudence and brushed up on the standard works. Re-examining Woyzeck would allow him to refute the new-fangled "psychiatry" he detested. Then, on January 12th, he held the first of his five two-hour sessions with Woyzeck. No one, and least of all Dr. Bergk who sat in on several of them, would dare accuse him of not having given the case his utmost attention.

As during their earlier meetings, though for different reasons, Woyzeck's relation to Clarus turned into a bizarre camaraderie. Previously, the murderer's self-destructive impulse had found a fitting echo in his cross-examiner's sarcastic temper; now Woyzeck's eager confessions, which he hoped might save his life, were in full, though deceptive, harmony with the cheerful inquisitiveness with which Clarus asked his questions. On February 21, the Herr Hofrath saw his victim for the last time; one week later, the second report was received by the Court. Although several times as long as its predecessor it reached the same conclusion: having at no time displayed unmistakable madness, the delinquent was to be held fully responsible for the murder. "Woyzeck's alleged apparitions and other bizarre events," it concludes, "have to be taken as mere sense delusions, occasioned by circulatory disorders and aided by prejudice and superstition; further, there is no ground for assuming that Woyzeck, at any time during his life, and more particularly *prior to*, *during*, and *after* the murder, suffered mental disorders so as to make him act from a compulsive, blind, or instinctual impulse or in ways

—40—

other than those dictated by our normal emotions, passions, and responses."

Nor would anyone dare assert that, after such painstaking labours, he had insisted inflexibly on his conclusions! People no doubt remembered how he'd backed Hänsel's request to the Court that Woyzeck be re-examined by a second expert. All he'd asked for then was that the Medical Faculty should have the final say in the case of a disagreement. In the same open-minded spirit he now requested that the Faculty respond to the second report, even if no major criticisms should be levelled against it from other quarters. No doubt such official scrutiny would turn his report into the model Clarus hoped it would be.

To most men involved in the trial, and particularly to Dr. Bergk, the outcome was a *fait accompli* as soon as Dr. Clarus was charged with the re-examination of Woyzeck; the lone exception was the delinquent who, full of hope, made an eager display of his mind to the man who sought his death. Dr. Bergk, of course, could have told him otherwise. But why fill Woyzeck's mind with anguish between now and the execution, a period which, depending on Hänsel's manoeuvres, could last for over a year?

As editor of the *Museum of the Occult*, Bergk had published innumerable stories of somnambulists, erotomaniacs, and pathological misers, of people who thought they were someone else, persons who had lost all sense of who they were, or others who had retrieved some alter ego from the depths of their psyche. On occasion, he had also spoken with patients at Leipzig's asylum. But never before had he been able to talk to a madman for months on end, and, what's more, make him reveal himself with such unexpected results. Here was a challenge both fascinating and full of frustrations! No doubt he should have devoted his life to such work instead of dabbling in dozens of diverse subjects. Now he was past fifty, however, and much too old to achieve what he might accomplish were he still young.

Discussing Woyzeck with friends, older ideas had suddenly coalesced into something like a new propaedeutic to mental science. Psychology had to be put on a new footing. Like any science in its infancy, it had to shed all the ballast of prior metaphysical and religious speculations. Everyone—Heinroth, Clarus, Henke—talked of the soul as if this mysterious entity could be simply taken for granted. But as Woyzeck's case had revealed to him, there was no soul to determine the individual's life. Indeed, the universe lacked all guidance by a primordial world spirit.

How absolutely a man like Woyzeck had always been driven by either his instincts or by the circumstances of his lowly position. To argue like Clarus that Woyzeck lacked moral freedom was both banal and misleading. For who, if anyone, ever truly enjoyed such freedom? Idealists took it to be everyone's birthright. If lost, it was the individual's fault, and insanity a direct result. How hypocritical! Or, at best, how naïve! We were all Woyzecks, circumscribed by our social status and driven by forces as large as this universe, forces with no concern for the individual. Man, while protesting his moral freedom, was like a skiff lost in mid-ocean, presuming to steer its own course, while, in fact, aimlessly tossed a-bout by the waves. All talk of moral freedom only obscured the true issues. To cross-examine a madman the way it was done by Clarus, could reveal very little as long as the questions were formulated around such assumptions. Let the madman talk by himself, the less handicapped by all preconceptions the better! This way he might well uncover secrets about the psyche never dreamt of in our philosophies.

A born raconteur, Woyzeck, once he got going, revealed much of himself, even when telling his pica-resque tales. Instead of him talking *about* life, life seemed to be talking *through* him. Gone was all bravado. Like a madman or dreamer he randomly moved back and forth in time: now going on about how much he loved his mother, then, the next moment, telling how he killed the Woostin. There was neither consistency nor coherence.

Such madness, however, might have its method, and Bergk had tried to find it. For several months now he'd analysed Woyzeck's new way of talking, and predictably he'd found the usual associations of causality, contiguity and resemblance. But just as often there were no links at all, or at least none to be grasped by the current psychological concepts. Might it be that people's fixed ideas, like Woyzeck's fear of appearing afraid, functioned outside the laws of association? Or were there certain subliminal links in man's thoughts making them move like a river temporarily submerged in subterraneous caverns?

There was small doubt in Bergk's mind that analysing Woyzeck had brought him close to discoveries which might revolutionize mental science. Never had he expected such amazing results! The Woyzeck talking now was a man, as it were, recreating his person through language. At last, after months and months of trying, Bergk had uncovered the hidden stranger who, when compared with his murderous double, must be the real Woyzeck. Probably everyone, even Bergk himself, harboured an estranged person only waiting to be set free! And no doubt the methods for doing so would be those he had developed with Woyzeck.

These methods alone, Bergk was convinced, meant a major breakthrough for science. Yet the greater work remained to be done—the task of uncoding the strange new language in which Woyzeck was now pouring forth his psyche. Just recently Bergk had read that a young Frenchman had done the impossible by deciphering the Egyptian hieroglyphics. Another such man would arise and unriddle the mind's secret script.

However, deep in his heart Bergk knew it would not be him. At the present time he had no ideas of how to approach that great task. Probably one should treat a few dozen subjects in some of the ways he had used with Woyzeck. While perhaps putting them into a trance like the mesmerists did, let them tell their life-story, first, in normal fashion, then more at random.

But who knows? His present efforts with Woyzeck might prove sufficient to crack these riddles. After all, it was less than four months since Woyzeck had changed his persona, and only eight or nine weeks since he'd started to ramble in this strange fashion. Perhaps, as he'd continue on these meandering paths, his words might on their own account spell out their hidden matrix. Bergk felt deep pangs of conscience for hiding the truth from Woyzeck; the man who looked at him as his saviour and visibly went through great anguish in acquiescing to his demands. But to tell him the truth at this point would merely plunge his visibly distraught mind into even greater despair.

Also, who could predict the future? "Man proposes, God disposes."* It was always possible that the Court, if presented with some new fact, might change the sentence. Perhaps Woyzeck's madness, so long held in precipitous abeyance, but nudged on to reveal itself by his talking, might come rushing forth like a landslide and call for a third examination. In short there was every reason for Bergk to continue what he did with Woyzeck.

So Woyzeck kept talking and hoping, while the mills of the law ground through their predictable motions. Hänsel's third defence argued that Clarus's findings, if viewed in light of current psychological theorizing (merely hinted at and dismissed by the Herr Hofrath), might lead to diametrically opposite conclusions. But the Court ignored Hänsel's arguments and refused his request that the Medical Faculty give its own report on

---

* A German proverb: "Der Mensch denkt und Gott lenkt."

Woyzeck's mental condition.

Undeterred by such contumelious disregard for his office, Hänsel continued to labour in Woyzeck's defence. In a further submission, he requested that the delinquent be granted another appeal for mercy and again demanded that the Faculty pronounce its views on the case. In this, he argued, he had the backing of Clarus himself whom he had recently spoken to on the matter.

To his great satisfaction, Hänsel's request this time did not go totally unheeded. On January 23rd, 1824, the Court, though voicing reservations regarding a third appeal, expressed itself willing to hear the Faculty's view.

Encouraged by such triumphs, Hänsel now requested that the city and country court of Stralsund, where Woyzeck had spent several years of his life, hear diverse witnesses. Particularly, there were his long-time mistress the Wienbergin and their daughter Marie. Also still living in Stralsund were his former sergeant, his landlord, and several friends. Once again, the Court granted Hänsel's request, but with dire consequences for the defendant. The six witnesses had a lot to say about Woyzeck's immoral nature, but next to nothing about his madness. The worst was that Woyzeck had hidden these facts from Clarus.

According to the new evidence, Woyzeck had lived in Stralsund under the false name of Wutzig. Notorious for his drunkenness, he had once been sentenced to six months in jail for a theft. He'd sometimes beaten his mistress and, more often, treated her with extreme harshness—both of which the victim ascribed to his drunkenness and pathological jealousy. She still remembered a letter from him full of strange and incomprehensible expressions which she put down to the same causes. Otherwise she recalled him as someone who tried to be good to her and their child and for whom, when he misbehaved, one felt pity rather than anger.

On April 17th, just two weeks after receiving these testimonies, the Court obtained the requested response by the Faculty. The outcome of Hänsel's efforts once again had devastating results for Woyzeck. The Faculty fully endorsed Dr. Clarus's report; it ruled, as a matter of principle, against consulting a second medical expert in cases like Woyzeck's, in which the sanity of the delinquent was in question; it finally recommended that whenever a crime was presumed to have been caused by blind impulse, Dr. Clarus's report should serve as a model.

The Court had no choice but to confirm its previous sentence. It did so on July 12th, after extended deliberations: the defendant would be notified of his fate on July 30th.

Meanwhile, Hänsel went to inform Woyzeck of recent events and of what he would do in his further defence. Woyzeck was incredulous and confused. This was the first time he had heard of the implications of Clarus's second report. Why had nobody ever told him about it? Especially, why hadn't Bergk? Of course, it wasn't Bergk's fault if Clarus, despite all his friendly inquisitiveness during the second examination, had been out to have him convicted. But why had Bergk kept all this a secret from him? Out of shame for having failed to save his life? Or was he simply making a fool of him after all? The man in whom he'd put such trust! Had he made him reveal the most embarrassing things in his life just so that he could write about them in his *Museum of the Occult* and to make people laugh about him after his death? And the agonies he'd been going through in thus turning himself into an object of ridicule.

Never before had madness been threatening him in such absolute fashion. He was not even hearing strange voices or seeing ghosts. On the contrary, there was nothing at all, only a gaping void—just this terrible fear, without focus, about to swallow him up. The worst was his sense that, once in its grips, it would never let him go, not even in death. Was this a foretaste of eternal damnation? This unnameable, bottomless anguish in which whatever he felt and thought, yea what he saw, heard, and touched—his very sense of his limbs and his body—seemed either removed to a far distance, or strangely transmogrified, bent, and dismembered.

Johann Christian Heinroth

Johann Christian August Heinroth (1773-1843)

WOYZECK'S HEAD
Childhood Memories

It was just after one of these attacks that the prison chaplain came back to Woyzeck's cell. The Reverend would be willing to forgive Woyzeck's past sins, he said, if Woyzeck showed proper humility and contrition. But Woyzeck found talking to him as unsettling as ever. With Bergk he'd learnt to speak without shame. But that was by no means what the Reverend wanted. When he tried to tell him about a dream, the Reverend barely let him describe its beginning. Yet the dream seemed important to Woyzeck—already he'd dreamt it three times. He was embracing the Woostin, when suddenly he realized that she lay dead in his arms. He shook her and shook her, until her mouth opened screaming: "You coward, come fuck me!" Then, as he ran to the staircase, her laughter reverberated behind him. What could a dream like that mean?

But the Reverend would not listen. He was horrified, bursting out: "My son, beware, these are the blandishments of the Devil sent to lure you into eternal damnation!"

But what could he do, Woyzeck protested. Was he not innocent of his dreams?

"You speak of innocence, my son, and yet confess to a horrible murder."

"But Dr. Bergk says I was mad then and didn't

know what I was doing."

"*Perniciosa simplicitas,*"* the Reverend muttered under his breath, as Woyzeck continued with his anxious protests.

At this point, he, the present Woyzeck, Woyzeck argued, could hardly recognize the other Woyzeck who, three years ago, stabbed the Woostin that fatal night in the hallway.

"But you yourself—horrid thought—implored God to give that she were dead, and Satan, for months on end, made you persist in this cursed defiance," the prison chaplain insisted.

Even that had been the earlier Woyzeck, a maniac haunted by voices, ghosts, and, yes, Satan.

"I have been a different person for months now. Dr. Bergk is my witness."

"He may well be lost to us forever," the Reverend muttered to himself. "How in God's name can I pull him out of his confusion?"

"Dr. Bergk with his Satanic ideas," he shouted, "has led you astray in the labyrinths of hell. Never again will he be allowed to come here."

Woyzeck was speechless. What could Bergk, who almost saved his life and who perhaps was still trying to save it, what could the soft-spoken doctor have to do with such matters?

"Perhaps you have heard of Dr. Heinroth, professor of psychic therapy here in Leipzig?"

"Yes, he once came to my cell with Dr. Clarus," Woyzeck replied.

"Did this learned man tell you that persons going insane merely reap the rewards of their sins? Yes, Heinroth is right, there is no lunacy that cometh not from the Devil." The Reverend found himself slipping into his pulpit rhetoric as he keenly watched for the effect of his words on the condemned man. "No, if the Heavenly

---

* Latin, "Pernicious simplicity."

Father striketh certain sinners with madness, it is so as to give them here on earth a foretaste of their everlasting tortures in hell."

Woyzeck was horrified. Once again he felt as if he was pushed down a bottomless void. He straightened up in his chair, with his spine about one inch from its back. His knuckles whitened as his hands clenched the seat. Thus he sat—for minutes or perhaps hours. Meanwhile the prison chaplain, after watching Woyzeck seize up with horror, silently left the cell.

Woyzeck's panic gradually gave way to despair. And to know that such horror might last forever! Then a hand, which took hold of his right shoulder, brought back a faint sense of where he was. Who was this unknown pastor who'd come to his cell? Woyzeck could hear his voice, but his figure seemed far, far away.

"The hidden sanctuary of God's plans is forever closed to man," the man said.

For one so infinitely small and distant, the pastor's voice was surprisingly clear and loud.

"The self-righteous, eager to break into these secret precincts, will stumble headlong and lose themselves in an endless maze. Their minds will be swallowed up and lost in eternal damnation."

Was he not already lost in this labyrinth of anguish? Then, once again, he felt the Reverend's hand squeeze his shoulder.

"But there is always hope for those, both sinners and righteous alike who, humbled and cast down, learn to tremble at the Almighty's wisdom and to esteem His infinite mercy."

The pastor fell silent still holding Woyzeck's shoulder.

"I'm the Reverend Gottlieb who's come to pray with you for your eternal salvation. Let us kneel."

Until his death, Woyzeck's waking hours were almost entirely spent in prayer. With pastor Gottlieb he prayed from books; when alone he simply repeated the Lord's Prayer or addressed Christ and the heavenly Father in freely improvised effusions. Then, lulled into somnolence by his rhythmical incantations, he would lose himself in his daydreams.

*   *   *   *   *

Praying brought back memories of childhood, particularly of the years when his father, shortly before he died, had drawn Johann into his more and more fervent devotions. He vividly remembered Herrn von Speen's dining hall where the two joined others at the oak table illumined by massive, seven-branched candelabra. At a sign from Herrn von Speen, they'd close their eyes, lower their heads on the table, and remain thus immobile, each person absorbed in silent prayer. How overawed Johann used to be when, after some twenty to thirty minutes, one of the devotees broke the silence to announce that he'd heard the voice of the Almighty.

Would God ever speak to Johann? As hard as he tried, he could think of little else than the table and how it pressed on his temple. His prayers were constantly sidetracked by pain and shameful thoughts. What could God's voice, which spoke to the others, possibly sound like? Did they also see Him, as He talked to them, in the way that Johann could, as long as he kept his eyes closed, see St. Nicholas who had come to his house last *Advent*? Would he ever find out? Or was he one of those who were born deaf to the inner Word?

Even more puzzling to Johann was Madame Guyon. Why did the mere mention of her cause his stepmother to start another of her endless rows with his father? The lady, Johann concluded, must be one of father's wealthy clients. A little later Johann found that Madame Guyon had long since died in a lonely dungeon. She was a saint and a martyr who had written the many

—52—

volumes which occupied a whole shelf in Herrn von Speen's villa. In fact, it was only due to her wisdom that von Speen and his brethren could hear God's voice.

But enough about Madame Guyon remained as puzzling to Johann as ever. Why had the lady been jailed? And why did mentioning her cause such distress to his stepmother, who each Sunday went to listen to Reverend Schulmann's sermons? But most confusing to Johann was Madame's idea that you had to enter Nothingness before God would talk to you. What was this Nothingness?

With his head pressed sideways against the oak table, Johann learnt to feel shame at his many strange daydreams. Even when, for a moment, no particular image sidetracked his search for this Void, there was his constantly gnawing stomach to conjure up visions of sausages and potatoes. As father spent more and more time at von Speen's, such fare had become scarce in their household.

"You cannot find Nothingness without killing your passions," father used to tell Johann. It was all his fault, said father, if he always grabbed more than he needed, and as this "greed" increased, his chances of ever attaining the Void were getting slimmer and slimmer. Johann's "greed" was a clear sign—a sign, father concluded, that Johann might be damned. To his surprise, even stepmother came to agree with him on this point. This happened when Johann revealed yet one more sign of his possibly damned state.

The children were strictly forbidden to enter the pantry, which made it doubly tempting to Johann. His hollow stomach made him dream up a land of milk and honey behind the locked door; but worse was a new, irrepressible urge to do precisely what was forbidden. How much pain he had already caused father who, at one point, had built such high hopes on his imminent conversion! Should he not try his best to regain his and God's favour? But the temptation of doing the opposite was much stronger. He knew where stepmother hid the key, and one day, when she and father were gone, he tremblingly unlocked the secret door. What he found—some bread and *Sauerkraut*, as well as about fifteen centimetres of sausage—was disappointing in the extreme. He almost relocked the door without touching anything. All the more strange was what followed. He had planned to just nibble here and there, so that his theft would not be detected; instead, he suddenly gulped down handfuls of *Sauerkraut*, bit off large chunks of bread, and, within minutes, swallowed all there was of the sausage.

Even afterwards, he merely felt a sullen contentment. No doubt his punishment would be severe; but he'd know how to clench his teeth in silence. Only after the first dozen strokes from his father's hazel-rod, did defiance yield to tears and contrition. Why had he done something so heinous? Johann didn't know.

"Don't lie!" The hazel-rod hit his back with redoubled fury and Johann began to scream for mercy.

"Tell me why. Why, why did you do it?"

"Because I was hungry!"

"Ungrateful glutton."

"I'll never do it again. Stop, father, stop!"

But Stephan Woyzeck's punitive fury showed no signs of abating. To Johann's surprise, it was stepmother, who, unable to stop her husband with screams, threw herself between father's rod and himself.

"Stop, Stephan, stop. You are killing your child!"

Then the three stared at each other in silent exhaustion. Never before had his father beaten him like this. Despite his pain, Johann felt almost sorry for him as he stood there, ashen-pale and shaking. And his stepmother, who'd protected him with her body!

That night he heard them whisper in bed. This is what Johann had expected; in fact, he'd stayed awake so he could hear what they'd say.

"How hard I tried to make Johann hear the inner Word," his father began. "And all the while Satan was building a citadel in his heart."

Would Johann, instead of hearing God's voice, now have to hold colloquy with the Devil?

"I agree with you," said his stepmother. And after some silence she added: "If Johann is lost, we can only watch and pray."

Was he indeed lost to Satan? From that day onwards, a marked change came over his parents. Instead of having their usual quarrels, his father and mother began to exchange knowing glances while apprehensively watching their son. At dinner, when he ate more than his due, his father would simply remove the food bowls, but not say a word. Meanwhile, he avoided Johann's searching eyes, resting his own in those eagerly turned towards him by his wife.

So Johann decided to abandon himself to his sombre fate. What else could he do, being lost to the Devil? He hardly washed and altogether stopped brushing his hair. At, the Free School* he picked fights with his former friends. When he couldn't hurt others, he took pleasure in hurting himself. Not that he had lost all impulse to be kind or to help! But if he did, it was somehow done hypocritically, as it were, in spite of himself. He would do it, but smile, convinced of the thoroughness of his deceit.

Most enjoyable, in the same way, were the forbidden games he played all by himself. Was it Satan who guided his hand, when out of some uncontrollable urge, he decapitated all the marguerites in the *Bösische* Garden one night? Once, he tried to torture a cat. But the beast, as he pulled it up by its tail, curved round in an arch, and severely scratched his arms, face, and chest. So, instead, he turned his attention to flies, swatting them not because they annoyed him, but because he enjoyed the

---

* Leipzig's elementary school for the poor.

killing. Then, after each execution, he rang a deathbell made of two brass rods suspended by strings from a stick.

Instead of the war games at school, he now fought fantasy wars, in which he acted as hero, victim, and lord of destiny all at once. He'd spend whole days in the fields past Johannis Valley, where the white and red flowers divided naturally into opposing armies. He'd watch these for hours, naming the large ones after his favourite heroes like Hagen and Siegfried. Then he'd jump forth wielding his stick and, closing his eyes like blind fate, wreak havoc among both armies. Later he noticed with both sadness and elation, that the flower he'd named the evil hero Johann Christian Woyzeck lay dying amongst the hundreds of dead and wounded.

But perhaps most exciting to him was to build paste-board houses, churches, and town walls. These he'd stack together so closely, that once one of the outside dwellings caught fire, all the rest would be slowly consumed by the spreading flames. Then he'd just sit there and imagine the screams of the burning men, women, and children. Once a real fire broke out on the nearby Corn Market and thick clouds of smoke came wafting into their windows. Johann was frightened. But deep in his heart he wished that the fire would not be extinguished too quickly.

Then, late in 1793, he fell ill. His tonsils swelled up so much they started blocking his throat; even swallowing liquids felt as if he were being sliced by razors. Never before had his parents paid him so much attention! Whenever he woke from his feverish nightmares, he found either father or stepmother there, wiping the sweat from his body, propping up his pillows, or spoonfeeding him liquids and gruel. Then they'd sit down beside him and look at him smilingly, but sadly. Sometimes the Reverend Gruber was there too, the three of them whispering by the window.

Around October, his fever diminished, though the pain in his throat continued. But then there was something more terrible. His nightmares, though less numerous now, somehow threatened to go on forever. At first, he just couldn't shake them off. Then, even after he did, a more abstract horror descended upon him. The dreams, which on waking left him with this anguish, all resembled each other. Out in the sky, two birds collided head on, and fell dead to the ground; two cannons brought mouth to mouth were both fired off together; Siamese twins sharing one skull were tossing about in their vain attempts to free themselves from each other. It was as if this horrible something at the core of these dreams now began to raise its monster head in plain daylight.

The worst, however, was still to come. So far, all such invasions of horror could be linked to a prior nightmare. But then, of a sudden, they began to appear out of nowhere. The first time it happened was one afternoon in November, while father was reading to him from the bible. Was his body dropping into a void, even though he could feel it lie so heavily on the mattress? Everything he could see and hear suddenly seemed far away. Even the razors slicing his tonsils, though painful as ever, were doing their work at some infinite inner distance. He was almost surprised to find that his hands, far out there at the end of his arms, could still shroud his eyes in darkness. Then he turned to the wall and cried.

When he emerged from his anguish, the room, cast in the evening's shadows, loomed closer than ever. His father was gone, but there was a book on his thighs, half lost in the folds of the blanket. He'd never seen it before. Johann glanced at its title: *Instructions on How to Fear the Lord*. No doubt his father had left it on purpose.

It was in three parts: "Instructions on How to Fear the Lord" for boys of six, of nine, and of twelve. Reading the preface, Johann was glad to find that even a twelve-year-old boy could still become one of the righteous. But as he read on, this task looked harder and harder. If only his parents had shown him this volume sooner! Already from six to nine, the pious boy, so it said, could not just double but triple this treasure of heavenly grace. How Johann had wasted his chances instead! Worst of all, instead of storing up treasures in heaven, he had grown more and more indebted to hell.

While the sections for six and nine-year-olds said next to nothing about damnation, the third part dealt with little else. Even the Reverend Schulmann, whose sermons could make one shiver with fear, had never depicted its horrors in greater detail. Hell was described as a prison, bounded by walls ten thousand miles in thickness. So crowded was its vast interior that all bodies formed one writhing mass of convulsions. Yet each of the damned was so utterly bound and helpless, that the hand could not pluck at the worm which was gnawing its way through the eyeball. Everything was plunged into darkness, for the fire of hell gives forth no light. Instead of air, there was the stench as from millions of fetid corpses, coalesced into a swarming jelly of putrefactions. Each of the damned, though massed in with all the others, was utterly lonely, engrossed in the diverse torments afflicting the different senses.

Now imagine yourself as one of these sinners! Your eyes lost in darkness, your nostrils inhaling putrid odours, your throat choked with boiling sewage, your skin branded with red-hot irons, and your ears deafened by your own screams and those of all others suffering similar torment. Then imagine—horror of horrors—that you'll suffer these torments forever. In all eternity, where time is, but never ends, where every minute will seem like an endless millennium of anguish, and each such millennium be but a prelude to millions and billions of such millennia. Never to end, but to last forever. Never, forever. Never, forever. Worse than all else will be your despair at the thought of such never-ending torment. If it would last for only a year, or ten years, a hundred, a thousand, a million, or even a billion! But no, it will last forever!

Reading on feverishly, Johann was struck by a frightening thought. No doubt his recent seizure of anguish was part of that boundless despair he was to suffer as one of the damned. Was there no hope for him at all? In turning the page, Johann was glad to find that the book was raising exactly that question. And there *was* hope, if now, once and for all, he would quit his evil ways. But what could he do after already wasting six years? Johann read on fearing that, once again, he would have to search for the *inner* Word. But no! Tears of gratitude blurred the page when he found that the possible remedy was much simpler. All he must do was kneel down and pray with loud and audible voice.

Never before had Johann acted more promptly. As far as his feeble limbs permitted, he threw back the blanket, jumped to his feet, but collapsed onto his knees right where he was, facing the bedstead. Then, with a voice hoarse from illness, and shrill with devotion, he loudly cried out *"Vater Unser, der Du bist im Himmel, geheiliget werde Dein Name.*"* Once finished, he simply repeated the same prayer, his voice sounding more shrill and hoarser each time. What if the sweat poured down his body! What if the razors slicing his tonsils executed their work in ever more rapid succession, as he gasped for breath and tried to moisten his dried-out mouth with spittle! The more it hurt, the more it would please the Lord! Reassured by this thought, each spasm, to Johann, became a moment of joyful triumph. Then he suddenly found himself chanting:

> *Ein feste Burg ist unser Gott*
> *Ein gute Wehr und Waffen*

---

* German, "Our Father, who art in heaven, hallowed be thy name . . ."

Er hilfft uns frey aus aller Not
die uns itzt hat betroffen
Der alt böse Feind
mit Ernst ers itzt meint
gros Macht und viel List
Sein grausam Rüstung ist
Auff Erd ist nicht seins gleichen.
Mit unser Macht ist nichts gethan
wir sind . . .*

Here, Johann got stuck. Another result of the six years he'd wasted in sin. But nothing could break his zeal now! He resumed humming the tune until a stream of private effusions came pouring forth from his mouth. Now at last he was talking directly to God and the Lord Christ. Meanwhile, his body and hands started acting in tune with his words. He'd cross his hands, palms turned outwards, in a protective screen before his face when addressing the Almighty in his wrath; or he would let his arms form a circle while rocking his body as if he were holding a baby when appealing to Little Jesus to intercede for him with the Father.

His father and stepmother, intrigued by the noise from the bedroom, found Johann, his back and footsoles turned towards them, in a pose of sudden, jubilant outburst, face and arms raised sharply towards the ceiling. They stopped by the door in amazement. By now, Johann's chanting had deteriorated to a string of barely audible squeaks. But to his parents he sounded more like one of the blessed angels in heaven. Their amazement increased when Johann, after casting a sideways glance

---

* German, "Our God is a castle strong/A good mailcoat and weapon/He sets us free from ev'ry wrong/That wickedness would heap on/The old knavish foe/He means earnest now;/Force and cunning sly/His horrid policy,/On earth there's nothing like him/'Tis all in vain, do what we can,/Our strength is . . . "

to the door, once more screwed his flagging fervour to the utmost of what his enfeebled body could render. What bliss if right at this moment, reconciled to his father and the Almighty, he might cease his life while intoning his prayers!

* * * * *

Now that Woyzeck was sure he had to die, a certain calm came back to him. Yes, he was scared of death, and even more scared of the execution. But gone, at least for a while, was that horrible, groundless anguish. In a way, it almost seemed as if that lesser fear had replaced the greater. Once again, he took pride in telling whomever wanted to know that, at bottom, he didn't care about dying.

"I always knew it would cost me my head," he'd say. "But what does it matter. I'll have to die sometime."

Like a madman turned saint, he seemed resigned to his death and to enjoy his remaining days. He had always known it would turn out this way, he said, when Staffmaster Richter came to hand him his sentence. Richter was visibly shaken at having to bring such evil tidings, but Woyzeck reassured him. He said it wasn't Richter's fault. The *Herr Stockmeister* had been good to him always, and, anyway, he was quite ready and willing to die. Everyone was amazed to see him so cheerful, and even eager to make people laugh with his jokes.

Woyzeck knew that during the last days before his death he'd enjoy special favours. Once again, he was transferred to the Poor Sinner's Chamber of the *Rathaus*, where he was given to eat whatever he wished, could ask the choir boys of St. Thomas to sing for him, and have whoever he wanted come visit.

That his cell-keeper treated him with unusual kindness seemed at first to be part of the same arrangement. But Gelbfuß was downright servile. Only once in his life, after donning the clothes of a nobleman whom he'd found lying dead by the roadside, had Woyzeck had people call him *mein gnädiger Herr*. Gelbfuß not only did that, but asked how he'd slept, brushed the crumbs from his convict's blouse as if it were a magistrate's redingote, and, in addition to shaving his beard, offered to comb and wash his hair. It was all rather strange, but Woyzeck was glad to accept it.

There was nothing so soothing as to have Gelbfuß comb his hair after a troubled night. Before long, Woyzeck looked forward to it every morning.

"I hope Your Honour spent a good night." Woyzeck growled assent as Gelbfuß' big hands were stroking his temples.

"I understand if Your Lordship does not want to speak to me," Gelbfuß said a little later.

Ever since he had been here, Woyzeck indeed had spoken no more than a few dozen words to him.

"I'm a poor man with a wife and six children," Gelbfuß continued, combing Woyzeck's hair with even more than his usual dedication. "And you could easily make us happy for ever."

Gelbfuß probably mistook him for somebody else.

"Like you, I believe in ghosts, although I have never seen one as you have."

There was another moment of silence.

"My family often goes hungry for days. So I'm playing the lottery. But no luck for me," Gelbfuß resumed. "Even when close, I am always short by one number. But with *your* help our misery could stop for ever. And I am not afraid of ghosts, Sir."

Woyzeck still had no idea what Gelbfuß was after.

"Anyway, here is my address," said Gelbfuß.

With trembling hands he pulled a scrap of paper from his breast pocket, unfolded it carefully, and handed it to Woyzeck.

"You know where it is: *Holzgasse 6*, three flights up, the door on your right. I'll leave it unlocked, Sir."

He stared at Woyzeck as if at some supernatural being.

"Even if Your Honour can't do it, please don't tell Staffmaster Richter that I asked you. It might cost me my job, Sir."

"Asked me *what*?" Woyzeck burst out.

"To visit me after the execution and tell me the lottery numbers for Sunday."

"Visit you?"

Didn't he know that the ghosts of recently executed men can foresee the future, Gelbfuß wondered.

No, Woyzeck didn't, though he'd heard that people about to die had prophetic powers. So why not those who *had* died? He'd always believed in ghosts, even before he had seen one himself. Now the mesmerists were capable of conjuring them up scientifically, Bergk had explained to him. What, then, would the doctor advise him to do? Could Gelbfuß be right and should he, Woyzeck, visit him after his death? Of course, he'd much rather tell Marie's mother. But the Wienbergin lived far away in Stralsund, and there was no way of making her buy a lottery ticket before Friday. Why, then, not help Gelbfuß?

Woyzeck's last prayer in his own hand. Facsimile.
German Literature Archive, Marbach.

WOYZECK'S HEAD
The Execution

Father, I am coming! Yes thou callest me,
my heavenly Father, thy merciful will be done.

During his last three days in the Poor Sinner's Chamber,
Woyzeck had composed a prayer. He would recite it on
the scaffold which was nearing completion down on the
town square.

> *Thanks,*
> *heartfelt thanks, praise and honour to thee, all*
> *compassionate one, who despite my great guilt lookest*
> *lovingly upon me and deignest to make me thine.*

Looking up from his table, he saw the men haul the
railings up the scaffold's steep wooden stairway. How
much effort had gone into the building of this massive,
house-size structure rising some five meters above the
cobblestone town square! Since Monday, a crew of five
had erected a box-like frame, then nailed down huge
planks to its sides and top, and finally added the twenty-
five step stairway facing the dignitaries' balcony above
the town hall's main entrance. Throughout the week, the
workmen's hammerblows had punctuated his prayers.

Thanks to you, that, after the many hardships I have

> *suffered, thou driest the tears,*
> *of which I have shed so many.*
> *Father, I commend my soul into*
> *thy hands! In thee I live, in thee I die, thine*
> *am I dead and alive. Amen!*
> *Help, Lord! Let it turn out right, Lord!*

For hours now he had practised how to recite his prayer. He'd kneel down on his right leg, keep the other flexed at a right angle, and while praying pause solemnly here and there. Then at last he'd stretch out his arms up high as if to embrace his Saviour. It was with those very gestures that Woyzeck, on August 27th, 1824, just before eleven o'clock in the morning, recited his prayer to the eager crowd on the *Marktplatz*.

The execution was a triumphant success of unprecedented pomp and precision. As early as August 20th, public excitement had become such that the *Rathaus* printed a leaflet threatening up to ten thaler fines to anyone who'd break the following rules: on the day of the execution, no wagons of any kind were to pass through the inner towngates; all carts, carosses, or other vehicles were to vacate the streets and alleyways leading into the town square; spectators must not stand on barrels, carriages, scaffolds, and similar contraptions; most of all, they must not unroof their houses, for falling tiles might cause death to others. Generally speaking, apprentices and servants should stay at home, and those present abstain from all pushing and jostling.

Further measures were taken to enforce, if necessary, what mere threats might not accomplish. All town soldiers plus officers were put on full alert at the *Grimmaische* prison. Equipped with long truncheons, all local scribes, city hall officials, leaflet distributors and blockmasters were strategically positioned in the crowd. But none of them had to make use of their weapons. Neither public officials nor spectators committed acts to detract from the traditional solemnity of the occasion.

At ten o'clock in the morning, the shrill metallic sound of the Poor Sinner's Bell of the clocktower sent shivers down the backs of the thousands of men, women, and children jammed body to body in the market place and crowding the windows of the surrounding buildings. Thrice rang the bell. Then the vanguard of the execution defile—a corporal, eight soldiers in twofold, quadrangled formation, and the bailiff on horseback, staff in hand—appeared under the pointed archway of the town hall's main entrance. These were followed by the major's two cuirassed and helmeted horsemen; the lamp-carriers, coal measurers and market broomsmen, in a group of eleven, each one armed with spear and bayonet; twenty pupils of the Thomas school, the carpenters, the wine and beer dispensers; the market surveyor, with glistening cuirass, morion, and pike; two town and two council officials; and finally Woyzeck, his face ashen but smiling, flanked by two priests and the sextons, behind him Staffmaster Richter, with the poor sinner's pitcher full of wine, therewith to refresh the delinquent. Also surrounding Woyzeck, as they emerged from the dark archway into the bright sunlight, were ten beadles, the deputee market surveyor, and concluding the procession, the Vice Marshall fully armed on horseback. The whole defile circled thrice around the scaffold, while all armoured personnel positioned themselves symmetrically on the outer edge of a vacant quadrangle cordoned off from the spectators. Then Woyzeck, the executioner, and his assistants ascended the scaffold. The two priests, clad in black robes, remained at the foot of the stairway.

All hearts were moved to hear Woyzeck recite his prayer and confront his death with such obvious trust in his salvation. Public sympathy reached its pitch when the delinquent, upon concluding his prayer, broke established protocol by embracing executioner Körzinger. Then he untied and removed his kerchief and sat down on the chair of execution. There were shouts of "See, the noble Woyzeck!" with women holding up their children while others broke down in tears and lamentation. But the fears of Vice Marshal Stürmer, who for a moment turned his helmeted head toward the crowd, proved unfounded. People were glad to relapse into passive awe as soon as judge Deutrich, rising from his seat on the clocktower's balcony, addressed executioner Körzinger with loud and audible voice.

"We, this city's judge, assure you of our protection in case that your sword should miscarry." The rest happened so quickly as almost to pass unnoticed. Körzinger's sword gave off a flash of sunlight as it swerved round in a semi-circle, while groans and sighs from thousands of throats reverberated through the town square. Contrary to previous customs, the authorities of the present, enlightened age had determined to expose the bleeding criminal for no longer than required. One spectator later claimed to have seen how Woyzeck's head skipped in an arc before it hit the floorboards; another, teacher, composer, and poet Ernst Anschütz, how the severed head stuck to the blade, until Körzinger turned round the sword. Be that as it may, the executioner's assistants hurriedly caught Woyzeck's trunk in black velvet and along with the chair and the head, quickly tumbled it down a trapdoor. Meanwhile, all eyes were focused on Körzinger who thrice whirled the blood-stained sword over his head, then, with his face turned to the clocktower balcony, shouted, "Have I done right, most noble judge?"

"Thou has done what was required by right and sentence," came the answer.

Thereupon Körzinger bowed thrice to the people before slowly descending the stairs of the scaffold.

Meanwhile, five men, who had obtained the town authorities' permission to test the dead man's responses during the seconds, minutes and hours after decapitation, busied themselves around the corpse. They were Dr. Clarus, Dr. Bergk, *Prosektor* Bock, Herr Schmitz, and Professor Dr. Ennemoser, expert in phrenology and animal magnetism as well as the author of a compendious *History of Magic*, who had not shunned the three day journey from Bonn in order to attend this occasion. The learned men let no time go to waste in their scientific endeavours. No sooner had the crowd's collective groan upon the deadly swordstroke abated, when Herr Schmitz picked up Woyzeck's head from the sawdust underneath the scaffold. He held it at arm's length in his stiffly outstretched hands so as not to dirty his shoes with the blood gushing from the neck.

The five men stood amazed: severed neatly from the trunk at the fifth cervical vertebrum, the head retained, even in death, its romantically sensitive air. An almost beatific smile which, as Dr. Clarus pointed out, had sometimes, for no apparent reason, lit up Woyzeck's face during the psychiatric examinations, seemed to have permanently settled in his otherwise deeply furrowed features. Was it possible that the dead man's head still harboured consciousness and emotions? Were those pupils under the half-lowered lids still seeing him as Herr Schmitz saw Woyzeck? As the former was to write in the thirty-seven page dissection report published in the third 1825 issue of Langermann's *Magazine for Psychic Therapy*, the much debated question as to the possible continuance of consciousness, will, and emotion after a head has been severed from its trunk can hardly be solved by galvanic and similarly dilettantish experiments. The appropriate answer could be reached only through first-hand, detailed observations as conducted by himself and his colleagues. As a result of these efforts, Woyzeck's post mortem beatitude was not allowed to endure for long.

At a heated, preliminary session before the actual execution, the five men had agreed upon the several stages of their experiment. They had also chosen the eagerly volunteering Herr Schmitz as their main agent. The latter now arched forward while bringing the dead man's left ear to about five inches' distance from his mouth and shouted: "Murderer!"

Then he moved the head, which still bled profusely from its carotid arteries, back to its previous, arm's length position. The effects, Herr Schmitz reports in Langermann's *Journal*, were instantaneous: "The eyes opened widely, staring fixedly at the observers, with an air of amazement but without any sign of grief. This lasted for several seconds, then the eyes tilted upward so that the pupils became almost invisible. Finally the lids descended over the eyeballs, and several tears trickled down the cheeks."

Is it possible that these observations were prompted by wishful, humanitarian thinking? Any such doubts about Herrn Schmitz's and his colleagues' objectivity are dispelled by their subsequent experiments. Woyzeck's ghostly pangs of conscience were given little time to unfold. Instead, his temporarily contrite face was put through a series of grimaces and contortions. As planned the day before, Herr Schmitz slowly revolved Woyzeck's head, while Herr Bock filled its nostrils with liquid ammonia, stuck his index finger up Woyzeck's windpipe, and finally poked at the marrow of his spinal cord. The results were as striking as unexpected. After severe twitchings of his facial muscles, Woyzeck's jaws opened wide while his trembling tongue stuck out as if to mock his observers. "Soon after the tongue retreated into the mouth but reappeared for about two seconds when further liquid ammonia was applied to the nose's pituitary membrane. . . . Repeated insertions of the finger into the spinal cord reproduced the previous results. When Woyzeck's head, after a total of six minutes, was finally put into a coffin along with the trunk, its eyelids were completely closed."

Once at Leipzig's *Anatomie*, the learned men dissected Woyzeck's body. They discovered diverse, noteworthy features. While all organs in Woyzeck's cranium, chest and abdomen were found to be in completely healthy condition, his heart was surrounded by inordinate layers of fat. His scrotum, of otherwise normal dimensions, was somewhat swollen and hardened on its right upper edge. As one would expect from someone noted for his "illicit indulgences of the sexual impulse" (Dr. Clarus), his oversize penis showed scars left by the pustules of past venereal infections. His prostate gland, upon some light squeezing applied to it by deputy dissector Bock, yielded large amounts of sperm along with a plentiful slimy discharge. Equally notable was his clearly overdeveloped *nervus sympathicus*.

The dissection of the body concluded, the men's attention once again turned to Woyzeck's head. Deputy dissector Bock started fingering the skull, a procedure insisted upon by Dr. Ennemoser.

Hofrath Clarus demurred at having such observations included in the report. Had not Gall* and his cranial bumps been long made the laughing stock of Europe? Had he not been, just like Mesmer** before him, hounded out of Vienna for his quackeries? Or how about "phrenomagnetism?" Clarus drew the syllables out with a distinct sneer. What else was phrenomagnetism but the most recent, Hydra-like offspring of these monstrous new superstitions? Ennemoser, though sceptical of phrenology himself, flinched at his colleague's denunciation of mesmerism.

"You forget that mesmerism is a fully accredited

---

* Franz Joseph Gall (1758-1828), Austrian anatomist and the founder of phrenology which studies the shape of the human skull with respect to character traits and mental faculties.

** Franz Anton Mesmer (1734-1815), German physician and founder of "animal magnetism," later called "mesmerism," the pseudo-scientific antecedent of hypnotism.

discipline taught at several German universities," he exclaimed.

"Which is a regrettable fact," replied Hofrath Clarus, deliberately turning to the other three men. "Our respected Bonn colleague has probably failed to peruse the new Grabe commission report from Berlin?"*

"Grabe's exorcisms have nothing to do with the noble endeavours of animal magnetism," Ennemoser protested.

"Gentlemen, please," intervened Dr. Bergk. "Let us go on with the business at hand and leave our learned disputes until after dinner."

"Here we are," exclaimed Ennemoser who throughout the dispute had continued to finger Woyzeck's skull. "A bump just slightly above the ear. Exactly where Gall locates the impulse for violence."

"And another bump there," replied Clarus, poking his index finger at another part of the head. "Precisely where Gall locates the organ for ideality."

"And why not? Think of Sand.** We know of several murderers guided by idealistic concerns."

"That depends on how we define 'idealistic'."

"Gentlemen, please." Dr. Bergk's gently persuasive voice once again had to intervene in the debate. "As you probably know, I'm no particular friend of Gall's theories myself.*** But I wouldn't mind if Herr Schmitz

---

* Grabe, a 29-year-old ostler, magnetizer, and quack, was brought to Berlin's *Charité* and asked to treat 85 patients under the scrutiny of a Commission specially set up for this purpose. The Commission's final report specified that the majority of these patients suffered marked deteriorations of their health in the process. As a result, Grabe was prohibited from further practising his skills by Royal order of August 28, 1824.

** Concerning Sand, see below, page 85, note*.

*** Dr. Adam Bergk had published an attack on Gall entitled *Bemerkungen und Zweifel über die Gehirn-und Schädeltheorie des Dr. Gall in Wien* (Leipzig, 1803) (*Comments and Doubts Regarding the Brain and Skull Theory of Dr. Gall in Vienna*).

would discuss the delinquent's cranial idiosyncrasies in our report."

"Then so be it," rejoined Clarus, attentively watching Herr Bock's powerful handsaw divide Woyzeck's cranium slightly above the noted bump.

But Clarus's pleasure in admiring his old friend's surgical skill was of short duration. If only he hadn't let himself be drawn into this experiment engineered by Bergk and Ennemoser. Hardly had Bock laid bare Woyzeck's cerebrum, when Ennemoser once more started spouting his pseudo-scientific theories: this brain with its numerous, small and bilaterally uneven convolutions, he argued with characteristic insistence, had a distinctly female constitution. Which was supposed to throw light on Woyzeck's insanity and the murder. What rubbish!

Though tempted to utter one of his well-known sarcasms, Hofrath Clarus decided to remain silent. Who was to stem the tide of these absurdities in the end? How much trouble he had had to oppose them during the past trial. Except that it had allowed him to set a precedent for the future cases of a similar kind, the entire second examination of the delinquent had been a total waste of time. Why play the psychic father confessor to mentally unbalanced criminals and make them spin out their sordid lives in self-indulgently embroidered detail, or worse, shock them back into normalcy in the Punishment Chambers of the new *Irrenhäuser*?* To Clarus, all that was another form of inquisitorial mania and a deplorable regress into the dark ages. But clearly he had had no choice. If he had dared go against the new trend, the Criminal Court would have been forced to consult an external authority who might have overthrown his verdict.

"Our dear Hofrath seems rapt in thought." Ennemoser's strident voice shook Clarus out of his reverie.

---

* German, "Lunatic Asylums."

"I was still thinking of Woyzeck's female brain," he replied. "Perhaps, my dear Ennemoser, we should venture the hypothesis that it was not the one he was born with, but some later surgical implant. We have recent accounts from England about such feats being performed by a certain Dr. Frankenstein."

Schmitz and Bock began to laugh.

"Maybe," Clarus continued, "we have executed the wrong man and should try to ferret out the mad surgeon behind the innocent Woyzeck. A notice in Dr. Bergk's *Museum of the Occult* might put us on the right track here." Even Ennemoser and Bergk joined the general laughter.

"The incorrigible Herr Hofrath," chuckled Ennemoser. "But let's discuss that in a more cheerful place. You promised to show me where Mephistopheles bewitched the drunken Leipzigers, Dr. Clarus. I hope you'll all join us."

The suggestion was eagerly accepted by the others, and the five men went to spend what was left of the day in the *Gemütlichkeit* of Auerbach's Tavern,* just a hundred yards from the site of the morning's execution.

---

* The locale of a famous scene in Goethe's *Faust* I, line 2073ff.

Woyzecks letzte Worte.

Vater, ich komme! Ja, mein himmlischer Vater, du rufst mich, dein gnädiger Wille geschehe, Dank, herzlicher Dank, Preis und Ehre sey dir, Allerbarmer, daß du bei aller meiner großen Schuld dennoch liebreich auf mich blickst und mich würdigst, dein zu seyn, Dank sey dir, daß du nach so vielen ausgestandenen Leiden die Thränen trocknest, deren ich dir so manche weinte. Vater! ich befehle meinen Geist in deine Hände! dir leb ich, dir sterb ich, dein bin ich tod und lebendig. Amen!

Herr hilf! Herr laß es wohl gelingen!

Woyzeck's last prayer. Broadsheet of 1824.
Museum for the History of the City of Leipzig.

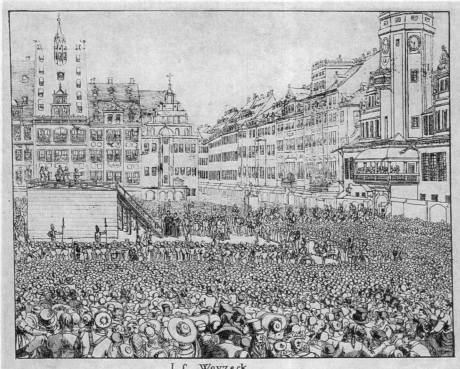

I. C. Woyzeck.

Geht seinnen Tode als reuevoller Christ entgegen, auf dem Marktplatze zu Leipzig, den 27 August 1824.

"Woyzeck faces death as a repenting Christian on
the market place in Leipzig on August 27, 1824."
Lithograph by C.G.H. Geißler of 1824.
Museum for the History of the City of Leipzig.

THE BERGK-SCHOPENHAUER
CORRESPONDENCE
Part One

Leipzig, February 5, 1820

Dear Arthur:

How strange, yet fascinating what you write about your
elusive encounter with the ill-famed poet-lord from England.* Meanwhile I met your old friend, the Olympian,
in Weimar. It was all rather strange. Chaperoned by our
boring, though highly regarded Hofrath Rochlitz, I went
to Weimar to hear Goethe talk of himself, but instead,
found him mostly talking about you. However, let me
tell you about my first glimpse of the great poet. You
know how much I rely on intuition! As when I saw you
on that first occasion by the sunlit window of the Dresden

---

* As Klaus told me, neither Schopenhauer's nor Bergk's letters
previous to the above were found amongst the papers he
discovered in 1938. But the mention of the ill-famed poet-lord
from England no doubt refers to Lord Byron. Schopenhauer
later recalled how he went to Italy armed with Goethe's letter
of introduction to Byron. "In Venice I wanted to go and see him
with Goethe's letter, when one day I abandoned the idea
completely. I was walking along the Lido with my mistress,
when this Dulcinea suddenly burst out in the greatest excitement: *'Ecco il poeta inglese!'* Byron dashed past us on horseback,
and my donna couldn't get over this experience all day. Hence
I decided not to deliver Goethe's letter. I was afraid of being
cuckolded. How much I have come to regret it since!"

Schloss Café (remember?) listening to a full-bosomed blond, with that charmingly contemptuous smile of yours playing 'round your lips. That large, rounded (may I say?) Promethean forehead, those fiery yet melancholy eyes, and that full, sensuous mouth. Looking at you, I thought: surely he is one of that new tribe of Romantic poet-philosophers who storm heaven and hell in search of the innermost secrets of the cosmos. But back to Goethe.

I confess that I felt rather nervous and ill at ease in his chilly and barren *salle de reception*. Waiting for him, we had ample time to look at Goethe's various busts and statues. Finally a door opened at the far end, through which a tall figure came striding towards us in utter abstraction. Everything about him—the long, blue *surtout* hanging loosely on the gaunt body, the heavily powdered hair, the neckcloth in disarray—seemed somehow grotesque, antique, and eerie. Without uttering a word, Goethe finally stood in front of me, his eyes looking through me rather than at me. Had a *revenant* appeared to me, I could not have been more dumbfounded. Like a true ghost, Goethe obviously wanted me to talk to him first. Just remembering it, still sends a chill down my spine.

All I could do was stare at his face, whose calm barely hides the volcanic energy smouldering beneath. Have you ever looked at his eyes, rather than lose yourself in them? His iris is of three colours, a blue outer ring surrounding the brown core which in turn encircles a pitch-black pupil, with a whitish *arcus senilis* forming the outer circumference of these three rings. How could I ever forget it after standing face to face with him in silence for what seemed like an eternity? Then I suddenly heard myself speak, while a kindly smile started lighting up Goethe's features. I thanked his Excellency for the honour of receiving me and told him about my attempts to acquaint myself with the newest metaphysical speculations.

"So you no doubt have read the recent work of my young friend Arthur Schopenhauer?" he wondered.

No, I hadn't, I admitted, but quickly added that I did know your earlier writings and that, in fact, I had met you during the years when you lived in Dresden.

Once active, Goethe's spectral appearance underwent a complete transformation. Would we like to see his prints, and coins, and minerals. Or his busts? Of course we did, so out from underneath his *surtout* came a heavy bundle of keys which he wears attached to a massive belt. But why tell you any of this? You must have seen it all yourself. There is something almost furious about how he does things: how he opens and locks his numerous show-cases, hands you his carefully ordered folders, or points out this or that precious item— like his small gold bust of Napoleon. It was as if he were trying to fill some gaping void that might engulf us, if only for a few seconds we fell silent or ceased being active.

As the morning wore on, Hofrath Rochlitz and I, of course, were not the only ones in his Excellency's presence. No doubt you have seen how Goethe holds court amidst his diverse employees, dependants and guests. In fact, after so much of his attention, which, in return for *his* time, solicits the utmost of what one's intellectual powers can render, I felt relieved in being relegated to one of several persons catering to his physical and spiritual needs. I am told that every other day Goethe has his hair reset with heated curling irons, and this was the day for having it done. But like a Napoleon of the spirit, he always seems to want to be both acted upon and active at once—have the outside world coddle, stimulate or prod him in a ceaseless and mingled flow of events while pursuing diverse simultaneous activities himself. Now we saw the hedonist contentedly abandoning himself to the skilful hands of his hairdresser, then the poet suddenly anxious to dictate some lines to his secretary, next the former statesman answering a knock on the door with a forceful "Come in!" turn his ear to a whispered message from his friend and sovereign, Grand Duke Karl August of Saxe-Weimar-Eisenach, and release the liveried envoy with a quickly formulated letter full of seasoned and elegantly articulated counsel. It was amazing to watch how, after this interruption, he went back to dictating lines of verse as if reading them from a typeset page. In between all this he asked his servant to fetch him your *World as Will and Idea,* all the while enjoying his hairdresser's assiduities with pronounced though dignified relish.

Then, leafing through your two volumes and reading here and there, Goethe, suddenly turning to me, said: "The German philistines will not like him, and, as he tells me, punish him with their silence. But I am sure that he will grow to be head and shoulders above us all."* Then after once again losing himself in your pages, he added: "He is a truly independent thinker who expresses his thoughts with honest and pleasing precision. At first I found his style somewhat forbidding; but once you get used to renaming things as he wants them, he can be read with great facility and pleasure. The same applies to his ideas, which are often not unlike my own—though given my German readers I make Mephistopheles take the blame for them rather than uttering them myself."

An almost imperceptible smile became more pronounced as he added: "If only people could see the things I have hidden in my *Walpurgissack!*"

"*Walpurgissack?*" I asked.

Goethe had obviously anticipated my question. "My *Walpurgissack,*" he explained with the solemn seriousness of a judge of hell, "is a kind of infernal bag, container, or whatever you want to call it. Originally, I

---

* Goethe's expression, "*der wächst uns allen noch einmal über den Kopf,*" of course, may imply some irony, since Schopenhauer was of relatively short stature.

simply hid in it poems related to the witches' scenes in *Faust*. But since then its function has somehow broadened—just like hell, which at first was a single abode, and later came to include purgatory and diverse limbos. Each piece of paper which ends up in this *Walpurgissack* falls down into hell, and from hell, as you know, there is no redemption. Sometimes I feel like tossing myself into it too. Down at its bottom burns an unquenchable fire which, once it spreads, spares neither friend nor foe."

By now the smile had disappeared from Goethe's face. "I would advise people not to approach this blaze too closely. I am terrified by it myself."

Everyone was abashed to hear Goethe reveal himself in this vehement fashion, while he reimmersed himself in your pages without paying the least attention to our consternation. Then suddenly he began reading from your book, his powerful voice vibrant and almost irate with emotion:

"What else is this world but a playground of tortured and anguished beings, who can only survive in that one devours the other; what else but a place in which every beast of prey is the living tomb of thousands of other creatures and its self-preservation a chain of painful deaths; a place where consciousness merely sharpens the sensitivity to feel pain, which reaches its highest degree in man, the more so the more intelligent he is."

Then after another moment of silence, Goethe added: "They call him a pessimist who hates life, failing to see the fierceness of his compassion. No doubt the time is not ripe for this young man's vision; perhaps it never will or even should be. Even Arjuna in the *Bhagavad Gita*, which he quotes like his bible, averts his eyes from the ultimate destruction as if to stare at it were the sin of sins. My own happier temperament finds refuge from it in the enclosures of fruitful activity and thought. I still remember the couplet I wrote in Schopenhauer's remembrance book.

Willst du dich deines Werthes freuen,

So musst der Welt du Werth verleihen.*"

As a smile reappeared on his face, Goethe continued: "But this, of course, is precisely what he will not do."

Then as the morning toilet reached its conclusion, Goethe's thoughts turned to other subjects. So I finally found time to fill in the notes I'd taken right before his eyes. I'd heard that Goethe is quite used to his visitors doing this. And how else could I've retained verbatim (as I quote them in this letter) all his precious words. Certainly not with this old tired brain of mine. Some of Goethe's comments strike me as rather cryptic, but I am sure you can make better sense of them than I.

There is much else worth reporting from Weimar, more of which perhaps in a future letter. But I should not forget to mention meeting your tender-hearted sister Adele as well as your brilliant and charming mother. (By the way, it is they who told me you had temporarily gone back to Dresden.) Both of them send their love and wish you success with your *Habilitation* in Berlin. Yes, good luck, old friend, and send more of your news, and of your growing ill fame in Rome!** You know how much I relish your colourful anecdotes and caustic humour. And now I will plunge into *Die Welt* which lies open in front of me as I write this.

Yours as ever
Adam Bergk

---

* German, "If you wish to enjoy your own worth / You have to lend worth to the world."

** Did Schopenhauer, in his lost letter to Bergk, speak of the notoriety he acquired in Rome? This is suggested by his sister's letter responding to his account (also lost) of the impression he left behind there. "Half jokingly," Adele writes, "you touch upon the bad reputation which you brought to Rome and, when you continued your journey, left there behind you. It is to my unutterable sorrow that I hear something of the kind. Stomp such calumny under foot if you have to; but I implore

—82—

Berlin, March 17, 1820

Dear Adam:

Just a note to thank you for your long letter. It reached me the day before my departure for Berlin. Goethe's comments sound familiar but are nonetheless welcome for their detail. I have not time to give my response in full, but after two recent encounters we had last August, Goethe knows all too well what it is. The jurist's motto is: *fiat justitia et pereat mundus,** my own, as I told him: *vigeat veritas et pereat mundus.*** But at least he understands what I am saying, and that's more than I can say of anyone else.

Here in Berlin I am busy preparing my *disputatio pro venia legendi**** on the four different kinds of causality. It will take place on March 23, 1820. Professor Dr. Hegel, that repulsive, platitudinous charlatan and unprecedented scribbler of nonsense, yesterday gave me his placet for the proposed topic. Once this is done, I shall lecture at precisely the time when Hegel dispenses his humbug on 'Logic and Metaphysics.' We shall see if there are students left with their brains uncorrupted by his contagious nonsense. Otherwise back to Italy and

---

you don't let it be your delight. I can guess at the accusations you mention. Let me confess, that out of mere cowardice, I often put aside your book when I read a particular passage in it. Your philosophical views are not altogether alien to me; and I am far from bigoted and not even truly and genuinely a Christian, the way we conceive of it these days: nonetheless I am afraid that your opinions and creeds differ from mine, and I dread the painfulness of such dissent."

* Latin, "Let there be justice and the world go to hell."

** Latin, "Let the truth prevail and the world go to hell."

*** Latin, "Disputation to obtain the permission to lecture." This was the academic requirement for becoming a *Privatdozent* or person who has the right to teach at a university.

*Lambe, ingrata, mihi nudas, Germania, nates!** Write me again as soon as you can.

Yours
Arthur

P.S. By the way, I have definitively broken with both my mother and sister and prefer to neither hear of nor talk about them, let alone speak to them, unless I have to.

Leipzig, May 28, 1820

Dear Arthur:

No doubt this will find you a well-installed *Herr Privatdozent* whose popularity is about to give apoplexy to Hegel. How much I would have liked to attend your *disputatio pro venia legendi!* Don't forget to let me know how it went. For this and other reasons, Berlin has been much on my mind of late. Did you follow the developments of the *Turnvater* Jahn** affair? I just had a long report about it from my friend, Varnhagen von Ense. You know how I keep my spies in every city. Varnhagen writes how Metternich, via Fürst Wittgenstein, is turning Prussia into a police state. Notables like Schleiermacher are accused of seducing the young while people from all walks of life are arrested. I have a feeling Sand's murder

---

* Latin, "Lick my bare behind, thou ungrateful Germany."

** F. L. Jahn (1778-1852), German patriot, active in efforts to free Germany from Napoleonic rule. His *Turnverein*, a gymnastic organization, purposed to build strength and fellowship among the young, became a centre for nationalism and the movement to unify Germany. Charged with revolutionary activities, Jahn was arrested in 1819.

of Kotzebue* only served the authorities as a pretext. That wretched Sand! Without him, Metternich certainly could never have pushed through his Carlsbad Decrees, which, by the looks of it, will stay with us for ever. But thank God, there is some resistance.

Varnhagen tells me that the King, about a year ago, appointed E.T.A. Hoffman** to his new Commission for the Investigation of Treasonable Organizations and Subversive Activities, but with unexpected results. You no doubt know that Hoffmann, apart from being a writer-composer-artist, is a highly regarded criminal expert who usually keeps his two identities neatly separate. But in this case, the artist seems to have gotten the better of his bourgeois double. Hoffmann's report on *Turnvater* Jahn (a man whom, by the way, he detests) made the Commission decide that the defendant was innocent and hence should be released from prison. Then, when Jahn sued the dreaded police chief, von Kamptz, Hoffmann's Commission again backed the defendant and (imagine!) summoned von Kamptz for a hearing. At that point, King Friedrich Wilhelm himself

---

* August von Kotzebue (1761-1819), popular playwright and librettist, but notorious for his reactionary propaganda, worked as an agent of Czar Alexander I when he was murdered by the student Sand. The assassination provided the pretext for the Carlsbad Decrees adopted by the ministers of the German states at a conference convened and dominated by Fürst Metternich. The decrees which remained in effect until 1848 provided for uniform press censorship, and close supervision of the universities, with the aim of suppressing all liberal agitation against the conservative governments in Germany. It was particularly directed against organizations like Jahn's *Turnverein* and the student organizations, or *Burschenschaften*, of which Sand was an active member. Sand was beheaded in Mannheim on May 21, 1820.

** E.T.A. Hoffmann (1776-1822), composer and novelist, mainly famous for his Gothic tales of madness, grotesquerie and horror.

had to come to von Kamptz's rescue. But the battle between him and Hoffmann rages on, with most Berliners siding with Hoffmann. You must have noticed some of this excitement. Varnhagen writes that news of Sand's execution (Teutonic style, with a two-handed double-edged sword) have further stirred the unrest. Will there be the revolution so much feared by the authorities? Torch-bearing students gathered in the *Hasenheide* for a nocturnal requiem in Sand's honour; a poem on his death is circulating amongst them, etc.

But enough for this time from your gossipy old Adam.

P.S. I am deeply immersed in *The World as Will and Idea* and will write you about it soon.

Berlin, June 2, 1821

Dear friend Adam:

I am sorry for being so late in replying to your last letter. Yet what is there to report but the eternal drudgery of life. No, I had no idea what political scandals were raging around me. Why bother? In principle I agree with Voltaire: *Point de politique en littérature! il faut dire la vérité, et s'immoler.** The true philosopher deals with those facts alone which affect mankind everywhere and at all times alike; he ignores the politics of the day; and (unlike Hegel whose state-employed sodden brain hails Prussia as the world spirit's final unfolding) despises kowtowing to those in power.

But you should hear that *pontifex maximus* of tomfoolery address the full assembly of his worshipful

---

* French, "Absolutely no politics in literature: one has to say the truth and immolate oneself."

dunce-cap followers. Says he: "I am inclined to say, like Christ, that I teach the truth and that I am the truth." During my *disputatio* he asked me: "What is the motivation when a horse lies down in the street?" I answered: "It's found in the horse's joint awareness of its fatigue and of the ground underneath its hooves," and added, amid growing laughter, "for the horse would hardly lie down if it found itself standing on an abyss." But our latter day Jesus Christ was not amused. "So you count the animal functions among the motivations?" he insisted, glaring sullenly at his jocular colleagues. I explained to this ignoramus, who obviously hasn't read Haller, that modern physiology separates unconscious from conscious animal functions. Once ruffled, the *summus philosophus* turned increasingly self-righteous. But no luck for him that day! When he kept on mumbling his inane jargon, a professor of medicine, impatiently jumping to his feet, put a sudden end to the debates. "You will forgive me, Herr Kollege," said he, "but Dr. Schopenhauer is absolutely right on this point. Our discipline *does* make the distinction he mentioned."

My lecturing has been less than triumphant. I hoped to find at least a few whose brains are not stuffed to the brim with Hegelian tripe, but in vain:

> Car tous suivront la créance et estude,
> De l'ignorante et sotte multitude,
> Dont le plus lourd sera reçu pour juge.*

The few students I had hardly made the drudgery worth my while. So I lectured till August, then even before the end of term decided *ecclesia missa est.*** The only result of my academic endeavours so far is a calumnious concoction of distorted quotes and critical inanities which one of

---

* French, "For they will follow the belief and choice / Of the ignorant and stupid multitude / whose dullest member will be welcomed as judge." (Rabelais, *Gargantua*, Chapter 68, V, 45-47.)

** Latin, "Church is over."

my students, F.E. Beneke, unsuccessfully trying to hide under the cloak of anonymity, published in the *Jenaische Literaturzeitung*. It might amuse you to read my recent letter to the editor, entitled "Necessary reprimand for mendaciously making up quotations."

Thus stripped of office and fame, I was also threatened with being cheated out of part of the fortune left me by my dearly remembered father, by the same smooth-faced scoundrel Muhl who, pretending bankruptcy, has already robbed my sister and mother of their share of the inheritance. But I decided to call his bluff and prove to him that one's being a philosopher does not mean that one has to be a fool. Muhl argued his insolvency whenever I asked for my money, so I taught this rascal the syllogism with which Kant proves the moral freedom of man, viz. how we conclude about what a man can do from what he ought to do. Or *lingua vulgi:** since he would not pay up willingly, I made him pay up in court.

Yours
Arthur

Leipzig, June 10, 1821

Dear friend:

What have you done to old Adam? Is it right that a man over half-a-century old should abandon his long-cherished beliefs. But I have no choice. If it is to be for better or worse, I know not: I only know it has happened. *The World as Will and Idea* has changed my life so irrevocably that the attempt to return to my former creeds would be like trying to make myself once again believe in the stork

---

* Latin, "In the language of the common people."

that brings babies. For you have more than just changed (or rather turned inside out) my *Weltanschauung*: I feel like a modern Lazarus come back from the dead, who has found out that all that the living ever felt, believed, and thought, is mere lies and self-delusion. Wilt thou, like a latter-day serpent, make us eat from the tree of life and cause our ultimate fall into a knowledge of things which should have stayed Nature's secret for ever?

I have to admit that before you convinced me, I was angry with denial, which lasted until well after I had reread your volumes. In fact, my Damascus did not occur at all while travelling through your pages. It happened, when least expected, while sitting on a bench in the *Bösische Garten* early one evening. At that moment your ideas were as far from my mind, or so it seemed, as they might be. There in front of me, on another park bench, were two young lovers, and I watched them as closely as modesty permitted. Our cosmopolitan "little Paris" allows the young some freedom on these occasions and, as you know, I am far from prudish myself. The sight of the two warmed my old heart. How tenderly they kissed and touched each other! And how they sat, oblivious of the world around them, looking into each other's eyes with tremulous affection! If there is a heaven on earth, I thought, then these two are in it. But I suddenly realized that what I saw was a hell.

For what else was their delight but nature's ruse to perpetuate suffering and death? What else would their moment of greatest bliss be, when his genitals would fuse with hers, but the birth of another life with its burden of misery and strife, perhaps even torture, captivity, and madness? Like these lovers in front of me, all others before them had vowed love eternal, while merely acting their short-lived part in the puppet show of Nature who cares all for life and nothing for the living.

Only half-way through this train of thought, as a profound sadness, yea, even nausea, took possession of my whole being, did I realize that I was looking at them through your eyes. At the same time, I recalled and suddenly understood your phrase about the genitals as the "focal point of the Will" which at first had struck me as rather contrived. The page is open in front of me as I write this: "Nature, too, whose inner being is the will to live, with all its might drives man and beast to reproduce themselves. Once this is done, Nature has reached her purpose concerning the individual, and is thoroughly indifferent concerning its destruction. For, to her, as the Will of Life, the preservation of the species is essential, but the individual nothing." As with this, so with the rest. I suddenly understand, or rather feel, your thoughts, as if they had been implanted in my brain. Is this how your fatal lore will creep up on the generations to come?

As I sat on the park bench, I also remembered Goethe saying that they call you a pessimist who hates life but ignore the fierceness of your compassion. And yes, I felt that too, a sheer boundless pity for those two, so caught in the snares of their delusions, while merely acting their narrow parts in the bitter drama of endless reproduction, misery, and death; and along with that pity a sudden rage against the philosophers, priests, and educators who reinforce these delusions in the name of their false idols. How true what you say about our cruel fantasies of hell as in fact applying to life's endless cycles here on earth, with each child atoning with its suffering and death for its parents' reproductive sins.

Or have I carried all this too far? Do write me soon. I am much in need of spiritual comfort.

Yours as ever
Adam

Berlin, June 18, 1821

Dear Adam:

Is Adam Bergk to be the first of my Apostles? I have a feeling that men like you—independent and courageous—will help bridge the rift between myself and the generations to come. Let University hirelings, priests, and scribbling scoundrels malign or ignore me as they will: by 1900 mankind *nolens volens* will have swallowed my basic ideas. Yes, you did see those lovers on the bench through my eyes. In truly Adamic fashion, you also hit upon the *punctum pruriens** of my system. Adam's fall is indeed but an allegory of man's sexual enslavement to life. I have adumbrated that much in my book but will expand on it in a separate treatise to be entitled "The Metaphysics of Sexuality." You know that I have suffered my share of such enslavement myself, enough to make me wish, with St. Augustine, that celibacy become the universal law of the race. *Novi quosdam,* writes he, *qui murmurent: quid, si, inquiunt, omnes velint ab omni concubitu abstinere, unde subsistet genus humanum?—Utinam omnes hoc vellent! . . . multo citius . . . acceleraretur terminus mundi.*** Have you ever seen a child with the croup, its little chest choking for breath, staring at you with uncomprehending and terrified eyes, until it dies under horrid convulsion? There you have them, the ultimate joys of sex!

At age seventeen while still devoid of all real education I was first struck by the misery of life—just like the young Buddha coming to understand illness, pain, decrepitude, and death. That truth, of which the world speaks so clearly and loudly, overwhelmed the Jewish

---

* Latin, "Prurient point."
** Latin, "I know some who grumble and say: If all were to abstain from sex, how could the human race survive? Would that all wanted to abstain . . . for thanks to that we'd arrive at the end of the world all the faster."

doctrines which, like everyone else, I'd been made to absorb. From then on, I concluded that this *"meilleur des mondes possibles"** cannot be the work of an all-benevolent Creator.

Yours
Arthur

Leipzig, June 25, 1821

Dear Arthur:

The big news here is that Leipzig has had a murder—the first in over two decades. On June 21, a certain Johann Christian Woyzeck, aetas 41, stabbed to death his 46-year-old mistress, widow of *Chirurgus* Woost, in the hallway of *Sandgasse* 6, an area well known for its low-life prostitution. *Un crime passionel!* You know about my special interest in such matters. The weapon was a broken sword to which the delinquent had attached a handle. The victim was dead on the spot, after being stabbed seven times both in the chest and lower abdomen. According to the official dissection report, the lethal stroke pierced her left bosom, then the first rib cage artery, both layers of the pleura, and finally the lower aorta at a place totally inaccessible to surgical skill. As an expert in criminal law I have, as you know, free access to Saxony's prisons, and I've made an appointment to visit Woyzeck tomorrow. We'll see what trouble I can stir up in order to save him from execution. My thoughts on the issue still remain those I expressed years ago in my *Philosophy of Penal Law:*** capital punishment, for what-

---

* French, "Best of all possible worlds."

** Adam Bergk's *Die Philosophie des Peinlichen Rechts* was published in 1802.

ever reason, is a form of institutionalized crime worse than murder.

I am glad you don't seem to think that I've misrepresented your deep thoughts. Meanwhile I have begun to see more of the positive sides of your system: the sharp breeze it will send through the stuffy chambers of our state-and church-employed educators and thinkers! Out of sheer spite I recommended your book to Heinroth at a local reception last Friday. Did you ever look at his *Disturbances of the Life of the Soul**—Vogel here in Leipzig put it out at the same time that Brockhaus published *The World*. Insanity, Heinroth argues, stems from "vice and sin," it's "the fruit of moral disease." A visit to his *St. Georgen* confirms one's worst suspicions about how such theorems translate into therapy. Heinroth's so-called Punishment Chamber in that hospital looks much like the torture chamber in the old town hall; only there is the new array of up-to-date technical machinery, like Langermann's cell or Reil's fly-wheel, added to the traditional ropes, pulleys and branding irons.

Heinroth, a professed Christian, is a staunch supporter of the "pain-inflicting method" of "the excellent Horn" at Berlin's *Charité*.** Non-specialists are unwelcome at his Punishment Chamber sessions, so I ignore what goes on there. But Heinroth, who boasts of having used Horn's "extremely attractive method" in "many cases of insane melancholia, rage, and even secondary idiocy," gives us a good idea. The method, he writes in his book, is either "negative"—when the patient is deprived of "food, air, light, freedom of motion, etc."—or "positive" in the sense of inflicting pain either externally or internally. "To the internal antagonistic remedies (he writes) belong purgatives producing nausea and vomiting, and medicaments stimulating salivation; to the ex-

---

* *Störungen des Seelenlebens*, published in 1818.

** A famous Berlin hospital.

ternal ones belong all the means which produce intense irritation of the skin and stimulate the peripheral activity: intense tickling, sternutators, the nestle whip, artificially produced skin disease, cauterizing and burning means, baths (preferably cold), drenchings, showers, immersion."

You should see this man with his large, brown, melancholy eyes, his benevolent airs and his fleshy, slightly smiling mouth. The worst about him is the genuineness of his convictions. Much like the inquisitors of old, he tortures his patients in order to save their souls. Yet one wonders if his praise of Horn's method would have been quite as lavish had his book appeared just a few months later. For meanwhile, the "excellent Horn" was relieved of his duties for killing one of his patients. The poor follow was put into the *Hornsche Sack* where he died of asphyxiation.

Thank you for naming me your first Apostle. I'll do what I can.

Yours
Adam

[Undated]

Dear Adam:

The study of psychology, as practised by most people, is vain, for there is no psyche; man cannot be studied alone, but only in connection with the world—microcosm and macrocosm combined. So I agree with you about Heinroth, but not re Woyzeck. Even Beccaria, whom you follow, grants that the punishment must equal the crime; to think we can replace punishment by education is one of our modern, philanthropic delusions. Education is powerless against the will, and honesty can be taught least of all. What greater lure to do mischief than the sight of our modern state prisons—here the potential rapist or robber can hope to enjoy the luxurious living denied to his poor, but honest compatriots.

Of course, none of this is a question of ethics. We must punish the crime, not the criminal. What Woyzeck did is what we all wish to do sometime or other. Napoleon or the assassin whose limbs are broken on the wheel are not more evil than us: many a coward would do worse than they did; what he lacks is the will to act out his wishes. But society must protect the lives of its members, and this can be done through forceful deterrents alone. To those who, like you, would abolish capital punishment, I say: "Let's get rid of it, but not before getting rid of murder first." But by all means let me know more about Woyzeck.

Yours
Arthur

[Undated]

Dear Arthur:

Perhaps I might save Woyzeck's life without getting rid of capital punishment first. Here is what happened. When I stepped into his cell Woyzeck simply pulled his cap down over his deeply-lined features. All I could see was his jaw slowly chewing tobacco.

"I've come to see if I might help!" My opening sentence was greeted with silence.

Then after about two minutes, during which I continued my overtures, he said, his eyes still invisible under his cap: "You sound like a priest."

"I am a criminologist come to find out why you murdered the Woostin."

"She was a pig and an animal, that's why."

"What did she do to you?"

I was taken aback by his romantically sensitive face when he suddenly looked at me with his large-pupilled greenish eyes. "I told you. She was an animal."

But instead of the anger that should accompany this remark, an almost imperceptible smile became visible around his slightly tremulous lips.

Then, in an accent and language markedly different from the lower class jargon he had spoken earlier, he added: "I confessed my crime and would like to be left to die in peace."

Naturally, I felt tempted to continue the conversation, but then, no doubt wisely, decided to let things rest. Meanwhile, Woyzeck had once again lowered his chin onto his chest.

But imagine what happened when I came home from the prison! There was my newspaper carrier, Haase, waiting for me in a state of barely concealed agitation. Woyzeck, he told me, had been his lodger for several months until just a few weeks before the murder. According to what he told me, I am quite sure that Woyzeck is a madman. That strange smile on his lips when he asked to be left to die in peace! Or that sudden change from a lower class jargon to the diction of the educated classes! He seems like two persons in one.

Here is Haase's story. Woyzeck lived in his house from last year's Johannis to a few weeks before Michaelis. He occupied a windowless attic where, with the help of a lamp, he did pasteboard work during the day. But Haase's wife soon became rather scared of her strange lodger. For one thing, she strongly disliked the Woostin, who, usually unannounced, came to see Woyzeck at any time of the day or night. Haase describes her as a swarthy, thick set, rather shortish creature of distinctly middle-aged features.

Was there anything in her appearance or manner

to explain her attractiveness to the younger Woyzeck, I asked him.

Haase couldn't tell. For her age, he claims, she was rather coquettish; there was something voracious, hyena-like about her. Her movements, especially of her hands, were of a strange, somehow calculated slowness. At the same time, she'd easily flare up in anger. She and Woyzeck were often heard quarrelling in the attic. Haase also recalls her foul language when once or twice he went up to call them to order.

But what really disturbed Frau Haase were Woyzeck's ghosts. The first time it happened, she and her husband had just gone to bed. Woyzeck as usual came in late and quietly walked up to his attic. But after a while they heard him run quickly back down the stairs. Then there was a knock on their bedroom door.

"The man I faced when I opened," recalls Haase, "looked much like a ghost himself. He was shaking, his face was as white as a sheet, and the hair on his balding head was visibly standing on end. With a squeaking, almost inaudible voice he told us that when he had lain down in bed, there had been a prolonged rustling, then a female voice saying: 'Oh come, come to me!' I instantly took my lantern and went up to the attic. There was nothing. But I felt sorry for Woyzeck and, for the next three nights, let him sleep downstairs near us."

Once back in the attic, Woyzeck had more of the same spectral visions. He felt that invisible hands were patting and pulling his blanket. The voices had become lower, but were nonetheless audible and distinct. One of them, he thought, was the Devil's. He felt as if his heart were touched by a needle, and as he tried to betake himself to his prayers, this voice shouted: "There you have him, your God of love!"* Eventually even daylight gave him no respite from his visitations. So, instead of doing his pasteboard work, he went roaming around the

---

* "Da hast du den lieben Gott!"

streets. Things came to another climax just a few weeks before he left the Haases. Roughly an hour before midnight, he was heard walking down the staircase shouting, "There it comes! There it comes!" At this stage even Herr Haase was too afraid to confront him. He refused to open when Woyzeck, once again, knocked on their bedroom door. Hence neither he nor his wife are quite sure what happened next. All they could make out was his voice shouting, "I am lost!" as his body seemed to be rolling on the floor planks. Then, until daylight started peeping into their window, Woyzeck's steps were heard pacing restlessly up and down the hallway.

What we might have here, then, is a murder committed due to mental alienation. But I am afraid that our local justice will not wish to bother with such niceties. Instead, they'll no doubt push for a speedy execution. After all, we've been famous for centuries for our decapitation procedures! However, Adam has already done his damnedest to stir up trouble. Two colleagues, county court physician Dr. C.M. Marc in Bamberg and Professor J.C.A. Grohmann in Hamburg, have been told what I am telling you and asked to monitor the coming trial. (Perhaps you have seen Grohmann's pieces on crime and insanity in Hufeland's *Journal* and Nasse's *Magazine for Psychic Doctors*.) I have also put a notice into the *Nürnberger Correspondenten*, briefly outlining the crime as well as the mental state of the delinquent. How much they'll love me for it here in Leipzig! But there is simply no other way to rouse our court system from its pre-enlightenment slumbers.

Hearing about Woyzeck's ghosts made me wonder what you think of recent mesmeric attempts to enter the world of spirits. Here and there in *The World* you allude to somnambulistic trances, or you quote, with approval it seems, from Kieser's *Archiv*.* How much I'd

---

* *Archiv für den Thierischen Magnetismus*, edited by Dr. C. A. Eschenmayer, Dr. D. G. Kieser and Dr. Fr. Nasse (later replaced by C. G. Nees von Esenbeck) during 1817-1822.

like to know what goes on in Wolfart's famous Mesmeric Clinic in Berlin! But given your hermit's life you no doubt wouldn't bother to go there.

Yours
Adam

Berlin, July 28, 1821

Dear Adam:

No, I have been to Wolfart's Clinic. I thought you knew how closely I've followed animal magnetism over the years—in fact, I suspect it might turn out to be mankind's greatest discovery ever. It's just that most of it still remains mere promise, or, as Goethe once warned me, mesmerism is still "too full of mouseholes and mouse-traps." Wolfart's clinic is a typical instance: the man himself, though well-intentioned, is no doubt corrupt, his conversation a hodge-podge of pseudo-scientific jargon and pious sentiments; his so-called clinic combines the seedy plushness of a Parisian brothel with the fake solemnity of a cure-all shrine for deluded pilgrims.

The great magus himself took me into his inner sanctum. It's a large, dimly-lit, oval-shaped room, all wallpapered in dark red, with two *baquets* at its elliptical centres; I won't bore you with a detailed description of these contraptions. Basically, each of them looks like a four-legged massive iron stove (somewhat inappropriately displaying Asclepius's serpent), which through a big hollow glass tube connects with a bowl, of proportionate size, supported by four, about twenty-five-*Zoll*-long, metal staffs; it's filled to the rim with a watery concoction of iron filings, glass pearls, seeds, and other magnetized ingredients. Via small holes on the upper edges of this container, the patients, about twelve of them around each *baquet*, dip iron staffs into the mesmeric strong broth, then apply these magical wands to their *epigastrium** and rub themselves until they fall into a trance. According to my chaperone, nearly everything from hysterical vapours to consumption and tape-worms has been cured by this ingenious method. He would like to cure syphilis as well, if it weren't for the fear of contagion which might be spread by his magical pokers.

For all his quiet, though somewhat fussy manner, Wolfart runs this outfit with businesslike efficiency. The poor, who come in great numbers, are treated in the morning, the well-to-do, in somewhat smaller hordes, in the afternoon. Thus they rub away in complete silence, the men around one *baquet*, the women around the other, while the newcomers are eagerly waiting to take their places. All preserve the same ghost-like silence. Then as the patients, one by one, become entranced, they are escorted to small sofas placed along the wall, each of them in its own little boudoir made of green curtains. Here our father confessor whispers a few words to each one of them in turn, then lends his ear to their somnambulistic effusions. It's hard to imagine that Schleiermacher, Wilhelm and Caroline von Humboldt, Fürst Hardenberg, plus his wife and brother, and many other celebrities, have subjected themselves to this treatment. I was allowed to talk to one of the entranced ladies, but came away unenlightened about the beyond. What she said to me bore the obvious imprint of her father confessor's ill-conceived zeal and platitudinous ideas. Like Wolfart himself, she struck me as unquestionably sincere, but nonetheless self-deluded.

Let me know what's happening re Woyzeck.

Yours
Arthur

---

* Part of the abdomen above the stomach.

Leipig, August 13, 1821

Dear Arthur:

After reading your graphic account it feels as if I'd been to Wolfart's clinic myself. How I wish we could resume our madcap escapades and heated debates of old back in Dresden.

Luckily, my efforts re Woyzeck are starting to bear results. As soon as the defence attorney read my notice in the *Nürnberger Correspondenten*, he asked that Woyzeck be medically examined. The Court consented, though with reluctance. What's more, they appointed precisely the man from whom they have least to fear. Hofrath Clarus, Leipzig's town physician, is full of contempt for the new psychic science, though he prides himself on knowing all there is to it. Like the Court officials, he feels that the law is the law and not to be meddled with by the "mad doctors." I've had my brushes with him at various times and know how he feels about concepts like Pinel's *manie sans delire* and Platner's *amentia occulta*. Patients afflicted by the former are immoral subjects, those driven by an irresistible impulse should be taught self-control and better manners, etc., etc.

Just yesterday, I sat in on one of his examinations of Woyzeck, which confirmed my worst suspicions. But there was something unexpected, and once again I would say insane, about Woyzeck. The man talking to us seemed to be doing everything in his power to speed up his conviction—as if he were using these examinations in order to commit suicide; what's more, he did it almost gleefully. But at least this wasn't the taciturn Woyzeck I'd met at first. So there is hope for my stratagems after all.

Yours
Adam

Berlin, August 20, 1821

Dear Adam:

Now Berlin, too, has its *crime celebre*. The culprit is a
gentleman of the best education, of decided accomplish-
ments as a philosopher, and one whom fortune has
favoured with ample financial means. This gentleman,
of otherwise spotless reputation, suddenly revealed a
heinous, yea fiendish side to his person: picking on a
mere pretext, he, a man in the prime of life, nearly
bludgeoned to death a hard-working, poor, and defence-
less old woman. All that was needed to prompt this
monstrous deed was his annoyance at being disturbed
by the woman, by profession a seamstress, as she was
innocently chatting with two friends in the *entrée* to his
apartment.

What happened on that fateful day of August
12th? Returning home, the gentleman asked the women
to vacate his lobby, and nearly accomplished his aim by
his inhuman rudeness; the mere sight of him, brandish-
ing his walking stick and screaming, was enough to make
the two friends take to their heels without further ado.
But the seamstress herself made the dire mistake to resist;
after all, she had the right of access to a drawer in the said
entrée and understandably felt reluctant to simply
abandon her poor belongings to this strange person. But
her persecutor was deaf to all argument. Instead, he gave
her five more minutes to vacate the *entrée*, but five minutes only, then vanished into his apartment.

From then on everything happened with an inhuman, clockwork precision. The gentleman came back
after exactly five minutes and, once again, asked the
seamstress to leave. When she refused, he gripped her
throat with his two hands and brutally dragged her
down the stairs. Then, rushing back up, he bombarded
her bruised body with her belongings from the top. The

poor woman, in gathering up her things, noted that one of them was still missing, and had the audacity to once again walk back up into the *entrée*—she will probably pay for her hardihood till her dying day, for the monster, who was lying in wait for his prey, first tore off her bonnet, then renewed his stranglehold around her neck and once again dragged the screaming and struggling woman down the stairs. When she finally collapsed, he continued to hit her with his fists, and finally trampled on her old body, all the while shouting his ghastly imprecations. It seems that he did not act like a man but more like some Indian Juggernaut or modern machine. Beaten unconscious and abandoned by her tormentor, the seamstress finally revived and dragged herself to a doctor, who found that she had suffered severe internal lesions.

You realize that this gentleman-monster is none other than your friend Arthur, as he is portrayed by a certain Caroline Louise Marquet and her lawyer in their plaint to the Berlin Court of Justice. Needless to say, the whole thing is a shameless fabrication. We know that women try to make up for their lack of intellect by cunning, but I had no first-hand experience of the extent to which such mendacity can be amplified when it allies itself with a lawyer's corruption. In honesty to my philosophical conviction, I admit that my feelings on the occasion were of a decidedly homicidal nature; but such emotions have nothing to do with the *facts*.

These are as prosaic and unsensational as can be: the woman had no right to be in my *entrée*, and since she refused to vacate it of her free will, I used my limited brachial powers to throw her out; but instead of gripping her neck, I tried (unsuccessfully) to encircle her unshapely body; instead of hitting or trampling on her, I simply warded off her windmill-like movements; instead of shouting "ghastly imprecations," I called her once and once only, in subject and predicate, "old bitch," which may be inadmissible from the point of the view of the law, but is no doubt accurate from any other. When she fell, she probably threw herself down on purpose; that she fainted is a complete lie; as for the rest: that her bonnet fell off her head; that her pulse was accelerated (to be explained in terms of frustrated female pride); that she received two bruises on her arms; or that she incurred the loss of a wart: all this is quite normal in such a fray. There was no further damage according to the report she hastened to get from her family doctor, a certain Kluge; but the cunning of such females is exceeded only by our society's permissiveness towards them; hence their intolerable arrogance; which reminds one of the sacred apes of Benares which, aware of their inviolability, think themselves free to do whatever they please. When it dawned on this creature that her two bruises and one torn-off wart might not be sufficient to carry her suit, she developed an inner malaise the next day and again ran to the said Dr. Kluge to have her ailment put on record. But no doubt the judge will see through these blatant fabrications. If only one could handle such matters oneself instead of having to put one's fate into the hands of rascally lawyers! The verdict is due by next April.

By all means let me know how you plan to rescue my fellow companion in crime.

Yours as ever
Arthur

[Undated]

Dear Arthur:

That Marquet sounds like trouble, so you'd better get yourself a good lawyer. Let me know if I can be of help.

A few years ago we had a similar case here in Leipzig in which the defendant was finally sentenced to pay a life pension to an astute and persistent imposter. Don't take it too lightly, my young friend.

Encouraged by your penultimate letter, I have been deepening my studies of animal magnetism in the direction of the spirit realm. It has always been my hope that mesmerism, once it outgrows its obscurantist phase, will one day allow us to conjure up and study ghosts in strictly experimental terms; and, if they let him live, Woyzeck might very well help us find out how. I knew of your interest in the mesmerists' venture but was unaware of its extent. Hence my reluctance to admit to such speculations. I feared your merciless wit!

Yours
Adam

Berlin, September 6, 1821

Dear Adam:

Another instance of how close my first Apostle's ideas have come to my own (or vice versa): what you say about mesmerism made me look up some notes jotted down in the original fervour of writing *The World*, and having reread these notes, made me plan out the main ideas towards a treatise to deal precisely with what you suggest: a *Prolegomenon to the Science of the Spirit World;* it is to show how mesmerism is turning up proof for my having cracked Kant's great riddle. For if pursued in proper fashion, animal magnetism can no doubt open the gates to the *Ding an sich* and let us inspect the Will's hidden workshop; its experiments will uncover the laws of the supernatural world just as the physicist's have revealed those of nature; they will accomplish in metaphysics what has already been achieved in physics. For even at this point no one who's read the mesmerists' writings can continue to doubt the authenticity of the spirit world (except he be some blockhead Anglican parson).

Crucial to the whole issue is that reason, as I have shown, evolved from the ganglia (i.e., nervous) system; that it's simply another of nature's tricks by which certain species, and primarily man, have learnt to fend for themselves in the eternal battle for survival; and that as this latecomer in the formation of life, it will forever remain the Will's bondslave. Yet while evolved by the Will and doomed to work in its service, reason is totally blind to its hidden master, who continues to work through the ganglia system. Only sometimes do we catch glimpses of the Will's hidden operations: for instance in madness which, by suspending reason, lets the Will erupt into the lunatic's visions; or in those big dreams dreamt, not by us, but by the Will, as it dreams through us. For there are two kinds: one which, as Aristotle observes, is but a continuation of thought during sleep, the other which lets us enter the secret realms of the *Ding an sich*. It's these latter dreams which enter through the gates of horn, while the former use the ivory gates (Homer, Od. XIX, 560). *Post mediam noctem, cum somnia vera* (Horace, Serm. I, 10, 33).* Cut loose from causality, time, and space, the person who dreams these big dreams fuses past, present, and future while drawing on memories deeper and larger than his; he is at home in the far distant future as much as in the immemorial past; he perceives things close by as clearly as those far away or hidden by mountains; he can affect (*actio in distans*) and be affected by (*passio a distante*) everything thus co-existent beyond time and space. In principle such vision is inaccessible to normal perception; the little of it which enters consciousness appears in

---

* Latin, "Past midnight, when dreams are true."

it riddled with allegories and symbols equally incomprehensible to reason.

It is only in sleepwaking that these deep dreams have direct access to the mind; for half awake and half asleep, the somnambulist sees the world, not with the eyes of the mind, but with his dream organ or *cerebrum abdominale*.* As he starts talking about these visions, they will, as the big dreams we try to remember, don the garments of conscious perception; but enough of the world of the Will, past causality, time, and space, as seen by the somnambulist's inner eye, will communicate itself through his words. Hence ordinary things from daily life may intermingle with spectral visions; a true ghost from the land of the dead (not one just made up as by our fanciful small dreams) will insert itself into the world of the living. Might Woyzeck's ghosts be of this kind? If they are, they are as real, or more so, than our so-called "real" experience. Let me know what you think. Perhaps you should try to do some more searching along these lines. Would they allow you to mesmerize Woyzeck?

Yours
Arthur

[Undated]

Dear Arthur:

I wish there were ways to explore what you suggest, but for the moment I can't even learn the basic facts of Woyzeck's life. The second time I sat in on him and Clarus (which also happened to be their last session) was even more frustrating than the first. Still, there's enough to make me suspect that Woyzeck's may be a case of

---

* Latin, "Abdominal brain."

psychopathia sexualis, a subject much neglected by our psychic doctors. Wouldn't you agree?

Sexuality and violence have been close companions throughout his life. When he used to beat up the Woostin, it was usually with a potentially homicidal intent. On one occasion, he brutally threw her down the stairs of a dance-hall where he had found her with another man. Another time he bloodied her face with a broken pitcher, for which he was thrown into gaol for eight days. The testimony of a certain Schindelin shows that these homicidal impulses towards the sexual object can be traced back to his mid-twenties. She and Woyzeck cohabited quietly for several weeks, when suddenly, while drinking and dancing at the Fire Ball, he hit her several times on the head, screaming: "Watch it, *canaille,* you're trying to cheat on me!" By reporting him to the town hall, the Schindelin simply provoked another such incident. Woyzeck, with his usual swagger, told us he simply wanted to "give her a love-token, which she'd carry forever." Other testimony points to more sinister intentions. Both Woyzeck and the Schindelin agree to the following: one night, he knocked on her door, and when she opened it he grabbed one of her breasts (she had merely thrown on a coat in order to answer the door), pulled her into the street, and hit her twice on the head with a sharp object (causing a wound about the size of a copper-coin), screaming: "Bitch, you must die." Their only disagreement relates to the nature of Woyzeck's weapon. Woyzeck claims it was his keys, the Schindelin insists it was a brick.

Further incidents mentioned by Woyzeck suggest the same basic pattern of *psychopathia sexualis*. But with Dr. Clarus present I simply had no chance to explore them. Whenever Woyzeck touched upon one of them, our Hofrath would listen only to the point where he could once again assure himself of Woyzeck's depravity, and then cut him short. This happened, for instance, and then cut him short. This happened, for instance, when Woyzeck told us of his exploits during the conquest of Lübeck. After the incidents with the Schindelin, he wisely decided to flee from Leipzig, spent ten weeks roaming the country as far as Posen and Berlin, then, after Jena and Auerstedt,* enlisted with the Dutch forces stationed in Grabow. Life as a vagrant and soldier naturally allowed him to widen the scope of his pathological proclivities. You've probably heard of the atrocities the French committed when they finally conquered Lübeck. As a member of the victorious Napoleonic army, Woyzeck played an active part on the occasion.

"August and I found a woman in a toolshed," he told us with routine matter-of-factness. "She was hiding. We told her to stop screaming. When she wouldn't, we gagged her and then. . . "

". . . raped her?" I burst out.

"Yes, and . . ."

"That's enough," Dr. Clarus interrupted. "I am here to investigate the delinquent's state of mind, not to listen to his sordid sexual stories. As it is, I have heard enough of them to last me a lifetime."

This was two weeks ago, and now the Court has received Clarus's report. Predictably, it finds Woyzeck sane and fully responsible for his crime, stressing his "moral degeneracy, his imperviousness to all natural sentiments, [and] his indifference to past and future." All through the report Clarus sounds conspicuously like Heinroth, who is taking a special interest in the case and has sat in on one of the examinations. I suspect this is Clarus's way of securing his colleague's backing in case his report should be challenged. For normally he prides himself on his urbane rationalism rather than on his moral sentiments. But listen to this: Woyzeck's life, Clarus writes, "has been summarily deficient in inner

***

* The sites of Napoleon's victory over the Prussian army on October 14, 1806.

sion to self-scrutiny, lack of willpower or the strength to rise above himself, an awareness of guilt without the urge to ameliorate or diminish it by adducing extenuating circumstances, but also without particular remorse, anxiety and pangs of conscience, and, instead, an apathetic indifference towards the outcome of his destiny: these are the traits which mark the mental state of the delinquent." At the same time, Clarus can hardly conceal his cynical, or shall we say, pragmatic view of religion as a means of controlling the illiterate and the poor. "The traces of religious emotion" in Woyzeck, he writes, "are far too frosty, weak and transient as to be granted a possible influence on his views and actions, particularly since he lacks all those scruples and urges thanks to which coarse and uneducated people are often kept within the enclosures of bourgeois order, even though their moral and religious convictions may be either flaccid or non-existent."

Dr. Clarus is not fictionalizing: according to what I saw and heard, Woyzeck behaved in precisely this fashion, while staunchly refusing to admit his madness. Of course, a doctor examining a criminal's state of mind should not take the man's words at face value; instead, he should probe behind whatever mask the delinquent might choose to wear. But in his zeal to have Woyzeck convicted, Clarus had good reason to ignore such niceties. The verdict is expected by mid-October, and there is small doubt about the outcome. But even if Woyzeck is sentenced to death, all hope is not lost. I'll let you know in my next what I might do to rescue him at the last minute.

Your old friend
Adam

Leipzig, May 10, 1822

Dear Arthur:

I hope your silence doesn't mean trouble. Let me know if that's the case. I'd like to help where I can.

Since I last wrote you, Woyzeck has been sentenced to death, the court has heard another defence with the result of confirming the earlier verdict, and Woyzeck has filed his first appeal for mercy. Meanwhile, I have been trying to gather more information about him—though not with quite the success I'd hoped for. Of all his landlords I have spoken to so far (and he had roughly half a dozen during 1818-21 alone), only one, beer tapster Haase's wife (not the newspaper carrier's!), remembers anything striking about him. Woyzeck used to tell her his dreams, making his own oneirological comments. Dreams of black horses, for instance, foretold him that he'd soon come to grief. Another incident told by Frau Haase throws quite a new light upon the defendant: once, when a beggar knocked on their door, Woyzeck insisted on sharing his food with him, even though he only had a few pennies left in his pocket. I have also established contact with the Schindelin, who still resides in this city.

However, more evidence will have to come from Woyzeck who *has* begun to volunteer such information. With death staring him in the face, he is proving more open to my suggestions. He still wouldn't confirm Haase's story about his ghosts, but said he was willing to write about his life—especially about his relations with women. Characteristically, I had to assure him that style, spelling, and grammar are of no account in this endeavour. He also told me about hallucinations directly linked to the murder. Just after buying the fatal weapon, a voice told him: "Stab the Frau Woostin to death!" At which he thought, "No, I won't." But the voice replied, "Oh yes, thought, "No, I won't." But the voice replied, "Oh yes, you will." Still, he seems to be hiding something essential. More and more I am convinced that under his picaresque bravado there lurks a totally different Woyzeck impatiently waiting to reveal his face. If only I knew how to get through to that hidden stranger. In the meantime, letter carrier Haase's story about Woyzeck's ghosts might in itself prove sufficient to stop the execution at the last minute—for if I waste my best ammunition right now it would simply be lost in the self-righteous momentum of the proceedings. And should my battle-plans fail, we'll still be enriched by the memoirs, told without art, of a German picaro gone astray. Write me soon.

Your friend
Adam

Berlin, May 24, 1822

Dear Adam:

Thank you for your letters. I shall arrive in Leipzig on June 2nd and stay for two to three days. Try to reserve me as much of your time as you can. I hope you forgive me for not writing earlier.

*Alia iacta est.** I have decided to leave this dreary city and to quit my academic career. My first plan is to travel through Switzerland and then to live in Italy. There, once again, I shall spend my days in the contemplation of beauty and my evenings shouting *Cameriere* and *Bottega*.**

But *Fortuna*, while proffering blandishments with

---

* Latin, "The die has been cast."
** Italian, "Waiter! " and "Bar!"

the Court dismissed her suit, the Marquet has appealed the verdict. This means that, during my absence, I have to appoint a lawyer, leave power of attorney, and even perhaps put up bail. Oh you prophetic soul, protector of demented murderers and dehumanized malefactors! I may indeed need your help after all. By the way, could you get me access to Woyzeck? To have actually seen him will enliven the perusal of your reports which, I hope, will follow me thick and fast during my Mediterranean peregrinations.

I shall stay at the *Hotel de Bavière* as usual. Hope to see you.

Yours
Arthur

Florence, September 30, 1822

Dear Adam:

Once again the Great Bear hovers low above the horizon; once again the dark-green foliage, hanging sullenly in the motionless air, cuts its jagged silhouettes into the dark-blue sky; once again I walk across the strange piazza full of sculptures, or past the campanile, the battistero and the cathedral, all washed clean by the rain and glistening in the sunlight; once again I dwell amidst these infamous people who have such beautiful faces, yet, O, such treacherous hearts. They seem so spirited, witty, yea even honest, while really being so dishonourable and shameless, that sheer amazement makes one forget one's anger.

What a relief nonetheless to be away from my country of jargon-mongers and inkwell pedants. One lives with Italy as with one's mistress, wrangling bitterly one day, and swimming in a sea of mindless bliss the next; while with Germany as with one's wife, neither smarting from jealousy, nor plagued by anger. Over recent years I often dreamt I was in Italy, but upon waking found myself back in my Berlin apartment. The other day, the dream came back to me once again, but this time continued through the day. I shall stay here for the winter: some trees have begun to turn yellow, but most of them know no seasons. Even the orange trees in the San Lorenzo cloister will cast deep shadows onto the inner courtyard all winter long. Their sight will ease my aching heart when it turns colder; the rest is silence, *Eldorado* is six feet under the earth.

Has Woyzeck been executed? Often when lulled into daydreams by the jolting stagecoach going South, his haunted green eyes and eager features would suddenly stare at me out of nowhere; but last night he appeared in a dream most patently in the guise of a ghost. I was back in my study on *Niederlagstraße 2*, as his form came soundlessly walking through the unopened door. He slowly approached my desk, halted just two feet before it, all the while staring at me in silence. Even before I could ask what ailed him I noticed the blotches of gore along the sharply drawn line which encircled his neck. Then a deep moan came from his barely parted lips.

"So speak to me, speak!" I pleaded, but in reply only heard one more long-drawn-out hollow moan. Then, as I listened more carefully, I could discern two words: "My soul," and again "my soul."

"What is it about your soul?" I asked him.

"You have robbed me of my soul."

"There is no soul," I shouted.

Instead of replying, the ghost fell silent, reached for my walking stick on the wall, and, his features distorted by hatred, was about to deal me a blow on the head—when I woke. I looked at my watch: it was six o'clock in the morning. So, my dream was probably no more than one of those in which what we wished and feared the preceding day has turned into a phantasmagory of the night. But who knows? I sleep fitfully these days, and perhaps fell into an early morning deep sleep, when our dreams lead us into the secret world of the *Ding an sich*. It is ten o'clock now as I write this, and already I have had breakfast down on the piazza with its beautiful Neptune fountain. Yet my dream is still as vivid as at six o'clock when I awoke. Resolve me soon. I shall not wrack my brains about it further until you tell me if Woyzeck is dead in the grave or alive in his cell.

Also please keep me abreast of the news, viz. what donkeys are appointed to the chairs of philosophy, or who else is making a fool of himself in reviewing my book. German publications, including mine, are hard to get hold of here in Florence. When I passed through Milan, they showed me *The World* as a recent entry in the *Index librorum prohibitorum*.

Yours
Arthur

Leipzig, October 16, 1822

Dear Arthur:

No, Woyzeck is still alive, but he might be dead soon. The King has rejected his appeal. It took some persuasion on my part, but Woyzeck has appealed again, and even revealed part of his secret. I have learnt since you saw him, that he dreads ridicule like the plague; and that due to a verbal confusion not to be weeded from his brain, he equates being made a fool of with being a genuine madman. You remember how I wanted him to confirm

Haase's story, and how he swore he'd rather deny it than save his life in this way. All he was ready to do was to tell a visiting chaplain that years ago he had seen an apparition and heard some strange voices. However, even that bit of information was sufficient to prompt the defence to request that Woyzeck be re-examined.

Meanwhile, I talked to the Schindelin, who confirmed my worst suspicions about Woyzeck's deep-rooted *psychopathia sexualis*. You remember what I wrote you about his verbal and physical violence towards her. As I suspected, the same brutality permeated their sexual mores. Thus Woyzeck often engaged her in intercourse just after beating her. Of course, one might argue that this is not uncommon amongst the uneducated lower classes. But even when the violence was not actual, it was always there, so to speak, *symboliciter*.

Be it said to the Schindelin's credit, that she was far too ashamed to tell me about these horrible acts directly. In order to draw them out of her, I had to wrack my poor brains in trying to recall all the very worst that is known of man's bestial nature from what I have read in diverse obscure and illicit publications. Then, with shame twisting my tongue, I described these heinous deeds to her, until she would indicate by her blushing assent that this or that monstrous perversion had been perpetrated upon her by Woyzeck. In reporting these indirect confessions I prefer the scholarly Latin to my mother tongue. To be brief, Woyzeck used to tie the Schindelin to the bedstead, then *penem suum in orem mulieris arrigebat** while simultaneously or independently performing *immissionem linguae suae in vaginam mulieris.*** Now we know that the urge to use force is, within limits, a natural part of the masculine sexual drive; just as the willingness (even pleasure) to suffer

---

* Latin, "Inserted his penis into the woman's mouth."

** Latin, "An immission of his tongue into the woman's vagina."

pain is a distinctive psychical peculiarity in the sexual comportment of women. But the excesses observed in this case hardly fit these normal patterns. I have trouble explaining the loathsome urge towards *cunnilingus*, but suspect that the act of *fellatio* is a symbolic enactment of the urge to suffocate the female. Whatever it is, it no doubt springs from pathological causes. In any case, I am sure you agree with me that it's time to break the taboos that stop us from discussing such matters.

Of course, none of the sexual roots of Woyzeck's insanity will be recognized by the Court. So in order to stay the execution (which, should the re-examination request be turned down, might be scheduled as early as November), I shall have to feed them the Haases' story of Woyzeck's ghosts even at the risk that Woyzeck himself might deny it.

Concerning your queries, I have seen no further reviews of your great work. But it might amuse you to hear that Wolfart's prestige in Berlin high society has fallen into sudden decline. After magnetizing one of Blücher's grandchildren, the young lady suddenly became pregnant. Less amusing is what Varnhagen writes me about the final act in the feud between E.T.A. Hoffmann and police chief von Kamptz. After resigning from the Commission for the Investigation of Treasonable Organizations, Hoffmann instantly went to satirize that Commission's work in his next novel, entitled *Master Flee*. This would have no doubt passed unnoticed, if Hoffmann had not bragged about it at parties and in cafés, thus bringing it to the notice of Herrn von Kamptz who, in the name of Prussia, ordered the Senate of Frankfurt, where the novel was to be published, to confiscate all the *Master Flee* papers. Von Kamptz had his worst suspicions confirmed when he recognized himself in the novel's Privy Councillor Knarrpanti, who is fond of saying: "The main thing is to get people under arrest; the crimes they'll be charged with can be easily made up later." Except for Hoffmann's sudden illness, this might well have become his own fate at the hands of his powerful opponent. Barely recovered from his illness, he was cross-examined, wrote a tongue-in-cheek defence of his novel, but in truly Hoffmannesque fashion escaped further persecution by his death on June 25th. Meanwhile, *Master Flee* appeared in Frankfurt, but in a expurgated version; so we probably shall never know the true story of Privy Councillor Knarrpanti.*

> Yours as ever
> Adam

[Undated]

Dear Adam:

I tried to escape Berlin, but now find it haunting me worse than ever. Although I left clear instructions, it took the Court over five months to inform me that on May 25th the Court of Appeal reversed the earlier verdict. I am now sentenced to pay 20 *Reichsthaler* to the Marquet and to no doubt defray a hefty part of the court costs. And I still haven't seen the actual sentence!

But this is by no means the worst of what happened. Encouraged by her unexpected triumph, the Marquet thought of yet one more ruse of extortion. She now claims to have been ill and hence unable to work ever since I threw her out of my *entrée*; ergo I am supposed to pay for all her medical bills as well as seven *Reichsthaler* per month for as long as her illness continues (no doubt until ripe old age.) The Court not only accepted this ludicrous suit, but also seized my entire

---

* The unexpurgated version of the novel was first published in 1908.

—118—

fortune in lieu of bail. I have sent instructions to my lawyer, but wish I had someone reliable who in my absence might monitor court proceedings. Otherwise, I shall probably have no other choice than to return to Berlin myself.

Yours
Arthur

Leipzig, November 6, 1822

Dear Arthur:

I am sorry to hear of your troubles. Probably Varnhagen would be the right person for you. Write to him (c/o Hartwig, *Turmstraße* 36), tell him I asked you to do so, and he will no doubt do his best to help you. Before he receives your letter, he'll have one from me outlining the problem. Varnhagen no longer wields the influence he once did as a Prussian diplomat in Vienna and Karlsruhe: his outspoken opposition to the Baden government on behalf of a liberal workgroup made him fall into disgrace in Berlin and earned him the enmity of his former friend, Metternich—since the Carlsbad Decrees have come into effect his story, alas, is one he shares with many others. He now lives as a freelance writer. But no one knows Berlin social life more intimately than he does. What's more, he really cares about his friends, and you two will no doubt get on splendidly, even if, for the time being, only in correspondence.

The main news here is that Woyzeck is to be executed on November 13th. Already they have started to build the scaffold, right in view of the delinquent who, as tradition demands, has been transferred to the Poor Sinner's Chamber on the second floor of the town hall overlooking the market. In short, the government, on October 28, decided that Woyzeck's new deposition did not warrant further examination. Instead of being re-examined, he has been put in the care of a local pastor who with his fire and brimstone rhetoric will no doubt try to scare him back into the fold. Next Sunday, all churches in the city are ordered to add a prayer for Woyzeck's salvation to their regular services.

Meanwhile I have done all I can to reverse the tide. First I told Woyzeck's defence attorney, a certain Herr Hänsel, about Woyzeck's ghosts (Haase's story). Then I went to see Woyzeck who, with death now so close, proved more amenable to my stratagems than ever. Not only will he corroborate the Haases' story about his apparitions; he also vowed that, should I manage to stay the execution, he will rewrite his life, this time by neither exaggerating his criminal feats nor by hiding his shame. All that remains now is to wait for the outcome.

But here in the meantime is Woyzeck's "Life," or as much of it as he was able to finish. Another transcript went to Goethe, who no doubt will relish its vagabond tales. He recently introduced a curious book called *The German Gil Blas or The Life, Travels, and Fortunes of Johann Christoph Sachse as Told by Himself*, brought out by Goethe's own publisher Cotta, no doubt at the poet's suggestion. Lesage's *Gil Blas*, Goethe writes in his preface, is a "work of art," its German counterpart a "work of Nature." No doubt this is even truer of Woyzeck's "Life," especially if one shares the Schopenhauerian or *Walpurgissack* under-standing of "Nature." I wonder what Goethe's com-ments will be, and am equally anxious for yours. Should Woyzeck be executed next Friday, I shall try to have Nasse publish the story in his *Journal for Anthropology*.

Yours as ever
Adam

Arthur Schopenhauer (1788-1860) ca. 1818.
Oil portrait by Ludwig Sigismund Ruhl.

LIFE OF JOHANN CHRISTIAN WOYZECK
AS TOLD BY HIMSELF

I may be mad, your honour, but I am no idiot. To tell the truth, I always wanted to find out about things and why they happened. I tried for a long time. Mother used to say that "God's mills grind slowly," or she'd warn me about His hidden ways. There was always some reason for things. When I was sick, she'd say: "God's punishing you for a sin." "But I've done nothing evil," I'd protest, and I hadn't. So she'd change her tune saying: "We don't know. Just trust in Him. It's all done for your sake. Something good will come of it in the end, though only God knows what it is." Meanwhile, she hugged me in her arms and kissed me on the forehead.

I believed her and kept on believing her for a long time. Whatever happened to me was for my good. Even a toothache. There was some reason why God caused me pain. But unlike mother, I wanted to find out about it. And I finally did. Take it from a man who has watched these things all his life: there's nothing, no reasons for things. Just yourself and the world. I went to pray to Him at St. Michael's two days before I murdered the Woostin. I asked Him to stop me. But what good did it do me? I don't care if they kill me. I'm not scared of death. Just scared of dying. Otherwise I'd have killed myself long ago. I tried several times.

Look at what happened to mother. She loved

father, and admired him. She was a small woman; he was tall and broad-shouldered, with a bushy moustache, and dark, singular eyes which made people nervous. He came to Leipzig from Breslau at twenty-three, spoke only broken German with an accent. At the fairs I sometimes heard him talk Polish. He seemed a different man then, noisier, laughing a lot and slapping people on the back; someone strange to me, like these foreigners. In Leipzig father worked as a wigmaker and barber—"same thing I've always done," he'd say, when people asked him. But no one believed him. Some said he'd been a bankrupt merchant, others an officer, or spy, or even perhaps an escaped convict. But that was all nonsense, father insisted. Everywhere in Leipzig, they called him the "handsome Stephan."

Father knew everyone. After I'd turned seven, he often took me with him, "make the rounds," as he put it, "to see the fine folk who have their hair done." People liked him, especially the women. I remember one, Madame S., wife of the wool merchant on the Barefoot Lane. Father did her hair each Friday. Such a fuss she made each time we went there. Mother used to kiss me at bedtime, but not like Madame did. Madame was a tall woman, older than mother, with half-naked breasts bulging from her décolté, smelling of perfume. She smothered my face in them, hugging me, all the while laughing and screaming, things like "Oh, what a pretty, pretty boy!" (your honour asked me to record all such trash) lifting me up to kiss me, smack on her painted mouth, then whirling me round till we both got dizzy. Then she'd fall on her sofa, still holding me pressed 'gainst her wobbly bosom.

Usually, I just waited till father was finished. But sometimes Madame would slip me a coin, saying: Here, little gentleman. You and Johanna go to *Jänichen's* Garden, for some nice lemonade and chocolate cake. You'll treat her. So run along both. And Johanna, be back at four, on the dot. Much later I found out that father had an affair with Madame S.

These were happy days, but things changed after mother's death. She'd always been weak in the lungs, and that year her grandmother died and left her some money which we needed a lot. But her younger brother cheated her out of it; I could never find out how he did it. Anyway, mother was very upset and drank too much *Schnapps*, which was unlike her, and got sick in the chest. She died a few days later, from consumption they said.

Father remarried: Geier's daughter, who was sixteen years younger than him, a hard-working, head-strong woman with eyebrows that met in the middle. From the beginning I remember her fighting with father. Each Sunday she went to listen to Schulmann's sermons at St. Thomas. She brought father some money and he made her buy a farm with it. He'd seen one near Paunsdorf, about three miles from Leipzig, with a cow and five pigs, several chickens, a vegetable patch and some grazing land. There we'd all live happily, away from the noise and bustle, father said. Father had always had schemes, but never the money for them.

We moved there one beautiful day in September, 1791. At first all went fine. Father set about his new tasks. He even got himself books about farming and read them at night. Stepmother worked even harder. The house needed lots of repairs, and the nearest well was at Paunsdorf, some twelve hundred yards from the farm. They hadn't thought of that when they bought it.

Things got worse towards winter. The house was draughty and cold. With the first rainstorm, water came down the rafters. We needed a new roof, which ate up the rest of stepmother's money. But watching the roof leak, they hadn't noticed the water coming in through the North wall, near the floor. Of course, the Paunsdorfers knew all about that, but father had only talked to the Leipzig salesmen. It turned out the farm had been up for sale for two years with nobody wanting to buy it. It was built on an incline near the lowest point of a hollow, which, when it rained, drew all the water towards it. The Erfurter who'd built it never bothered to talk to the Paunsdorfers; so they watched on in silence until he was finished. Of course, even then a ditch just north of the farm to let the water run off around it would have easily taken care of the problem. But that bit of land belonged to the *Schultheiß*,* who wouldn't sell it. He was angry about the Erfurter who had built his farm right on the edge of his lot without asking.

But that wasn't father's fault. Why should he suffer for it? That winter he spent lots of time with the Paunsdorfers, playing cards with them at the Golden Lion and taking care of the women's hair for Sunday. So at last the *Schultheiß* relented. Of course it would cost us, and so it did, with a loan stepmother managed because of her parents' good reputation. Father was happy. As soon as spring came round, he started digging the trench that would "end all our troubles." The Paunsdorfers still wouldn't give him a hand, but lent him their tools.

In February stepmother gave birth to a daughter. With the damp and all, it made her so ill she nearly died. Father took care of her and the baby day and night. "I'll go to bed later," he'd say laughing. In April stepmother's breasts went bad, so he sucked them to extract the poison, then spat it on the floor. Towards May, she got better, enough to again start fighting with father, though she still had to stay in bed.

He said they should sell the cow and use the money to hire a farm-hand. But stepmother wanted none of it. He was out to ruin her, she said. He had no right to sell it, the cow was hers. They badly needed the money from the milk to pay off their loan. He had no choice, he said, with her being sick for so long. He hadn't slept for weeks. With the help of a farm-hand he could turn some

* German, "Village mayor."

of their grazing land into a garden and then buy back the cow with the money they'd make from the crop. But she called him a fantasizer and fortune hunter. She should have listened to father Geier and never married him, he'd be the death of her. Father turned white, slammed the door, and went on digging his trench. Then one afternoon, while she was sleeping, he took the cow to Paunsdorf and came back with a fellow called Michael.

For weeks afterwards stepmother hardly spoke. Then father admitted he'd been wrong. With the milk sales gone, they fell behind with their payments and the creditors threatened to confiscate our farm. Stepmother then was back on her feet, so father said he'd go back to Leipzig each week to make money, while she and Michael should run the farm.

"You'd like that, wouldn't you," stepmother said, "dump me here in this hole while you lord it with your Madames and von So-and-Soes."

"Then damn it all," he said. "I'll go back anyway. You can do what you want. I don't need your money."

She realized that he meant it, and gave in. So father set out for Leipzig each Monday and came back with food and presents Friday. Things went alright again for a while until stepmother found out about Madame S. She and father had been at it again when Geier got on their trail and told his daughter who told pastor Schulmann who told Madame's husband. Then the Reverend started preaching sermons against adultery at St. Thomas, not naming names but talking about this hairdresser who abused his profession to seduce respectable women. So people knew he was talking of father.

With the scandal father lost most of his clients and stopped going to Leipzig. He tried to make up with stepmother, but she wouldn't listen. We abandoned the farm and moved back to Leipzig. Father was miserable, with no work and all the gossip about him. So he got morose, cursing God and the world. It's at that time that

I first started playing games by myself. For instance, I made a tool to kill birds, like no one had ever seen before. I called it my *Peinstrument*. I worked on it for a long time on Sundays and in the evenings, then found out it didn't work, so I buried it, but later dug it up again. I also killed frogs, cut their heads off, and nailed their bodies to a plank in the sun, with sharp nails. I called that *verpeinigen*.*

Then I got sick, so sick they thought I'd die. I had a fever, and lots of nightmares, and then started thinking that I was lost. I can't describe it, just lost, full of fear, which grew worse even when I got better. Then my father died—it was his lungs, they said—just a few days before I turned thirteen, late in December. I got healthy again soon after we buried him.

We went back to Paunsdorf for a short time so mother could sell our farm. I was glad to be back in the country; life there was more fun than in Leipzig, where I had to go to the Free School with all the poor kids.

In the summers I used to help with the farm, then from Michaelis to Mayday I went to the village school. There were around thirty of us, boys and girls between six and fourteen, all together in one smoky room at the *Schultheiß's*. Our teacher, Schelte, truth to tell, smelt of *Schnapps* day and night. He often dozed off in class, while still clutching his stick. We kept quiet as mice while he slept, just made faces and held up our slates with dirty words and drawings on them. For if Schelte woke up too early, he'd thrash one of us on some pretext. Otherwise, he'd just snore on for fifteen minutes, then straighten up, hit the desk with his stick, and pretend to carry on with his lesson. Once me and Paul made snoring noises like his when he woke. Everyone laughed, but not Schelte. He pulled us up by the ears, held us, head down, facing the class, then suddenly shouted "Watch out!" and knocked our heads together with a crack.

---

* Like *"Peinstrument,"* *"verpeinigen"* is a German nonsense word containing the word *"Pein"*—"pain."

No wonder he scared us. You never knew what he was up to: cane your palm or whack your shin where it hurt most. Or make you write a sign saying "I am an ass," pin it to your back, and leave you standing in a corner for hours. "Play donkey," as Schelte called it, or "The Paunsdorf idiot," as we said. That usually was Anton's role, the cobbler's son. But once, just after I joined them, I had to play donkey myself. Then, after class, the children jeered

> Shame, shame, double shame,
> Idiot is his second name.

As I ran home, they came after me throwing stones.

Only boys had their bottoms caned, but with both boys and girls watching. First time I saw it it was my friend Paul's turn. Schelte made two of the older boys hold him down, rolled up his sleeves, then started, slowly counting each stroke. He finally had to pause and wipe the sweat off his face with his tasselled cap. What got me most were Paul's screams. It made me so sick I had to vomit.

Two months later, it was my turn. To my surprise it was nowhere near as bad as I'd feared. I got twenty the first time, and forty the second, two weeks later. By then I knew they admired it if you held out a long time without screaming. I did as long as I could, which also, I knew, would anger Schelte. Then, after class, the carpenter's Waltraut came up to me saying I'd taken twelve without screaming, and they'd like me to join their group; they'd meet me at five in the hayloft of Wehner's barn. Then she just stood there and stared at me.

First thing they made me do was put my right hand on a skull and swear, by my life, that I'd keep all their secrets. They called themselves the Skullheads. Next the blacksmith's Christoph renamed me Loki and told me the code-names of all the others. He himself was called Odin. Including myself we were seven in all, with

Waltraut or Frigga as our only female. Finally, Frigga bared my neck and put a band with a death's head around it. But they'd still have to test me, they said. Then my family moved back to Leipzig until father died; I have already written about that. When I came back to Paunsdorf, Frigga told me that the Mockau Blackhands had raided our Northern tree-house, and that we'd strike back this spring. That's when they'd test me. First we'd burn down their headquarters on the Parthe and then strike deep into their territory. There was a hill, called the Mount of Good Fortune, which people said was full of tunnels that lead to a treasure. On a spying mission last August, Odin and Balder had found the entrance. But it was too dark to go in when they got there. That would be my task.

They'd been planning the raid throughout the winter. Our small raft, built from the wood of an old barn, was hidden near the river just opposite the Blackhands' stronghold. It would carry our clothes and armour, an oil lamp, a flintstone, and a spade. With the camp being two miles from the nearest bridge, it would be hard to approach it undetected. But no one would expect us to swim across the Parthe in early April.

Yet that's what we did, at sunrise, the first Saturday in April. It was freezing, with all of us naked except for Frigga, who swam in a shirt that clung to her body. The Blackhands' stronghold was unguarded. So we hacked down their look-out, pulled down their palisade, and burnt their cave-house. We also slaughtered their rabbits: five of them. Then we slipped away towards the Mount of Good Fortune, the flames flaring behind us. After unloading the raft, Odin let it drift downstream past Mockau, where we'd find it again later in a sharp turn of that river.

The Mount of Good Fortune isn't much of a hill, just a slight rise above the plain. We found the tunnel and cut down some bushes to get in. I was to go first, alone, with the oil lamp, an axe, and trailing a thread which Frigga had tied round my waist. She kissed me farewell in the name of the Skullheads, and I went to meet my test and perhaps find the treasure. There were lots of bats flitting past me, but I was more scared of the big serpents, which I'd read would be guarding the treasure. I stumbled on for ten minutes, carefully lighting ahead for each step, then twice pulled the thread to tell them things were alright. (Three times meant "Help!") As I went on, the tunnel got narrower, and full of a sulphurous stench. At one point I had to squeeze past two boulders. Before I did, I put my lamp through the hole: two beady eyes were staring at me, with a squeal they disappeared in the darkness. Later the tunnel got even tighter, but I could see that it widened again further ahead. Before I went ahead, I thought I'd once again signal "alright," but found that the thread round my waist had disappeared. As I tried to squeeze by, some earth came loose, extinguished the lamp, and plunged everything into darkness. I wriggled back to light the lamp, when more earth came tumbling down on my head. That's all I remember.

First thing I noticed when I woke again was Frigga's eyes staring at me: next the night sky above the mossy hollow where we lay; then her chest and belly pressed against mine.

"Don't talk," she said. "Just get warm again. Poor Johann, how you're shivering! The others have rushed back to Paunsdorf for help."

Then slowly, while rubbing my body, Frigga told me. It had taken them hours to dig me out of the tunnel. There had been a landslide. It was a miracle it hadn't killed me. So I got warmer, quite warm, until (pardon your honour)*penis meus Frigga officienti inveniebat vaginam suam.** Just like that, no talking, no fidgeting either. She

---

* As in his letters, Dr. Adam Bergk, in transcribing Woyzeck's autobiography (the original ms. seems to be lost), translated all matters of an overtly sexual nature into Latin.
** Latin, "My penis, guided by Frigga, found her vagina."

must have done it before, but not me.

We never did it again though. I tried to, but she wouldn't let me: one day she'd promised to meet me at a treehouse I'd built for us. It was May, a beautiful day. I'd cut some turf and made a bed. There I lay, waiting, all eager, *cum erectione** (with your kind permission) dreaming, though wide awake, of how I'd slide my right leg between hers (I beg your pardon), *uti apprehendit penem meum, vaginaque sua iniecit.*** It was almost as if she was there, but she didn't come. I waited till sundown, then later met her by chance back in Paunsdorf.

"We can't do it again," she said. "I don't think Christoph found out. But he's been strange to me since then, and we want to get married."

Which they did, five years later. They're still there, in Paunsdorf, Christoph and Waltraut Wenzel, with their six children.

I got over it after we moved back to Leipzig. With father dead I was glad to leave home and turn apprentice. Like him, I'd become a barber. Despite father's bad name, wigmaker Stein took me on, and I soon found out why. For weeks I never got near a comb or wig. Instead, I washed mistress Stein's dishes, fed their pig, changed the baby and watched the two older children. But all day Monday and every night for two hours I was free to roam around Leipzig.

I soon found there were easier ways to make money than at my master's. Franz, a former classmate from the Free School, showed me how. There were beautiful horse-drawn Viennese carriages, all upholstered and plush inside, which the rich could rent at Peter's Gate. I had no idea what went on in them in the evenings. For two *Groschen*, a couple could rent one, pull down the blinds and go to it. Meanwhile Franz and I

---

* Latin, "With an erection."
** Latin, "How she grabbed my penis and slipped it into her vagina."

would be watching outside for constables. If one came near, we'd knock on the carriage, so he'd find the couple just sitting there as if ready to leave.

Lots of them were regulars—usually once or twice a week. After a while I could tell each one of them by their sighs and moans or the way they'd rock the carriage. One of the ladies always exclaimed "Ai, by my saviour, what a thick one you have." Always that sentence, just before the carriage would start rocking. One day, Madame S. approached the coaches with a uniformed Hussar, blushed when she saw me, and quickly turned away without saying a word. My favourite was Madame M. whose lover was tall and moustached like father. He always gave me an extra *Groschen*. I fell in love with Madame, and as soon as they'd start (how else can I put it) *penis meus tumescebat bracciis meis*.* So I'd hide behind the carriage *masturbans* (with your honour's permission). I soon learnt to time it *ut semper ejaculatus sum*** just when Madame made her final moan inside the carriage. Till one evening, *dum masturbabam ad tergum vehiculi*,*** a blow on my head hitting me like God's thunder knocked me flat to the ground. It was stepmother's father. I can still hear him: "So that's what your father taught you. The apple never falls far from the tree." Then all went black before my eyes.

I came to again with my head in Madame's lap. But I never went back to watch coaches. To tell the truth, I was bursting with shame and for weeks dreamt of revenge: I'd hit father Geier or insult him in public. I even wrote letters to him, defending father and challenging him to a duel. But how would we fight? In the stories I'd read they used pistols. I had no pistols and no doubt he had none either. I never sent the letters.

Then I found a new master, wigmaker Knobloch

---

* Latin, "My penis would swell in my breeches."

** Latin, "So that I always ejaculated . . ."

*** Latin, "While I masturbated behind the carriage."

and almost forgot about Geier. Weeks later I met Geier by chance, walking towards me on Butcher's Lane. When he saw me I glared at him, stopped, and spat on the sidewalk, while he just went on, shaking his head. I'd show them, him and his daughter! For over four years I worked hard with Knobloch who never talked much, but was good to me, and taught me: how to make wigs, fit them on, comb, powder and brush them; how to trim whiskers, file nails, spray perfume, and make curls with hot tongs.

But mostly I learnt how to please. One had to imitate people's manners, yet seem humble. Though not servile either; clients don't like that. They came to be stroked and fondled. Some liked to give orders; others to grumble; most just to be touched and peer at themselves in the mirror. If they wanted to talk, you'd talk; if laugh, make jokes; if tell you their worries, listen, though not in complete silence. One had to show one's concern, perhaps sigh with pity, or grunt with protest at what they'd suffered.

I have to admit, I liked it all, ambling round my clients, swishing the sheet before fitting it round their bodies; or holding the handmirror up to their backs, three seconds each side, while they'd crane their necks nodding approval. But I'd say: "This side needs some more pruning," flashing the comb and the scissors. After a while I got bolder, as with Madame N., saying: "What an exquisite head you have," swishing the sheet with a special flourish, "Let me bring out its beauty!" Before long I was widely known as "charming Johann."

One of my regular clients was the Frau Woostin, Knobloch's stepdaughter. Otherwise there was nothing between us. She was a strange one, but not at all pretty, and married, to town surgeon Woost, since her fifteenth year. When I first did her hair I was fifteen myself, while she was already over twenty. Anyway, clients liked me and I liked my work. Soon I'd have my own salon, I thought.

But I quickly found one needs more for that than to be liked. I tried once I got my licence, but no one would lend me the money. I couldn't even find work. By 1798, Leipzig had over a hundred wigmakers, and lifestyles were changing. Wigs were less fashionable now; folks went for the old German look. Old Knobloch let me stay in his house while I kept looking. But there was no more work for me in his salon. There was hardly enough for him.

So I packed my hairdresser's bag to try my luck elsewhere; but it was the same old story. People were going to war, not to the hairdresser. It's because of the rabble, they said, who had taken over in France, and then chopped off the sixteenth Louis's head in Paris. At first, everyone thought they'd quickly put down that mob. But they got beat up instead, first the Prussians and then the Austrians. We saw the Prussians march back to Berlin, a lot of them sick and wounded. So people got scared and began talking about war at Knobloch's. That's when I first heard of Bonaparte.

I set out in 1798, to Dessau and Berlin, then back to Hannover and Hessen; but no work for me anywhere. While at Knobloch's I'd saved twelve Louis d'or, but the money went quickly. No more coaches, for instance. Once, hopping the baggage rack of a mail express, I found it was spiked with nails, which sent me reeling into the dust with my hands and coat torn. A few days later, two ruffians pounced on me from the roadside, tore my bag off my shoulder, and with a cudgel blow left me unconscious. I was found by a farmer ambling home on his haycart. Back in the village, the *Schultheiß* asked me: "Where did they go?" "Towards East," I answered, so five men with a gun and three dogs went after them. Before robbing me, they had tried to break into the miller's house, but had never gotten past taking the lead frames off one window. They found them spending my money, eating and drinking in nearby Königsdorf.

From then on I kept off the main roads, walking straight through the fields and forests. One evening I sat by a fire, smoking my pipe, when I heard wolves howling nearby. Seconds later I saw their eyes, about ten of them, sidle towards me through the bushes. I knew the fire would keep them at bay, but how could I keep it ablaze until morning? I took a firebrand, walked backwards to the nearest oak tree, climbed up, then watched them prowl around underneath. I was scared that I'd drop down amongst them if I fell asleep. And I did fall asleep, then woke up in plain daylight. I was hanging on to two branches by my armpits, all soaked from a freezing drizzle. The wolves had gone.

Now good advice was dear.* I had to go West, but with the sun hidden behind dark rain clouds, I couldn't tell where that was. So I just guessed, and kept walking, frozen and starving, found a brook and followed it, hoping to find a water mill, but didn't. Then it turned dark again, pitch-black, I had to feel my way past the tree trunks, imagining wolves eyes' staring at me from everywhere. Each time I stumbled and fell I felt more like just staying there with my face down in the soft moss. The last time I did, I fell asleep, I was so exhausted. I woke up screaming just after the wolves in my dream were about to tear me to pieces.

I stared around: all was quiet. It was just turning light in the forest. I was frozen stiff, but felt peaceful, not wanting to move, not even my little finger. Perhaps I would die before they'd get me. Then I suddenly heard the far away tolling of church bells. One. Two. Three. Four. Perhaps I was dreaming again. But no. One. Two. Three. Four. Five. It was five o'clock in the morning. I was saved. The dear Lord had saved me, I thought. So

---

* *"Jetzt war guter Rat teuer."* Here and elsewhere, Woyzeck's knack for speaking in proverbs is often difficult to render in English.

I got to my feet and stumbled towards the church bells. And yes. There it was again. This time a single knell and then five. A quarter past five. So I went on, uphill, towards a ridge that opened onto a clearing, where I suddenly saw the towers of Eisenach down in the valley, glistening in the sharp morning sunlight. The town gate was locked, so I went back to a farm I had seen on the way. There was smoke in the chimney. I knocked, then the watch-dog came bounding towards me. He bit me just below *testiculis meis* (pardon my language).* Thank God they heard me scream, threw open the shutters, and ordered the dog to let go, which he did, crawling, tail down, towards his master.

"Why are you roaming around here?"

"I got lost in the forest," I replied, "I'm no vaga-bond but a journeyman. My trade's hairdressing. I was robbed."

Inside the house his wife washed the wound, put some dog's hair with balsam on it, fed me broth, bread and sausage, then let me sleep.

When I woke, I found the farmer, his wife, and someone else standing round my cot talking. The third was the Eisenach town physician who told me he'd have to take me away. My leg was swollen, and I had a fever, so bad I'd been raving for hours, they told me. But that was not it. There was an epidemic around, and I'd probably caught it, they said.

The hospital wasn't the place to get better. The stench alone could have killed you. And all the howling and whining. It was like being in hell. There was no escaping it. I tried to the third day, but two guards got me at the front gate and hauled me back, squeezing my arms so hard it made tears rush to my eyes. There I was back with the others, side by side on our straw bags in the main hall, almost as big as the St. Thomas in Leipzig—some writhing under their blankets, others with half-rotten

---

* Latin, "My testicles."

limbs or wallowing in their excrement, most just waiting for death. But that didn't save them from the surgeon, who always had someone howling, usually from cutting their legs off. Luckily I got better before he found out about *my* leg. That's probably because the town physician looked after me.

"Your trade is hairdressing, isn't it," he said to me one day.

"Yes," I answered.

"He's healthy again and had better be leaving. There's no work for him here in town."

I began packing my knapsack.

"Except if he doesn't mind helping the *Todtenfrau* fix up the corpses. We need someone like him, and there's money in it."

They gave me five *Groschen* per corpse, and people were dying like flies. Those who died from the epidemic, most of them in the *Spital*, were dug under instantly, with just the priest and the gravediggers present. Their coffins were sealed with pitch and lowered five feet deeper than normal. Most others got the full treatment. Each time someone was dying, we'd already be there, waiting for it. The pastor would tell us before he'd go feed the candidate his last holy supper, as they called it: like the dish he loved best, not just a wafer or something, the way the Catholics do it. That's the dying man's last chance, they said. He'd either die or get better, though all of them died, at least all those I saw.

Then we walked in: I with basket and lantern, the *Todtenfrau* with her barber's utensils. I'd help her clean the corpse, shave and wash it. Then we packed it into the basket, head on a pillow, put the lantern beside it and left it till midnight, when me and some other guy carried it to the *Todtenhaus*, next to the cemetery. There it stayed for a couple of days, with a ring on its thumb and a bell tied to it, in case it should wake again.

Shortly before the burial, me and the *Todtenfrau*

would be back to get the corpse dressed, usually in its best Sunday clothes: the women in white, often a wreath in their hair; the men in full gear—coat, trousers, cravat, boots and white gloves. If they owned them, that is. For an extra *Groschen* or so, we'd even fix them up special: like the town musician who got a wreath round his head and a gilt lyre on his chest.

"Oh, how pretty," people would say, parading past the corpse and describing it all. They liked what I did, but I got fired once the epidemic was over. So I had to move on again. But the money I'd saved kept me going for a while.

From Eisenach I went back to Leipzig. Perhaps I'd find work there, get married, have children—but nothing. I couldn't even find anywhere to sleep. The main fair was on, so beds were either taken or cost a fortune. I wouldn't waste my money that way if I could help it. At least I'd get some fun out of it: like drinking and dancing at the *Funkenburg*, and then spend the night at some woman's or in a barn outside Leipzig. When it turned winter, old Knobloch got me a place with his friend, wigmaker Bärwolfinger in Wurzen: no real job, just helping out in his salon and 'round the house. That was easy but boring, so early the next year I went back to Leipzig to get a new passport. There was no problem with that.

"Does he want one or two years?"

I tried to explain that I couldn't find work and so forth. But they knew. There were lots of them like me and the faster they got rid of us the better.

I once again headed East, mostly camping out-side, except when it was pouring and I couldn't find shelter. Clean hay or moss was much better to sleep on than some flea-bitten mattress. I always carried my thick old paletot and a blanket, and when it got really cold I stuck an old newspaper under my clothes. It's amazing how warm that keeps you. It was early March when I set out, and often still freezing at night. Once I slept in a haystack and found three inches of snow on me the next morning!

An old farmer came by with his cart and a pitchfork: "Poor fellow! Have you been here all night?"

"Yes," I said. I had not woken up once all night. He gave me some coffee and bread, and two *Groschen*.

At least I had learnt how to travel. When you had to share your lodging house cot, for example: a fellow in Breslau taught me how to go about that one. Just as we were dropping off he told me he'd kick and bite like a horse in his sleep, because his mother had been frightened by vicious horses while she was pregnant with him. And sure enough, he began whinnying a few minutes later, so I got frightened and lay on the floor, while he was snoring. He never once whinnied again all night, so I knew he'd fooled me, as I later fooled others. At first I was nervous about it, until I saw how it worked. And I never whinnied just once, but whenever I woke, even gnashing and grinding my teeth.

Later that year I ran into trouble in Prussia. A beer-carrier gave me a ride for helping him load and unload his barrels. At night we got drunk at a Waldenburg Inn, and next morning he took off without me, with the bag I'd left on his packrack. I never did things that stupid unless I was drunk like a pig (pardon your honour). Thank God I had most of my money sewn into my trousers, but my passport and service report book were in the knapsack. I tried to catch up with the carrier, but gave up in Schweidnitz. Nobody had seen him pass through. The swine, I thought (with your kind permission), took a different route so he could steal my knapsack. It also had my blanket and paletot in it.

It was freezing cold that night, so I went to an inn. But no way the host would let me in without papers. I explained, but he mumbled: "Police orders. There's a garrison nearby," standing there, grinning and fat in the warmly-lit doorframe, while I had the snow drifting around me. Thank God there was a barn with some hay in it two miles East of the village. But a cannon blast woke me again, then the village bells rang. I checked my pocket watch. It was just after nine, and the bells kept ringing non-stop. Perhaps there's a fire, I thought, but then heard the dogs and the hue and cry. They can't be after me just because of my papers, I thought, but the sounds came closer and closer. Then the barn door burst open: the dogs first, behind them the serfs with their truncheons and lanterns, one of them armed with a pitchfork. That thing nearly killed me, as the serf kept jamming it into the haystack. I can still see it, coming closer and closer. The next jab would have gone right through me, so I screamed.

"Stop! I am just sleeping here."

"We've got him! We've got him!" they shouted, tying my hands behind my back. They wouldn't listen to me.

"A fine story," they said. "Tell it to the major when we get to the garrison." There they took me, all the way talking about what they'd buy with the money I'd fetch them. They thought they'd caught a deserter.

The major was furious when he found out. "Cursed pack! They find a tramp in a haystack and want the King's premium for him," he shouted, thrashing them out of his office. But he kept me anyway, for vagrancy without papers. They stuck me in the garrison gaol overlooking the exercise yard. I'd be transferred to the Breslau House of Correction, he said.

Early next day I woke to shouting outside.

Rest your firearms!

Shoulder your firearms!

Rear rank, to the right double your ranks!

March!

I looked through the grates. The soldiers lined up in two rows facing each other, about four hundred of them. They moved like those jerky automata you see at fairs. The one screaming was the major who was furiously riding up and down behind their backs.

Front rank, face to right-about!

Order your firearms!

Bring your firearms to your left-sides!

Then the provost marched through the ranks handing bundles of rods to each soldier. I had heard about "running the gauntlet" but never seen it. The six deserters, their hands tied, had faces white as bedsheets. Now the first was untied and started running, each soldier hitting him as he passed and the major caning the soldiers' backs for not laying on hard enough. There was lots of screaming, most of it drowned out by the drums. As the deserter collapsed at the end of the line, the major screamed:

Throw away your rods!

Order your firearms!

Then the next one came on, and the next, and the next. Same orders, movements and screams. Then the first one again, followed by all the others, each one ten times. They were at it till late afternoon, when some of the prisoners couldn't stand on their feet any longer. So they just pulled them up, hit them, and shoved them along, right to the end and out into the dust, where they lay, their backs one bloody mess. Three of them had to be carried back to their cells on stretchers.

The next day all six were back for another ten rounds. On the third day, two were missing, and a third on the fourth day. One of them died, I heard later, which wasn't surprising. None of them now ever made it to the end of the line, but collapsed again and again, with their flesh exposed to the ribs, and black from the dust. On the fifth day, the three that survived were tied to posts where all the soldiers had to hit them once more. Most of them didn't like what they did, you could tell, except for the officers with their canes, and the major screaming his orders. Watching it from my cell, it felt like I'd be next.

How I loathed that major and all the officers! Why didn't the soldiers just shoot them? They could have, and wanted to, just like me, I could tell by their faces, but they didn't.

They let me go on the sixth day, after someone had brought in my knapsack. The beer-carrier had left it on his way back from Breslau with the Waldenburg host, who'd heard what had happened to me. I was free again. How great it felt to just walk along with the road under my feet and the clouds in the sky! Instead of heading for Breslau, though, I went back to Berlin. Even with my papers, the Breslau police might find some reason to lock me up in their House of Correction; or pressgang me into their army—I'd rather have died. I knew the Major had written to them. The whole countryside started to look like a gaol once I thought about it. I wouldn't go near one of those villages. Berlin was different, more like Leipzig, with lots of brothels, dance halls, and cheap lodging houses where no one asked for papers.

After a while there you got to know people, and stuck together. A brothel keeper let me do his *mamselles'* hair for a while, so I found out how they worked it. Some of the girls had permits and got themselves checked for syphilis every month. But most of them didn't. There were back exits in case the police came, and if the whores couldn't run fast enough, they had holes dug for them in the backyard which they'd jump into, covering them with some twigs or garbage. And what if they did catch a few! There wasn't much they could do with them, except lock them up at the *Charité* until they got rid of their syphilis. You could never have jailed them all, there were just too many.

There was no real work for me, but life was fun again. Only the money went too fast, and jobs like the one at the brothel were hard to come by. Once you got to know the women, you didn't pay them for it, though it always cost something, like you have to buy them food and beer. Eventually I took care of one, as her "lover" and bodyguard, her name was Leni. I collected the fifty per cent for the brothel keeper from her. But he complained that I let her cheat on him, so I got fired again.

One day Leni and I joined a crowd in Potsdam watching four so-called "French patriots" doing a pantomime. That's the first time I ever saw Frenchmen. Someone told us they had been captured at Verdun, before their comrades clobbered the Prussians at Valmy. But that was some time ago and all forgotten now. France was at peace with Prussia and things French were the rage in Berlin, especially with the ladies who liked to wear *tricolore* ribbons and *à la carmagnole* headgear. Sometimes the Potsdam *Gardes du Corps* played the *Ça ira* on their trumpets, while a street boy sang a translation of it. Once released, those French soldiers had just been hanging around Prussia doing their shows.

Take it from someone who's been around: I had never seen anything like it. God, they were raggedy— like out of some hobgoblin's tale. Hell seemed to break loose when they danced. You felt like joining them, which is what the kids did. Then they stopped and one of them brought out a bucket, a second a scaffold with a black blade at its top, and a third two puppets, a man and a woman, costumed as aristocrats. A fourth sang a ballad in French, while the others went through their motions, slowly, but with precision. It was eerie, but also funny. One knew exactly what they were doing. They finally stuck the puppets into that scaffold, let that black blade rush down and chop off their heads, first *monsieur's*, then *madame's*. Everyone heaved a groan when a red liquid came spurting from the puppets' necks right into the bucket; they must have had swine's bladders inside them. Then all four of them washed their hands in the bucket and, with their hands dripping red, danced again, screaming in triumph. Afterwards they pulled out miniature scaffolds—they called them guillotines—and sold them. The Berliners bought them like bread loaves.

Through Leni I met Wolf von Adelungen, who was one of her clients. Wolf was a *Junker* and student at Wittenberg. He looked much too old for a student, but Leni explained he was working on a big doctorate, which takes years, she insisted. He needs a servant, she said.

"What if he finds out about us?" I wondered.

"He won't mind at all," she said.

And he didn't. I'll come to that in a minute.

When you saw him walk down the street, Wolf didn't look much like a *Junker* either: a torn old blouse, worn leather pants stuck in his boots, and swinging his sword. "Who's a real man?" his drinking companions would bawl at the tavern. One, came the answer,

> Who shits on professors and philistines,
> Who gets thrown into gaol
> and struts along like a swine.*

Wolf hated the philistines, which was everyone but his friends. If someone annoyed him, he'd hit the ground with his sword, screaming *"Pereat,* down, *pereat, pereat."*** I remember him once after midnight hitting the cobblestones in front of a house so that the sparks were flying, screaming *"Pereat* Rudolf, the cur, *pereat,* the filthy swine, *pereat,* down, *pereat!"*

On and on, for about fifteen minutes (pardon your honour, I am just repeating Wolf's words): "Rudolf, the swine, cur, bastard, *Wichser, Schlappschwanz, Arschficker,**** etc." Always the same *"Pereat, Wichser,* down, *Arschficker, pereat, pereat!"* Rudolf finally came down, white in the face. Otherwise Wolf would have been there screaming forever. The philistines were too

---

* *"Der die Philister schwänzt, die Professoren prellt, / Der stets im Karzer sitzt, einhertritt wie ein Schwein."*

** Latin, "Perish!"

*** German "Masturbater," "limp prick," "arse fucker." As a German native, I had little trouble reconstructing these familiar swear words from Dr. Bergk's Latin circumlocutions.

scared to complain, or he'd smash their windows. They pounced on each other like bulldogs, but Rudolf was no match for Wolf, so he was lucky the beadle arrived, who threw them both into gaol. I don't know what happened that night, but Rudolf became one of Wolf's great admirers.

Wolf was very tall and usually looked down on you, and past you, when he talked: never straight in the eye. But he'd be watching you as soon as you weren't thinking of him. He had eager, protruding eyes, with a glint of contempt in them. Except for my women, I never knew anyone more closely than him, not even father; I could tell stories about him, and me, for hours—we spent several years together. But even now I can't really picture him, he was always pretending at something. There were several Wolfs.

He never got them mixed up though. Once when his father came, he had me dress him up with his cane and riding boots. He loved to be barbered and waited on! It was like serving some sultan. "Come here, *canaille*?" he'd scream, though with a smile on his face. His father was satisfied, which was important, I knew, for Wolf was in debt, and our fun would have stopped without his allowance.

The Wolf I didn't like was Wolf the officer, who once a month put on his uniform to join his fellows at the casino. Usually Wolf liked my stories but when I told what I had seen at Schweidnitz he got impatient, bursting out:

Front rank, face to right-about!
Order your firelocks!
Bring your firelocks to your left-sides!

with no smile on his face. He looked exactly like those damned officers on the exercise yard.

Then there was Wolf the philosopher, discussing God and the world with Ulrich. A real cur he was, that Ulrich, always reading some book or else cursing or sneering at someone. First time I met him, I was with Leni, at the Ramrod Cellar. There was Wolf, Ulrich, and their crowd.

"That's my new servant Woyzeck," Wolf told him. "Johann Christian Woyzeck."

"So Fotzeck's his name," Ulrich squealed.

"Woyzeck, Ulrich, Woyzeck," Wolf corrected him.

"Oh, it's Fotzfick!"* Ulrich went on. "He must excuse me, Fotzfick, my hearing's bad."

Everyone was roaring with laughter.

"Fotzfick! A proper name! He must be proud of it!" Ulrich continued. "But why not Fickfotz? We'll call him Fickfotz, Fotzfick. I'm sure he won't mind. Johann Christian Fickfotz. Leni's sweetheart, I gather. I should greet him with some little improvisation of mine. A love poem."

"Yes, Ulrich, but make it a swinish one," shouted the friends.

"How about this one," Ulrich replied:
> *Der Fickfotz und die Leni,*
> *Die treibens wie die Säu,*
> *Was scherts ihn, so lang sie's Geld heimbringt,*
> *Daß sie ihm nicht hält die. . . .* **
Daß sie ihm nicht hält die Treu," the friends shouted in chorus.

"That's too tame," protested someone. "We want something to make us puke." (God knows, I'm only writing down such filth because your honour asked me to. So, please, pardon the dirty language.)

---

* The most rudimentary knowledge of German will make clear this obscene wordgame with Woyzeck's name, playing on "*Fotze*," "vagina," and "*ficken*," "to fuck."

** According to his usual practise, Dr. Bergk renders the obscene parts of Ulrich's "poems" in Latin, which, with the help of the rhyme scheme, I have reproduced in what may be assumed to be the original German. "The Fickfotz and his Leni / Are at it like two pigs / He doesn't care that she's mere trash / As long as she brings home the cash."

"What's his trade, Fickfotz?" Ulrich asked me, and before I could answer he added, "We know he's Wolf's male valet, and Leni's pimp! I mean his profession, Fickfotz, his calling, his vocation."

Everyone was laughing again.

Wolf told him.

"A hairdresser! Go shift, Fickfotz, it's a vile trade, Fickfotz, there's no money in it. Let's see":

> *Der Fickfotz frisiert die Damen,*
> *Er schmeichelt jeder Gans,*
> *Hätt' er fünf hundert Thaler,*
> *Ihm schleckten alle am. . . .**

"*Ihm schleckten alle am Schwanz,*" roared the friends.

"Cheer up, Fickfotz, he's making a face like ten days rainy weather. There's hope, Fickfotz. Follow Wolf! You'll find your master in him. Poor Wolf is bored. His nose tells me, it looks so contemplative these days. Cheer him up, Fickfotz, be Wolf's aide-de-camp in the battlefields of lust."

"Tell us about Wolf!" shouted the friends.

"Tell them," Wolf commanded.

"But that's the last one today," Ulrich replied.

> *Kreuzweis mag er's am liebsten,*
> *Gern schiebt er'n ihnen ins Maul.*
> *Und sollten sie protestieren,*
> *Kriegen sie's auf allen. . . .***

"*Kriegen sie's auf allen Vieren,*" roared the others, except Wolf who was watching us. I hate to be made a fool of, and felt as if everyone else was in on some secret.

A few days later—I thought Wolf was at his casino—he walked straight in on us, *dum concubui Leni*

---

* German, "When taking care of their hair / Fickfotz calls each raven his Venus / If he had 500 *Thaler* / They would all suck his penis."

** German, "He likes most what's upside down / He loves to shove it into their mouths / And should they protest, those whores / He gives it to them on all fours."

*retro.** I pulled out when I saw him, but he abruptly ordered, "Continue!", but I hesitated, confused, so Leni, who turned around on the sofa, *apprehendit penem meum inseruitque vagina sua, tunc apprehendit penem Lupi oreque suo concepit.* ** her head dangling backwards over the edge of the couch. *Erectio mea prope conlapsus restitum est dum observavi penem Lupi arantem orem Leni, dum penis meus arabat vaginam suam, tandem synchronicite,**** Leni groaning.

"Wolf? I loathe him," she said to me after. "He's a swine. You'll see. But he pays me a lot, and promptly. Poor Johann, you looked so startled when he walked in. Wolf and I planned it all a few days ago but he ordered me not to tell you."

So that, too, became part of my job. During our sessions, Wolf spoke to neither me nor Leni. Just gave us his orders, like "Tie her hands behind her back, then, Leni, kneel down *et suge penem suum labiis tuis.*"**** (It's exactly in those same filthy words that he put it, your honour.) Or, "Tie her and gag her," then he whipped her, quite hard, until blood came, then asked me *concubinare cum eam a tergo,***** while he just stood there watching us in complete silence. It was never more than the three of us, but Wolf must have told Ulrich. For Ulrich kept teasing me about it, and always in front of others.

"Don't sneak out, Fickfotz, we need his advice," he screamed at me once as I was leaving the Red Rag.

---

* Latin, "While I was cohabitating with Leni from the back."

** Latin, "She grabbed my penis and inserted it into her vagina, then seized Wolf's with her mouth."

*** Latin, "My erection after a near collapse was restored when I watched Wolf's penis plough Leni's mouth while mine did the same to her vagina, both of us moving synchronically."

**** Latin, "And suck his penis with your lips."

***** Latin, "To cohabitate with her from the back."

"This French author* Wolf and I were discussing, argues that God is dead. There's only Nature, and Nature's a monster, he writes, destroying all she creates. Ergo we, too, he writes, should act like monsters. What does he think of it, Fickfotz. Does he believe in *den lieben Gott*? What, no answer Fickfotz?"

I can still hear him squeal.

"Does he not say his prayers at night and repent himself of his sins? Let me see. Tell us the third commandment."

"I can't remember," I said.

"Never mind, Fickfotz. The commandments are lies invented by people who want to enslave us—says our French author. Let's free ourselves and fulfil Nature's commandments instead. Do mischief, fornicate, rape! Yes, Fickfotz, he has reason to smile. Rape, torture and kill! He's on the right track. To hell with the ten commandments!"

I was fond of Leni, but glad to get out of all that. That's when Wolf decided to resume work on his thesis. I could never figure out what he was doing: something like study the old folks and their customs. We trudged all over Saxony and Thuringia, Wolf in his old German clothes, talking to people, and myself taking notes in blue notebooks. Wolf told them I was his *famulus*, whatever that is, I'm sure those people didn't know either. We went to fairs a lot, first studying them and then dancing and drinking, *et concubinantes cum puellis rusticis*.** Wolf had a way with them, and I'd pretend to be his younger friend so I got my fair share. Sometimes we even got round to doing some of the things we did with Leni, except whip them.

They sure were eager, with Wolf acting so friendly

---

* Ulrich's "French author" no doubt was the Marquis de Sade whose anonymous *Justine, ou les Malheurs de la Vertu*, along with others of his works, were current in numerous, though underground editions.

** Latin, "Made love to the rural girls."

to them, a *Junker* and scholar like him, but they always came with us in twos, for protection, I guess.

Ulrich was right. Everything had to be upside down with Wolf. Even when he was acting the scholar. How complicated he made things! At one time he got all excited about Easter eggs. Just as if no one except him had ever seen one. Of course, his Easter eggs had nothing to do with Easter. They were symbols, he told me, of death and rebirth. Then we found special Easter eggs at the Eisenach summer fair made of sugar, with ribbons wrapped round them; they opened up and had little baby dolls inside.

"That's it!" Wolf said. "That baby certainly isn't Christ."

Then once, at the *Thüringer Hof* in Eisenach, we found a strange figure dangling from our ceiling. It looked like a two-headed eagle.

"That's the holy ghosts," said the laundry girl. "They'll protect you for as long as you stay here."

"That's nonsense," said Wolf. "There may be one holy ghost but not two."

That bird was Thor, he explained, the old Saxon thunder god, his two heads stood for summer and winter, life and death. Wolf, I realized, hated everything Christian, but loved whatever was teutonic and pagan; such as the straw figures made during the summer fair that they threw into the river singing:

Old Thor we carry far away;

His grave shall be the stream today.

Or they'd tie them to wheels, set them on fire, and send them spinning down the mountain slopes late at night hollering:

Old Winter's course is fairly run,

For Summer hath the battle won.

Wolf's favourite was the story of Venus and Tannhäuser. Venus, he told me, was the goddess of love, Eostre in German, from which comes Easter, that is, the real Easter. We spent two whole days walking along the Fischbach road to the Venus Hole close to the top of a cliff near Eisenach. It does look *uti vaginam*.* It's just a crack in the rocks now, but in former times that's where the gate was through which Tannhäuser went to join Venus in her big palace inside the mountain. The Pope cursed him for fornicating with Venus. He stuck an old dried-up stick in the ground saying, "Just as this stick will never grow again, so God will never pardon Tannhäuser." But, after three days, the stick grew fresh leaves, so the Pope sent messengers all over the world to find Tannhäuser. But he couldn't, for Tannhäuser was inside the Venus Hole, *cuncubinans cum Venere*,** and there he stayed. I liked that story.

In March 1806 we were back in Berlin, waiting for Friedrich Wilhelm to call up the army. We spent most of our time with Helmuth, another *Junker*. Like Wolf, he was eager to fight Bonaparte, who'd been chasing the Austrians around. Several thousand of them had been captured at Ulm, including officers and generals. The rest were finished off later. But the Prussians, Helmuth proclaimed, would make mincemeat of Bonaparte and his Frenchmen. All that was stopping them was their own King, that coward. Helmuth and Wolf were of the war party, like Queen Luise and the Duke of Brunswick who fell at Saalfeld. The King finally called up the army, so they went to the French embassy and sharpened their swords on its stone steps, screaming insults. They thought they'd beat Bonaparte's soldiers just like they beat up the "Philistines," but they didn't.

Helmuth was a loudmouth, always fussing about something, giving orders and scolding me like a servant. I complained to Wolf, which made things worse. Wolf told me I had to obey Helmuth just like himself. I could never figure out why he'd make friends with such swine. Even before it happened I knew there was something sick

---

* Latin, "Like a vagina."
** Latin, "Cohabitating with Venus."

about Helmuth. He was a big, fleshy fellow, as if he were padded; even his fingers, with their pink skin bulging out from under rings he was wearing.

It happened one night at the Red Rag. We were drinking in competition, or *floricos* as they called it. Helmuth challenged me to it, and I thought, I'll show you, you swine. I had no idea how much Helmuth could take, though I wouldn't give up. I vomited twice in between, but then passed out, just fell under the table— then came to again on a couch in one of the backrooms they have at the Red Rag. First thing I noticed was someone *defricantem sugentemque penem meum.** (That's what it was, I swear by God.) I thought it was Leni, and reached out to touch her but felt a beard, opened my eyes and saw Helmuth's big body looming above me, *penis suus testiculaque sua*** just in front of my eyes, bursting out of his fly. My head was between his knees, which he closed like a wrench when I tried to get free. *Postquam ejaculatus sum ore suo,**** (it was disgusting, your honour) he straightened up, *et defricavit penem suum manu dextra,***** while still holding mine with his left, then tried to force *penem suum ore meo,****** (that filthy swine, pardon your honour) cursing me when I clenched together my teeth, and squeezed mine with his left, so hard it made me howl, while his went in all the way down my throat, *ubi ejaculatus est;****** it nearly choked me, with his fat body collapsing on mine. Then we just lay there panting, when I saw Wolf in an armchair watching us with his ugly cold eyes.

I felt so disgusted I wanted to die, thinking this was somehow all my fault. Now I know, of course, there

---

* Latin, "Rubbing and sucking my penis."

** Latin, "His penis and testicles."

*** Latin, "After I had come in his mouth."

**** Latin, "And rubbed his penis with the right hand."

***** Latin, "His penis into my mouth."

****** Latin, "Where he ejaculated."

are many like Helmuth, specially in the army; some of them became friends of mine later. But I still hate that Helmuth, and hope to God the French killed him. I should have run up to him, hitting him as he stood there talking to Wolf. But I just left, packed my knapsack and walked straight back to Leipzig.

All I wanted now was some woman, like Tannhäuser's Venus. And I did find one, the Schindelin; I moved in with her at the Richter's. I wanted to marry her, and asked her, but she said, "How can we get married, you have no job. They won't let us without it." I looked for one, did all sorts of things, worked at the warehouses or illuminated engravings. My friend Heuß, the coachman, found me some of these jobs. But none lasted. Saxony was getting ready for war, though no one knew till the last minute which side they'd fight on. Later in August they joined the Prussians, and their soldiers came pouring into the city. I could have joined the army right then, but no way I'd fight under swine like that Helmuth and Wolf.

Meanwhile, the Schindelin found a good job with Herrn Buschendorf and moved out of the Richter's to live at Engler's. All *I* could find was a servant's post out in Barneck, with councillor Honig. I still came in nearly each day to see her, but she didn't want it anymore, me having no money and no real work. Also, I thought, she must have found someone else. Later I met them once at the Fire Ball dancing together. I got into a fight with them, and I hit her. Next day she reported me to city hall, but I took off before they could get me. I went East to Berlin, then to Posen, then back to Berlin, where I tried to find Leni. I asked for her at the Red Rag, and they said she'd left with the soldiers. I got back to Leipzig just three days after Jena and Auerstedt and on the way met the Prussians fleeing as if they'd met the Devil. Next day the French arrived in Leipzig.

Most people were scared, but I was just curious;

I had nothing to lose. We were out at the Peter's Gate waiting for them. Then the first, some two hundred yards ahead of the others, came ambling towards us. We expected the French to come marching in like the Prussians during their parades. Here instead was this raggedy fellow looking more like a vagabond than a soldier. The sight made my heart dance. He was tall, haggard, and tanned, with wild curly hair, and a crumpled old hat with a lead spoon pierced through it.* A plucked goose dangled from his rucksack, and a loaf was stuck on his bayonet. He walked as proud as a king, looked at us briefly with his black eyes, then threw a piece of the bread to the poodle he lead on a leash, and said something to him in French. Fellows like him had defeated the Prussians!

I would have joined them right there, but it wasn't that easy. The battalion which occupied Leipzig did not enlist recruits. I was told that my best bet was to contact the seventh Dutch regiment enroute to the North. There were lots of us trying to join. I got to talking to one, named August. We headed North the next day. Each French garrison, we'd been told, would know where to find that Dutch regiment. We reached it the third day, at Grabow in Mecklenburgh, on the twenty-third of October. I still remember the date from my draft card.

They were awaiting instructions from Bernadotte who was chasing Blücher up North. Meanwhile they didn't waste time with us either. I thought they'd first teach us some French, but you never saw the French or the Dutch. The fellows in my regiment were fresh recruits like me, or Prussian deserters; except for the officers and the major: they were French, but spoke to us in broken German, mostly just bawling their orders. To them we were all deserters, and that's how they treated us. Even the French and Dutch soldiers did. Later on we

---

* The soldier must have been part of the famous Davout corps who wore lead spoons as their insignia.

had fights with them, but it was always we who got punished.

In those days, the French guns were different from most others, much faster they said. So the first thing they taught us was to shoot, all of us, even those who had served with the Prussians. For days we did nothing else till our mouths were as black as coalpits from biting the bullets. "Poise your firelocks!" "Cock your firelocks!" "Present!" "Fire!" "Half-cock your firelocks!" "Handle your cartridges!" "Open your cartridges!" "Prime!" "Shut your pans!" "Cast about to charge!" They wanted us to know how to do these things in our sleep, they said. But God, they drilled us. It wasn't much different from what I'd seen at Schweidnitz. After ten days, two fellows deserted. They were caught near Ahrendsee and shot on the spot. "Martial law." At least they could have let them run the gauntlet.

Everyone was ecstatic when we were ordered to leave. Anything but that garrison drill. Bernadotte and Soult were closing in on Blücher at Lübeck and our regiment marched up to join them. We arrived the day after they'd stormed the city. I'd never seen anything like it. Dead soldiers all over, some still staring at you. And the dead horses! Some with their intestines spilled on the pavement. It was night when we got there, so you just saw what was lit by the firebrands of the plundering soldiers. But you could hear them smash windows and doors; then the screaming, shouting and crying; wardrobes and cupboards crashing on floors, spilling papers, clothes, dishes, and once in a while a gunshot, although the fighting had ended. A cavalryman was riding straight through a hallway. Watching him, I stumbled over a corpse and lost my cap. I was groping for it in the dark when, turning the corner at the end of the street, came a whole regiment, marching in rank and file to their drums and flutes, their music for a brief while making all else fall silent.

But then it started again. It scared me at first, but August and I just got pushed along, into a doorway. August ripped a gold watch off an old man, who turned white—I can still see him. But most of the good stuff—money, rings, watches—was gone already. Then we heard the screams of a woman from inside a house and rushed in: there were five of them, *stuprantes feminam*,* one at a time, while the others were pinning her down on the floor, each one of them grabbing some part of her: thighs, shoulders, breasts. They had torn off her clothes, and she couldn't move much, but she was screaming, so they finally gagged her with her blouse.

You have to have been in that situation to know: all I wanted to do was join them, and so did August who was already trying to grab her. But they didn't like it. One drew his sword and pushed us out, cursing. So we took off, just desperate to find our own, which wasn't easy, all the young ones were hiding. But August got us a torch, so we finally found one behind some planks in a toolshed. We wouldn't have hurt her, but she put up a fight, so we gagged her. I held her first *simul August concubuit ea*,** until she quietened down, *hinc linteo ore suo ablato penem meum ibidem immisi*,*** holding her throat with my hands just in case (God forgive me!). Afterwards she just lay there whining. But we certainly didn't kill her, your honour, which happened to others. Some guys even looted the madhouse, *stuprantes mulieres insanas*.**** This went on for three days until Bernadotte stopped it: anyone looting would be shot.

Then the drill again, the same as in Grabow. At least the women were after us, because they were starving. The problem was how to get the bread to them. We

---

* Latin, "Raping the woman."

** Latin, "While August cohabitated with her."

*** Latin, "Hence, after removing the rag from her mouth, I inserted my penis in it."

**** Latin, "Raping the mad women."

were frisked at the garrison gate, and if they found food on you, you got two days arrest, with no food at all. But necessity breeds invention: there was an unwatched part of the wall where we could throw the bread to them. Then we went out ourselves, *copulantes cum illis** (pardon me) in some dirty room, none of it was much fun. We were glad to get moving again, this time to Pomerania.

Early in 1807 Marshall Mortier had crossed the frozen Peene, pushed the Swedes back into Stralsund, and built redoubts around it. That's where we joined them early in March. It was still freezing, sometimes the temperature dropped below minus twenty. Our headquarters were at Greifswald; but we spent most of the time in those fortifications: under the guns of the Swedes. Then Bonaparte ordered Mortier to move part of his army to Kolberg.

A few days later the Swedes launched a barrage before dawn. We thought Doomsday had come. Everyone was scrambling for cover. The earth shook, then one detonation nearby sprayed us with earth, another tore the head and left shoulder off the man next to me. At first I was sick with fear, but then fear turned to rage. We were all waiting for them, looking towards their batteries. They came in the early dawn, running towards us with glistening bayonets, hundreds of them, the guns had gone silent. All we could hear were their shouts, then our major screaming, "Plant your bayonets!" "Point your guns!" "Hold!" And when they'd come within 100 yards distance: "Fire!" Out it went like one big stroke of lightning. I'd never have thought there were so many of us. But we had no time to look. Once again our major screamed: "Prime and load!" "Point your guns!" and: "Fire!" After the third round they started to run, so we shot at their backs, while here and there screams of *"Vive l'empereur!"* went up from our redoubts. I, too, screamed *"Vive l'empereur!"* Never before had I felt that excited.

---

* Latin, "Copulating with them."

But that wasn't the end of it. In the afternoon they began firing again, this time from two sides. The swine had used the morning attack to move several twelve-pounders onto our left flank. From there they now hit us sideways, while we kept waiting for their attack. We waited and waited, while their cannonade went on and on, even at night, causing more and more slaughter amongst us. On the third day a special platoon tried to wipe out the battery on our left but it was beaten back. On the fourth day we began our retreat. We'd hardly left our redoubts when they came swarming out of the city, now several thousand of them, in two major columns.

At first we managed a proper retreat, reached Greifswald and went on towards Anklam. But there were just too many of them, pushing us from two sides. As we reached Anklam, part of their vanguard had already passed us, so now everyone was just running. Ours didn't even have time to blow up the bridge. Or perhaps they didn't want to cut off stragglers like me and August. After crossing the bridge, we entered a house on the market place which had windows in two directions. As we'd lost touch with our column, we figured we'd best just take a stand where we were. There were twelve of us, each at a window to see what was happening. I held watch in the bedroom. The pillows and blankets were all crumpled up, and the cradle still rocking. They must have fled when they heard us. The only one left was the dog who looked at me from under the table, wagging his tail; it seemed like a dream.

Meanwhile we saw the Swedes approaching from all directions. Towards the North-West they were placing their cannons close enough to reach any point in the city. Then their *tireilleurs* started firing at us from the other side of the market place. But they were too far to hit us. To really get at us, they had to come through an alley which we could watch from a window. They tried, and we shot two of them dead, three others we wounded.

They crawled back to their fellows, and we let them, two of us standing by the window. When the man in front saw someone coming, he'd step forth and fire, and if he missed, there was always the second, standing ready behind. We got all of them in this way. But we couldn't get out of the house.

As it turned dark, our main army was gathering to the South, just outside the city, forming a single big carré. The Swedes moved slowly towards them. Then suddenly everything was lit up: our carré had begun firing—first the front row, then those behind, and again those behind them. Then a lull, after which they fired again, then the shouts of *"Vive l'empereur!"* Then all fell silent. That's how they fought their way out of the trap.

Watching that, we hadn't noticed the Swedes crawl in through the roof. Suddenly they were right behind us, one of them shouting: *"Levez vos bras!"* They thought we were French. Two of us tried to shoot at them, but before getting their guns in position, they were. . . .

HANS MARTENS' STORY
The Woyzeck Circle

Editing the above papers was to be a labour of love in memory of two friends. One of them, Klaus von Bergk, died (or was reported missing in action) near Trondheim in 1940; the other, Carl Kuhlmann, seems to have perished as a political prisoner of the DDR regime. But my initial, fervent devotion to this task never recovered from the sudden onslaught of doubt I succumbed to at the German-Swiss border. Then I realized that to carry out the project would betray our joint resistance against Nazi terror which for the three of us—Carl, Klaus, and myself—had somehow come to focus around Büchner's *Woyzeck*. For what I'd managed to read and transcribe of these papers, before the Kattowitz Gestapo made me flee from Klaus' home, was suddenly revealed to me as the very ground in which Hitler's ideology had its roots.

Even decades later when, under circumstances I'll relate in due course, my ideological misgivings peeled off me like the skin of a snake, I never recovered the original enthusiasm for my task. Hence, all I managed to do was to render an account of a lifelong obsession and tell a story of failure. Now that I'll soon have to confront the horrid, cosmic spider of which Schopenhauer speaks, I'll leave to fate whether my scribbling, along with my translations of the Woyzeck documents, will ever see the light of day. Let the person decide, who may find them amongst my posthumous papers.*

I'll start from the beginning. Georg Büchner's *Woyzeck!* It was Carl, or rather his would-be girlfriend Else, who first drew my attention to it.

"Why don't you get off my back with your Woyzeck," I heard her say as I checked in on Salzwedel's *Café Kruse* to see if any of our gang was around.

"Yes, I *have* read it," she continued, raising her voice while throwing me a sideways glance. "And I don't like it," (slowly articulating each word). "What's so great about this madman, underdog, murderer. Though I can see how he fits in with your crazy ideas. You ought to watch out, or you'll soon run into trouble preaching this nonsense to Hinz and Kunz."

"I thought I was amongst friends," Carl said bashfully, after listening with rapt attention, his face seismographically registering every one of Else's threats and insults.

"Let's see what your friend thinks; he should read it too," Else said, ostentatiously turning to me while I settled down at their table. "He's got more brain in his skull than you have."

Patently, this was one of Else's typical manoeuvres. She was sexy alright—everyone who ever put eyes on her instantly raved about her—but sexy in a self-reflectively languid way that made all she ever said or did seem so calculated. Like the remark that I had more brain than Carl. To say so was downright perverse, and Else knew it. Although she certainly wasn't in love with Carl, she was enamoured with his brilliance, which, like everything else she coveted, she seemed determined to destroy so she could possess herself of the ruins. Even at our tender age I'd developed a sixth sense warning me against falling in love with girls of her prematurely exploitative sexuality. But Carl—my small-bodied, awk-

---

* For the rest of this story see the biographical note on Hans Martens at the end of this volume.

ward, hypersensitive friend, the last of all teenage boys at the *Gymnasium* likely to conquer Else's cruel heart—had fallen for it hook, line, and sinker.

"What are you talking about?" I asked defensively, made nervous by Else's overbearing flirtatiousness. For I knew that deep down she didn't like me, precisely for being armed against her charms.

"Why don't *you* tell him!" said Else, turning back to Carl.

At this point two neatly uniformed SS men from the new NSDAP headquarters on the *Schillerstraße* sat down at the table next to ours.

"Coffee with whipped cream and the usual slice of tree cake?" asked Ulrike, the high-bosomed, dirndl-clad waitress who had completely ignored my arrival. Ulrike, daughter of leather Schulze's tanner, had recently risen to the rank of headwarden of Salzwedel's *Bund deutscher Mädchen*.

"Let's go elsewhere," said Carl, "and I will tell you."

And tell me he did. Büchner's *Woyzeck* had struck him like a long-awaited revelation. There was no doubt in Carl's mind that Marx had unearthed history's blueprint towards the future. In spite of the rise of Hitler's fascists. That was simply an event like the coming of the Anti-Christ, preceding the final victory of the Communist revolution and the beginnings of a socialist paradise on earth. To call in doubt these developments predicted by Marx would be like denying the stellar movements.

But what troubled Carl was that Marx should have been alone amongst the great ones of his age in making these discoveries. Hadn't anyone else guessed intuitively at Marx's insight, or at least probed into the social circumstances of the period like Shakespeare and Cervantes. Reading Heine, Börne, and other poets of the *Junge Deutschland* had been just as disappointing to him as the study of the pre-Marxist Socialists like Saint-Simon and Fourier. Unlike Marx, all of them still clung to residual religio-humanitarian values, the appeal to self-improvement, or displayed a self-congratulatory irony and flippancy.

But then, via an article by Friedrich Gundolf in the *Zeitschrift für Deutschlandkunde*, Carl had discovered Büchner, and in a whirlwind of excitement devoured every scrap of the poet's published writings: *Danton's Death*, his drama about the French revolution, *Leonce and Lena*, his comedy, *Lenz*, his fragment of a novel about the *Sturm und Drang* poet, *The Hessian Messenger*, a revolutionary pamphlet, as well as Büchner's letters, school essays, scientific writings, and last, but not least, his *Woyzeck*. The more often he reread that fragment, the more he convinced himself that its author was the only German poet who would, but for his untimely death, have come to rival Shakespeare.

But Carl had further reasons for his hero-worship of Büchner. For this poet had anticipated several major Marxist insights. Both men, for instance, believed that the humanization of the individual was dependent on the improvement of man's social condition; and that the first step in this process would be the overthrow of the present order which, by the use of terror and oppression, kept the great mass of the people like work bees satisfying the unnatural needs of a minority of degenerate drones; or in Büchner's words, "let this superannuated modern society go to hell."

Also, Büchner had fought for his revolutionary ideas. Particularly dear to Carl was the image of the poet writing *Danton's Tod* in his parents' backyard, always ready to escape via a ladder leaning against the garden wall should the henchmen sent out to arrest him make their appearance in the house. This was after he'd personally distributed his *Hessische Landbote*, a pamphlet inciting the peasants to rise against their oppressors. In doing so he'd risked imprisonment, torture, and death.

A several times reissued arrest warrant featuring Büchner's personal details ("age: 21, forehead: strongly curved; peculiar characteristics: short-sighted") requested authorities in Darmstadt-Hessen and abroad to apprehend and extradite the wanted man for subversive activities against the state. His comrade, pastor Weidig, was captured, tortured, and driven to commit suicide in gaol. It was only thanks to Büchner's bravado and cunning that he avoided the same fate by fleeing, first to Straßburg, and later to Zürich, where he died at twenty-four, partly no doubt due to the exertions of his fugitive life. In his final agony he repeatedly fantasized about being betrayed to the police.

To Carl, Büchner's crowning achievement was his unfinished *Woyzeck*. Written in exile, it was the fruit of the author's by now fully developed revolutionary consciousness as well as of his mature poetic genius. Even Bertold Brecht, according to Carl, the greatest among contemporary playwrights, had never written a work as great as *Woyzeck*. While Marxist in the deepest sense, this play was totally undidactic.

Yet only people who had not read *Das Kapital* could fail to recognize that poor Woyzeck—underpaid soldier, alienated psychopath, and a dehumanized scientist's guinea pig—was in every way the victim of capitalist, bourgeois society. Everything he does, even when he murders his mistress Marie, is prompted by the oppression he suffers. The fit of jealousy in which he does the deed is but his final act of rebellion. Marie and their child are all he has in the world, and when Marie sleeps with the tambour major, there is nothing left for him to do but destroy himself. The murder, Carl argued ingeniously, was a form of suicide. It was Woyzeck's final act of defiance against the society which exploited him.

The strength for this final act came to him from the inner core of his mind which had remained intact in spite of all the tribulations he'd had to live through. The very madness of a mind driven insane by oppression is made to speak the truths others deny or cannot see. Clearly, Büchner put into his anti-hero's mouth some of his own deepest insights.

WOYZECK. *When you're poor like us, sir . . . It's the money, the money! If you haven't got the money . . . I mean you can't bring the likes of us into the world on decency. We're flesh and blood too. Our kind doesn't get a chance in this world or the next. If we go to heaven they'll put us to work on the thunder.*

CAPTAIN. *Woyzeck, you have no self-control. You are not a decent man. Flesh and blood? Why, when I'm lying by my window after a rain-shower and I see all those pretty white stockings twinkling across the street . . . damn it, Woyzeck, I feel love! I'm flesh and blood too. That's where self-control comes in, Woyzeck. The things I could waste my time on! But I say to myself: you are a decent chap, [maudlin] a good chap, a good chap.*

WOYZECK. *Oh, self-control. I'm not very strong on that, sir. You see, the likes of us just don't have any self-control. I mean, we obey nature's call. But if I were a gentleman and had a hat and a watch and a topcoat and could talk proper, then I'd have self-control all right. Must be a fine thing, self-control. But I'm a poor man.*

Although I had trouble following some of the more extreme points of Carl's interpretation, I was instantly captured by Büchner's poetic genius and read everything by and about him I was able to lay my hands on. My friend planned to do a thorough search of the play's historical sources. He had found that *Woyzeck* was based on an actual murder case, and that Büchner had drawn on the psychiatric dossiers of a certain Dr. Clarus who had been appointed to examine the original Woyzeck's state of mind at the time of the murder. Clarus' verdict—finding the delinquent sane and hence accountable for his deed—lead to Woyzeck's decapitation in 1824 but did not remain unchallenged. The exchange of often acrimonious reviews, articles and pamphlets pro and con Woyzeck's insanity which survived the murderer for several decades made his case famous in the annals of early European mental science. Even if one didn't bring to it Carl's peculiar point of view, the task proposed by him promised to be fascinating in the extreme.

Also to my liking was the idea of, as it were, labouring underground and digging up subversive facts. I knew that in all this my efforts would be harnessed by Carl's superior intelligence, but I was glad to accept that. For though I was not a devout Marxist like my friend, I had ample reasons for supporting his essentially anti-Hitlerite endeavours. The main one was my partially Jewish ancestry on the paternal side, a fact I'd only become aware of with Hitler's rise to power. Suddenly, this Jewish grandmother I'd never met and rarely heard of became the anxious topic of our tabletalk during lunch and dinner.

The events of January '33 had left my parents and the small but influential group of Salzwedel Jews in a state of stunned surprise and anguished expectation. Would Hitler implement the anti-Semitic threats he had voiced before his *Machtergreifung*?

Altogether, Salzwedel's comfortable citizenry was rudely shaken out of decades, if not centuries, of bourgeois reverie. Before '33, to talk politics was simply thought of as bad manners. Things were the way they were and bound to stay that way. Hence, even Carl's father, a former Spartakus combatant and Thälmann associate, with his widespread international contacts, had found few associates for his socialist ideas in our hometown. But all this changed in '33. Those eligible for collaboration with the new regime were called upon to demonstrate their allegiance in both word and deed. All others tried to make themselves as inconspicuous as they could. Then, by the time of the *Reichstagsbrand* and the *Röhm*

Putsch, those of Salzwedel's Jews who could afford to do so escaped abroad, while my father sat poring over *Mein Kampf* and every available pronouncement made by Hitler and his cohorts to find out if the family of a man with a (by now deceased) Jewish mother was to be subject to the same persecution threatened to *Volljuden*.

It was in this atmosphere that Carl and I embarked on our task with all the incorrigible enthusiasm of the young and naïve. From the beginning the undertaking was fated. As if by some secret magic, it quickly enmeshed a third victim in its sticky web. This was because of a discovery I made—the first fruit of my reading and rereading of Clarus's densely argued psychiatric dossiers, with their often incomprehensibly convoluted prose. I had drawn up chronological tables and alphabetical lists of all major events and persons involved in Woyzeck's life and, in doing so, had come across a person who, although only once named by Clarus, seemed to have played a crucial, if not heroic, role in the unfolding of the court drama. It was due to this certain Dr. Adam Bergk's well-timed intervention in the case that the appropriateness of Clarus's psychiatric dossier was first called into question, causing the Leipzig authorities to order a second, more detailed examination of the delinquent.

"It can't be an ancestor of our poet Klaus," said Carl when I whisperingly announced to him my discovery in our *Gymnasium* schoolyard behind the *Katharinen Kirche*.

"Who's our poet Klaus?" I wondered.

"Klaus von Bergk," answered Carl. "Don't ask me about him. I'm biased. What arrogance and conceit! Although I grant he's gifted as a poet. Have a look over there. The older fellow with the sharp profile. I dare say, he looks somewhat crestfallen these days. Thanks to brownshirt Meyer, he's recently fallen from grace. Like everyone else who shows any brain. Let's see how we'll approach him."

I suggested that I do so by feigning interest in his verse. Such pretence turned genuine fascination after I'd read his small collection of poetry entitled *Kreuzfahrten in ferne Reiche* * which had been published in '32. Clearly, Klaus was writing in the vein of Stefan George and Gottfried Benn, who, as Carl informed me, had publicly extolled the young poet's talent. At the same time, Klaus' poetry spoke in a voice all its own. In spite of its formal polish, it searched out the crude and ugly. Its favourite subject being Medieval and Renaissance history, it rendered the factual in such detail that reality at its most concrete seemed transmogrified into nightmare, like the best of Altdorfer and other early German painters, especially of the Danube school.

"I concur," said Klaus who was pleased with my analysis. I'd approached him after school as both of us were walking down the ornate stairs traversing the cloister-like interior of our *Gymnasium*. Klaus stopped, looked at me, listened, and then, with a smile, began talking to me as if he'd anticipated this encounter all along.

"The art of the coming years must have an intensity of the concrete to make it immune against all ideological intrusions." That's the one phrase of his I recall verbatim. I also remember that everything else he said was of the same determinate precision: like paragraphs of a well-wrought manifesto. Meanwhile he was standing there, one step below me, his right hand nonchalantly perched on the heavy bannister, totally oblivious to the other schoolboys bustling past us in their rush to get home.

But Büchner? Yes, he'd read him some three years ago when he'd been my age. What had particularly impressed him was the portrayal of Lenz's mental anguish. But since then he'd been disenchanted with Büchner's writings. There was passion, yes, and detail,

---

* German, "Crusades into Far Distant Realms"

but also a lack of formal finish. To Klaus, the primary events in life had to be enacted ritualistically. Even then, as I was looking at him so decorously poised on the step below me, I thought that one would destroy his life if one were to deprive him of these rituals.

When I mentioned Dr. Bergk, Klaus' fading interest in our conversation revived sharply. "An early psychiatrist, you said?"

"As well as a philosopher, historian, and jurist. A real Romantic factotum and polymath. I looked him up in the *Nekrolog*. He wrote or edited over one hundred books, as well as several journals. One, in some twenty volumes, is called the *Museum of the Occult*."

"And you said he lived in Leipzig?" Klaus's previously languid pose had hardened into keen attention.

"Yes. In fact, the *Nekrolog* lists his address. Something like *Burgstraße*. But I may get that name mixed up with our *Burgstraße* here in Salzwedel."

"*Burgstraße 135!*" said Klaus, his voice sounding fatalistic, as if he had resigned himself to some evil news. "That's our ancestral home," he added. "My grandfather lived there until last year, although he recently had to join us. Why don't you come and see me this afternoon and show me Clarus's dossiers. We live at *Gertraudenstraße 13*. Just across the bridge. The house built right into the *Dumme*. I'll introduce you to my grandfather."

Grandfather Bergk inhabited the top floor of this *Empire* style mansion. Its regulated voluptuous splendour complete with multi-branched candelabra, stained glass standing lamps, thick curtains, and bizarrely figurative furniture, was strangely at odds with the surroundings this old man had fashioned for himself. He wore felt slippers, a threadbare dressing gown, and wire-rimmed glasses through which he peered into a microscope. All around him lay open tomes, vials, flasks, little boxes, as well as scraps of food. Even at first sight the room seemed a relic of a former Spitzweg-like period that I'd begun to associate with the original Dr. Adam Bergk. There were heavily-bound leather tomes on divers haphazard shelves, woodcuts, charts, globes, measuring instruments, a nonchalantly pendulous skeleton, and a hollow-eyed, grinning skull on the window sill.

After eagerly listening to what I'd had to say about Woyzeck and the psychiatric dossiers (which Klaus was reading in a downstairs boudoir overlooking the *Dumme*), the old man screamed: "Tell me once again, but louder" (which I did), "my hearing's almost gone." Then, when I asked him another question, he said, quietly now: "Oh, I don't know, my dear fellow, I can't remember a thing," and stared past me with his childlike, whimsical smile. Meanwhile he'd repeatedly brush clearly non-existent crumbs off the table in front of him with a brisk though random sweep of his hand, as if every time he'd finished doing so, more imaginary crumbs sprouted like mushrooms from the table top.

When I brought my attempt at conversation round to his present pursuits, his hearing and memory were miraculously restored. He invoked a bizarre medley of mesmeric and alchemical authorities in support of an endeavour so persuasively fantastical as to make me wonder if not he but I had lost my bearings. Grandfather Bergk, if I understood what he told me at the time, was looking for the liquid capable of inducing mesmeric, that is supernatural, states in minds otherwise immune to the usual hypnotic practices deployed by animal magnetists.

Baffled as I was by it, the man's sudden euphoria encouraged me to ask him another question. Was there a portrait of his illustrious forebear?

Looking at me like a diver who'd re-emerged from scanning the ocean floor fauna, Klaus's grandfather smiled and said: "Of course, there is. In the attic next door. I insisted that they be brought here: our ancestors right down to Bergk, the organ builder, who became

Leipzig's *Bürgermeister*. No one wants them in this house (emphatically insisting on 'this'). This place is of the devil." Then, while sweeping the crumbs off the table-top with renewed vigour, he added: "But I'll drive him out."

"Drive out whom?" wondered Klaus, who had suddenly appeared in the doorway.

"The Devil ruling your father," said the old man, making Klaus smile as if to acknowledge some secret bond.

"Why didn't you ever tell me about this Dr. Adam Bergk?" Klaus asked.

"Because you weren't interested," said the old man, removing several open tomes blocking the door behind his chair. He opened it, entered, and, in the dusty twilight shot through by sun rays, pointed to one of some twenty heavily ornate frames stacked up against a wall. While Klaus and I tilted back about half of them, the grandfather pulled out Dr. Adam Bergk's with astounding octogenarian vigour. The portrait showed a man in his fifties, wearing old German clothes as were fashionable during the Romantic period. The warps in the crudely executed canvas made his features appear strangely bloated. Although his head was bent to the side, his eyes were focused upon us. This, no doubt, was meant to give the man an air of contemplative sagacity, but it really made him resemble a fugitive looking for those out to catch him.

"You don't mind if I hang it above my desk downstairs," said Klaus, in reply receiving a wave from his grandfather's hand like the flapping of a penguin's wing.

A little later, the old man said: "But you'll let me see that Clarus dossier!"

"Yes, I will," said his grandchild.

"What was all that about your father and the Devil?" I asked Klaus after I'd said goodbye to his grandfather.

"Well," replied Klaus, but without the smile that had lit up his face in the attic, "my father recently joined the ranks of the SS whom grandfather hates with a vengeance. The first few days he lived here he caused such a scene in front of SS visitors that father decided to lock him in the attic."

"How embarrassing for your father," I said, still not sure if I could entrust Klaus with the secret of our subversive scholarly labours regarding Woyzeck.

"As embarrassing as my poetry!" replied Klaus bitterly. For the first time since our meeting on the *Gymnasium* stairway he looked at me with a warmth that gave me hope that he would join our little cell.

Which he did, bringing to it all the power of his mature intelligence and poetic talent. He quickly read through the materials we'd gathered already, particularly the more readily available writing of Dr. Bergk, Hofrath Clarus and their Leipzig contemporary J.C.H. Heinroth who, as the first man ever to teach psychiatry as an academic subject, acquired fame on an international level. Then within weeks of initiating his own line of research which, unlike Carl and I, he kept to himself, Klaus embarked upon writing *Woyzeck's Head*. "I'd like to complete what Büchner left unfinished," he said, his familiar lack of modesty leaving Carl to cringe with embarrassment.

Klaus let us witness the unfolding of his work which I, for one, watched with growing admiration. As far as we could tell, Klaus wrote it down word for word, sentence for sentence, and paragraph for paragraph, with a deliberateness of premeditated effort which only here and there called for the crossing out and replacement of the odd word or phrase. At the same time, he staunchly rejected Carl's ideological suggestions. Carl was convinced that Dr. Bergk, in his diverse writings, had displayed not only pre-Freudian but also proto-Marxist leanings. Klaus acknowledged the former to the point, I think, of overemphasizing Dr. Bergk's ingenuity in psychoanalyzing Woyzeck. But he steadfastly refused to turn his ancestor into a pre-Communist hero. Somewhat rudely, it seems to me, he shrugged off as a provocative *jeu d'esprit* Dr. Bergk's suggestion, made in his *Philosophy of Penal Law*, that governments should be punished for crimes of mental cruelty to their subjects, which Carl, in all the flushed excitement of the proselytizing ideologue, took as proof of Dr. Bergk's pre-Marxist advocacy of the concept of alienation.

To Carl, art could be great only if, like Büchner's, it embodied the Communist understanding of life. By contrast, Klaus argued with Stefan George-like intransigence that art told of truths beyond the doctrinaire superstitions of religion, metaphysics or recent ideology—whether Communist or Fascist. The latter two, he declared, were retrogressive barbarizations of the human mind. In spite of these often acrid debates, the hate-love relationship between Carl and Klaus gradually deepened into a friendship based on genuine respect for each others' intelligence and impassioned convictions.

HANS MARTENS' STORY
The Woyzeck Papers

I could never find out if the arrest of Carl's father was linked to our *Woyzeck* research. But it certainly put an end to it for several years—that is, until my visit with Klaus in Kattowitz and my subsequent flight via the German-Swiss border. But let me tell my tale in due order.

First trouble arose when Carl, no doubt in competition with Klaus, set out to produce *Woyzeck* for the year's end of school celebration. During rehearsals in our *Aula*, Carl took the lead role of Woyzeck, while casting Else as Marie, Klaus as the tambour major, and myself as the scientist. Thanks to Carl's heart-rending impersonation of the downtrodden, half-demented, yet resilient protagonist, the production promised to be a big success—until Carl, much against our advice, insisted on inserting a brief, interpretive statement with quotes from Büchner's most inflammatory anti-authoritarian statements into the programme brochure. Sadly, our principal got wind of it before the first night.

Not a single copy of that brochure has survived, so I don't know what most aroused brown shirt Meyer's indignation. But he was no doubt right when in his reprimand (for which Klaus and I took the brunt jointly with Carl) he accused us of treacherously trying to undermine Germany's rebirth in the National Socialist spirit.

The performance was cancelled and the three of us threatened with instant dismissal if ever again we'd be caught engaging in similar activities.

What I remember vividly is our subsequent, anxious meeting in Carl's father's secret library. A door disguised as bookshelves led to its windowless, cramped interior. None of us, except Carl himself, had been aware of its existence. I stared with awe at the arrays of thick tomes on the wall-to-wall shelves. For the first time, I was allowed to enter the inner sanctum of that secret brotherhood which, as an initiate, I'd only peripherally inhabited. Most prominently exposed were the solidly bound works by Marx and Engels facing the desk. Beside these were tracts by Lenin, Trotsky, Stalin, Bakunin, Saint-Simon, Fourier and many other names still unfamiliar to me at the time. So here was the intellectual powerhouse from which our joint labours around Woyzeck had taken their initial impulse and which, before long, was to plunge us into disaster. Obviously, Carl had chosen the locale to give this critical meeting a symbolical framework.

Predictably, he pleaded for continued, active, though clandestine resistance, while Else, as usual, warned him against the inescapable calamities that would ensue. She did so pleadingly, and less provocatively than usual. Was that because of her visible awe of Klaus? Of all the teenagers known to me he seemed to be the only one totally indifferent to her sexual charms. I personally sided with Klaus who argued that the most dignified way of surviving these barbaric times was through a kind of "inner emigration."

But I wasn't allowed to entertain such fantasies for long. What happened soon after convinced me once and for all that "inner emigration" would be open only to those on whom Hitler's henchmen turned a blind and contemptuous eye.

They came at 3 o'clock in the morning, four days

after our meeting in the secret library: a black Mercedes and two armoured trucks. While machine-gun toting soldiers surrounded Carl's house, three men wearing boots, hats, and topcoats forced open the front door. They were obviously from out of town, probably Magdeburg. No one who witnessed the raid, like Carl and his mother, had ever seen them before. Carl's father was torn out of bed, barely allowed to put on shirt, pants, and shoes, then locked in the truck. *"Schutzhaft"* or protective custody they called it. Within a few days they took him to Dachau where he died eight years later, of a "heart attack" his family was told.

Through the hidden door, which obviously was no secret to them, they then proceeded to the library, tore the books from the shelves, trampled on the mutilated, torn, and bent volumes with their boots, then re-emerged triumphantly with half a dozen stacks of letters tied by reddish string: Carl's father's correspondence with comrades in and outside Germany from several decades, all of which he had planned to publish towards the end of his life.

Had someone in our group betrayed Carl's father's secret to the Gestapo? For a long time I most suspected Else, although I could never think of proper reasons why she should have done so. Why, if she'd had plans to betray Carl's father, would she have warned Carl himself of the possible consequences of his pro-Marxist proselytizing?

Or had it been Klaus, who in ultimate loyalty to his SS officer father, had revealed to him the existence of the secret library? Naturally, Carl in turn must have suspected both Klaus *and* me, while the possibility of a betrayal on Else's part apparently never crossed his mind. Hence he avoided us, and instead, more than ever searched out Else's company with an insidiousness to which she responded with a kind of pained embarrassment. Unlike Carl, Klaus and I, Carl and Else somehow managed to stay together and then got married at a time when, for a period of some two or three years, Carl seemed a rising star on the firmament of Ulbricht's young DDR. This was partly thanks to the fame of his father who had died as a Communist martyr at Dachau, but also due to his own intellectual brilliance and his unwavering, though ultimately fatal commitment to the Party.

With our Woyzeck Circle disbanded, my active interest in Büchner ceased for several years. Hence, there is no need to record my life during that period. What's alone relevant to this tale is that I quit school before my *Abitur* and moved to Berlin where I fell in with a small group of kindred spirits who, for reasons similar to mine, thought it best to resist rather than to passively suffer persecution. Pretending to be inspired by an ardent wish to join the card-carrying Nazi rank and file, we attended every possible rally, particularly those held by Goebbels, Himmler, Goering, and the Führer, then reported back to others who would wire our accounts to London. I never knew though through what round-about channels. Even amongst those attending the actual rallies, there were only two, my friends Emil Kasten and Peter Kindler, whom I knew by proper names. All others used aliases or no names whatsoever.

My original intention had been to follow my parents who early in '39 had gone to Paris in search of escape routes. But the speed with which Hitler, from the Polish *Blitzkrieg* onwards, implemented his expansionist *Lebensraum* policies, ran ahead of most people's plans. It threatened to cut me off from my family and entrap me in my more and more oppressive homeland. In this situation without visible exit, Klaus once again entered my life.

Over the years since the arrest of Carl's father we'd maintained a kind of distanced and non-committal correspondence. I thus knew about the main events in his life. Since getting married to a woman called Gerda shortly after his *Abitur*, Klaus had studied chemistry, then taken on a prestigious posting with the *IG Farben* research team in Kattowitz. Here he had quickly risen in the ranks due to his brilliant scientific achievements. Evidently, the writing of poetry and prose had been renounced as a thing of the past.

Klaus must have been guessing at my plight from what I'd told him about my father's Jewish mother and from what my letters had hinted at between the lines. For suddenly, without my asking, there was a letter of his with a request. Would I call him the following Friday towards eight o'clock in the evening?

The phone was answered by Gerda telling me that Klaus was still at his office. But he'd left me the following message—what he needed to push my application for a job with *IG Farben* were my personal details as well as two passport-size photographs. Barely able to stop myself from giving vent to my confusion, I promised to send what Klaus had asked for as soon as I'd obtained the photos. Gerda hoped that I'd not changed my mind about visiting them this coming Christmas. Yes, I replied, I'd be delighted, by now ready to follow up on each of her suggestions. She was so much looking forward, she said, to meeting her husband's old friend. How often Klaus had told her about their Woyzeck Circle! Her husband hoped that I was still interested in Büchner. Klaus had a big surprise in store for me, she said, but he'd rather tell me about that in person.

What I most remember about that Christmas at Klaus's home in Kattowitz is my anguished heart whenever the doorbell rang: my heart contracting in spasms imagining the stomping of boots towards the library where I sat copying the Woyzeck Papers. Was I about to be taken away like Carl's father? Caught in the same ingenious trap laid for him five years earlier? As I tried to listen to what was going on downstairs, holding my breath so as to steady my wildly beating heart, I couldn't help thinking that Klaus might after all be some monster of intellectual depravity who liked to play elaborate cat and mouse games with the victims he had entrapped already. I suspected him in spite of everything he'd done for me.

Klaus had come to pick me up at the Kattowitz railway station with his brand new, black Mercedes. The person I remembered used to be reticent, withdrawn and aloof, but this Klaus, his face marked by several barely healed fencing scars, talked incessantly, compulsively, with, as it seemed to me, a twang of fear in his voice.

"That's Dietrich's *Kindergarten*," he said, as his limousine turned a corner. "And there's the *Monopol*, one of the best hotels in the place: you probably read about it in the papers. They caught about thirty insurgents on its roof, several of them women, a couple of days after the occupation. They were sniping at German soldiers. Retaliation was swift. And severe. Too much so, I'd say. To set an example, they said."

Then nodding towards a massive gate flanked by two steel helmeted soldiers, he murmured: "That's the SD headquarters."

"Have they forced you to join the SS yet," I wondered.

"Not yet. But the pressure is on. And I'm scared of what will happen to me if I don't, as well as to Gerda, Dietrich, and Peter. Get fired from my job or forced to work in one of their camps? They are planning to build one right nearby in Oswiecim."

Then, after a brief silence, he turned around to look me straight in the eyes: "And yourself?"

Could I trust Klaus? Since he'd joined *IG Farben*, his career had been truly spectacular. How had he managed that while refusing to join the SS? He was brilliant, of course, so they needed him. But there were others like him, just as gifted, and everyone else joined.

"Of course, you don't have to tell me," he added. "Who wouldn't be suspicious seeing me drive a tank like this." (It was the heavy metalled model preferred by top ranking Nazi officials.) "It's a company car which *IG Farben* gave me, 'in acknowledgement of my outstanding contributions to German science,' as they put it. But it hurts me to see that I am losing the trust of old friends. Friends like yourself. Meanwhile, I don't distrust *you*. I'll even let you in on a secret. And ask for a favour. Anyway, here's my own little favour to you in this bargain. I thought you might need it."

With that he reached for his inside pocket, took out a mid-size envelope, and handed it to me. I could hardly believe my eyes when I pulled out its contents: a slightly-worn Swiss passport with the cross on it, issued in the name of Hans Bährmann but with my personal details and complete with the photographs I'd sent Klaus. I stammered thanks, asking him to forgive my distrustful silence.

"No thanks!" said Klaus. "And no questions! It was meant for a distant relative of Gerda's who unfortunately can no longer use it. Someone with your problems. So we both decided you should have it. Courtesy, so to speak, of the von Bergk household."

"But the favour for which you'll ask me. What if I can't do it?" I burst out, firmly holding on to the passport which promised life and freedom.

"Don't worry. If you can't, it's no matter. Just an idea I had since I thought you might be leaving anyway. For old memory's sake." Then, after another moment of silence, he added: "How much I envy you!"

"But why don't you leave yourself? I'm sure everyone abroad would welcome you with open arms."

"I'm not a bachelor, Hans. I'd never get out. Not with Gerda and the boys. And I don't even want to think what would happen to them if I were to flee alone."

Klaus was right, of course. By now we'd reached

Kattowitz's Southern, residential suburbs.

"So what's the favour I am supposed to do for you?" I asked, just as he was pulling into the driveway of a small, tree-encircled villa.

"I'll show you after dinner," he replied. "I was going to take the three of us to the *Savoy*. But Gerda insisted. She's making cabbage rolls. I remember how much you used to like them."

As promised, Klaus showed me after dinner: the Woyzeck Papers. It was Klaus's grandfather who had found them a year earlier. Klaus's father, who'd been researching his ancestors for their Arian racial purity, had asked him and Klaus to help. So the three of them had gone back to *Burgstraße* 135 in Leipzig, had reopened the house, and gone rummaging through everything from albums, books, old bills, to boxes, suitcases, trunks, and wardrobes. Klaus's father quickly grew impatient with the thousands of dusty, mouldy, and dank items, often crumbling in his hands, and went back to Salzwedel. But grandfather Bergk seemed in his element. And so was Klaus. The attic where as a child he'd been too scared to play even after his parents had installed lights in it, turned out to be a treasure trove of family reminiscences. And here they were: several shelves full of Dr. Bergk's publications including a complete run of his diverse journals. And, crammed between the volumes of his old and new *Museum of the Occult*, a large-sized, square, beautifully decorated metal box, the same box that was sitting in front of us on Klaus's desk.

"I've kept it all exactly as we found it. Here look! The original copy of Dr. Clarus's first psychiatric dossier of Woyzeck. And here the second! Next the attack by Bamberg Phyikus Dr. Marc on Clarus. Then Heinroth's defence of Clarus plus Clarus's own rejoinder. But that's not it. Look here, inside this yellow folder, marked "The Woyzeck Papers." The way it is all arranged, with the copies of Dr. Bergk's own letters, my great grandfather must have thought of publishing this himself," said Klaus while pulling out the contents. "I can't imagine what stopped him."

I quickly leafed through the stack of frayed, yellowish papers. There were the letters reproduced above under THE BERGK-SCHOPENHAUER CORRESPONDENCE, PART ONE, followed by THE LIFE OF JOHANN CHRISTIAN WOYZECK AS TOLD BY HIMSELF, transcribed by J. A. Bergk, *anno domini* 1823. Then more letters from Schopenhauer and Dr. Bergk, plus several smaller items as well as an envelope containing some strangely charcoaled and water-stained pages full of wild, oversize scrawls.

Klaus was wondering about what could have stopped Dr. Bergk from bringing out these papers. But why wasn't he doing so himself, I thought, having so much more reason for it than his forebear. As he knew all too well, Büchner's *Woyzeck* had been hailed as one of the great works of world literature for several decades; Schopenhauer, though suffering ignominious neglect for most of his life, had been recognized as one of the major philosophers of all time since the 1860s. Surely, there would be enough Schopenhauer enthusiasts who'd avidly devour this unknown treasure and who would definitely consider it a literary crime to keep it hidden.

"Who'd be the editor?" Klaus asked in reply to my question.

"Well, yourself, of course. I could never understand why you didn't publish your Woyzeck novella either."

"You must be joking, Hans. The Nazis might tolerate me as a chemist, and probably have forgotten that other Klaus von Bergk you knew. But as a writer I have long been on their blacklist. Especially since I was publicly associated with Benn."

I liked Gottfried Benn as a poet, but detested him as a person. All I could think of when Klaus mentioned him was Benn's notorious "Answer to the Literary Emigrants" (like Thomas Mann) from 1933. In it, Benn had called Hitler's vision of a biologically superior German race mythic and deep. It made the Führer an even greater man than Napoleon. Also, Bonaparte had imposed his will on the world, whereas Hitler embodied history's very spirit: a spirit which was geared towards breeding a new race of masters, Nietzsche's twentieth-century barbarians.

"Since Benn vowed allegiance to Hitler," I said, "he should be doing splendidly with the *Reichs Schrifttums Kammer*."

"Look at our well-informed friend," Klaus replied, turning to Gerda with a nervous chuckle. "Lives in Berlin and has no idea what the Nazis are doing."

I guess that due to my loathing for Benn's Emigrants' Letter, I had simply paid no attention to him since '33. So Klaus showed me. Like all his papers, he kept his Benn file in a neat folder: first, a couple of letters from Benn himself praising Klaus effusively and, it seemed to me, fulsomely, for some poems he'd written; second, the newspaper clippings of an attack on Benn, published first in the SS weekly, *Das Schwarze Korps*, then reprinted verbatim in *Der Völkische Beobachter*, the official party organ. The piece was entitled "The Self-Stimulator."

"It's bad enough," Klaus said, "if that kind of attack appears in *Das Schwarze Korps*. But when *Der Völkische Beobachter* picks it up the next day, it's like a death warrant or deportation order."

I only read the piece once, there and then, so I don't remember the details. But some of the words in it have been etched in my brain forever. It called Benn an "unnatural swine," "faggot," and "Jewish bastard." It said he should pack up his filthy scrawls like his comrades Kerr, Tucholsky and Kästner before him.

"So what happened to Benn after that?" I asked.

"Inner emigration," Klaus replied. "It's General

von Johst who saved him. Since Benn's an army doctor, the military had a major say during the subsequent investigation held by Goebbel's *Reichs Schrifttums Kammer*. Von Johst is supposed to have said: '*Das Schwarze Korps* is such a scum sheet that it can't possibly insult an officer—it would be different if it had praised you—the matter's closed, you stay with us.' But that was by no means the end of it. Via a frustrated would-be artist called Willrich, the Rosenberg faction of the *Reichs Schrifttums Kammer* had another go at Benn. Willrich wrote a book entitled *The Cleaning Out of the Temple of Art. An Artisticopolitical Combat Treatise Towards the Sanitation of German Art in the Nordic Racial Spirit*. In it, he repeated the diatribes from *Das Schwarze Korps*, adding that Benn was also guilty of insulting the Aryan race for having praised a Jewess and cultural Bolshevik like Else Lasker-Schüler.

"As a matter of fact," Klaus continued, "I knew nothing of all this until Benn himself told me. During a meeting at his home in Berlin, I asked him to put in a word for me with his publisher for some recent poems I'd written. He looked at me silently with his hamster-like, enigmatic face—you never know if he is smiling at or contemptuous of you. 'A recommendation from me,' he said, 'rather than get you published would have you damned. Do you know what happened when, under orders, I called Willrich's publisher Lehmann to account for printing Willrich's attack on me? Lehmann answered that I'd better shut up. Did I ignore the fact that my books were kept under lock and key at the Munich *Staatsbibliothek*? Didn't I know that they were accessible only to researchers with express party documents to prove that they were specializing in artistic decadence and spiritual perversion? And I *didn't* know,' Benn concluded. And neither did I," Klaus added. "I guess I was just too busy getting on with my career."

What could I say?

After a moment of silence, Klaus continued: "And you know, of course, how much Büchner's fallen into disfavour with the Nazis. In spite of the efforts made by some pro-NS critics like Pfeiffer to turn him into a National Socialist. In general they treat Büchner as a Bolshevik."

"But how about the Schopenhauer letters?" I wondered.

"They'd no doubt print those," Klaus answered, "though not without editing them the way they've edited Nietzsche."

Klaus was right, of course. So I was more than willing to do him the "favour" he asked me, which was to copy the Woyzeck Papers, take them with me abroad, translate them, and eventually have them published, perhaps in France, perhaps in England or America—anonymously, of course, so it couldn't be used against Klaus. All I insisted on was that we'd include his novella in this venture; he agreed with reluctance. I set to work the next day, until two Gestapo visits put a premature stop to my efforts.

My visit with the Bergks had been incognito, so to speak. But it later turned out that one of the helmeted guards in front of the SD headquarters had noticed me as someone unknown in town when we drove home in Klaus's limousine from the railway station. They first came on the 27th when, to my eternal good luck, I was out for a walk.

"A routine visit," they said. "For your own protection."

They had noticed some undesirable elements round the house. Polish insurgents, no doubt! Hadn't *die gnädige Frau* noticed them? (Klaus was out for his first day back at the office after Christmas.) No, she hadn't, Gerda replied. One man in a bluish raincoat had been actually seen walking in and out of their house. Surely, the *gnädige Frau* was aware of that.

"That's a friend from Berlin who's been staying with us over Christmas," Frau von Bergk replied.

"No offence. Just keep watching for anyone roaming around your house! We'll keep an eye on it ourselves. *Heil Hitler!*"

As a matter of fact, we'd already taken precautions. Klaus had noticed two SD agents walk past the house several times on Christmas Day. So we'd agreed on a number of signals. If I was out for a walk, Gerda would leave the front door ajar to signal that they were inside the house. Should they come to the door while I was in Klaus's study, she'd cough three times, so I could crawl up into the attic and stay there till they were gone. Given Klaus's prestige, they'd be unlikely to search the house. Nonetheless, now that they had come, I'd have to leave as quickly as possible or risk being arrested. And I still had to transcribe over a dozen Bergk-Schopenhauer letters as well as the fragments from Woyzeck's second autobiography, not to mention several other, smaller items.

On the 30th they were back. I could still hear them as I tiptoed up to the attic.

"Just another routine check, Frau von Bergk. Nothing to worry about. But if you don't mind we'd like to have a quick word with your guest."

"He left yesterday," Gerda replied. "On the evening train to Berlin."

On that too we'd agreed. Then, two days later, at two o'clock in the morning, that is New Year's morning, I left. It was a good day for flight. Everyone would be drunk, including, we hoped, the Gestapo agents. Through Johanna, their Polish servant, Klaus had managed to hunt up a taxi plus Polish driver who'd take me to Gleiwitz where I could safely take the train back to Berlin. I'd meet the man at exactly four o'clock in the morning, in the *Hindenburg Gasse*, a predominantly Polish district of town, some two kilometres from the Bergks' home. I'd have to walk there, through the back streets— Klaus had made me an exact itinerary with all the street names. Taking his limousine or accompanying me would have been too conspicuous.

Before I left through their backdoor, we said goodbye to each other inside the house.

"Remember we're in this together," Klaus said. "Don't you dare not tell them if they arrest you who made you carry this stuff in your suitcase. I'll know how to muddle through if that happens. It would hurt me far worse to know that you came to harm on my account. As for the rest of the papers, I'll get them to you somehow."

Then I turned up the collar of the coat he'd given me and walked into the night with my suitcase. One of the last things Gerda had done was to undo the lining, put the Woyzeck Papers I'd managed to transcribe inside, and sew it back on. She did a superb job. Without it, I'd no doubt have been arrested at the border near Schaffhausen when I crossed over into Switzerland and freedom. I have already given an account of that incident and how it made me realize that what was hidden in my suitcase was a part of that pernicious Nazi ideology from which I was trying to escape.

No wonder I began to question the authenticity of the papers, though at the time I did so from an unconscious urge to rid myself of their burden. Maybe the Schopenhauer-Bergk correspondence, or even Woyzeck's autobiography, were the fabrications of some ingenious brain. Perhaps Klaus's brain. No, that was unlikely. Under normal circumstances, one could have forgiven such a deception. But not in this case. To make me risk arrest, torture, and death, all for the sake of promoting his literary ambitions? Impossible. Yet perhaps Klaus had fallen victim to someone else's falsifications himself.

But whose? Perhaps the original Dr. Bergk. I pondered the possibilities for a moment, but there were none. Everything spoke against it. Who would have laboured to make the historical Woyzeck the focus of a number of carefully crafted and researched falsifications long before the incomplete manuscript of Büchner's play was acclaimed as a major work, let alone published?

Perhaps Klaus's father. The same man who caused his son (maybe deliberately) to find the manuscript in the attic of their Leipzig home. But everything I remembered, mainly from what Klaus had told me about him— his slavish devotion to Hitler's early National Socialist

Party, his highly successful, but notoriously ruthless business practises, his contempt for his own dilettante-*littérateur* father who'd brought the family to the brink of bankruptcy—everything spoke against it.

But how about grandfather Bergk? Yes, I concluded: that's the man who in a whim of elaborate fantasizing had produced the fake documents after Klaus and I had drawn his attention to Dr. Bergk years ago in Salzwedel. What intense interest, peculiar for a man in his eighties, he'd shown in the Clarus dossiers once Klaus had asked him for permission to put up the Dr. Adam Bergk portrait in his study! Perhaps this half-demented fantasizer had chosen to fabricate these papers in revenge for failing to establish himself as a poet after a lifetime of frustration. And no doubt it was he who had finally placed them, along with the other Woyzeck documents, in the colourful box neatly placed between the volumes of his ancestor's *Museum*. And what if Klaus himself should have failed to find it? Grandfather Bergk would still be haunting that attic as a ghost, when some child or grandchild of Klaus's, made curious by the folder inscribed "The Woyzeck Papers," would eagerly open it and begin to leaf through its pages with growing amazement. And how could grandfather Bergk have anticipated that his whimsical joke would be played upon persons who, as a result, would suffer anguish, disillusionment, or even death?

Before long, the idea became an obsession, and by the time I crossed over to France at the end of February, I was carrying with me a second suitcase. It was full of tomes which I'd spent some two weeks hunting up in the second-hand bookstores of Zürich and Bern: the six-volume Brockhaus edition of Schopenhauer's *Works*, his *Life* by Gwinner, an edition of his letters, Goethe's *Dichtung und Wahrheit* (which I'd never read), the poet's conversations with Eckermann, etc., etc.

The best way to find out if the Schopenhauer-

Bergk letters (and with them the rest of the papers) were fakes, I decided, was to test what they said about Woyzeck against what's known of him from Dr. Clarus's two psychiatric reports. Since I didn't have copies of them, I spent two full days at Bern's *Nationalbibliothek*, transcribing the two reports word for word from Henke's *Zeitschrift für Staatsarzneikunde*. All these papers and books, which over the years have grown into a sizeable Woyzeck research library, are still surrounding me as I write this in my university office.

Then I went to work, day and night, in hotel rooms and cafés, on buses, streetcars, and trains, checking dates and facts, and especially looking for (though secretly hoping not to find) statements by Schopenhauer and Goethe which might parallel those pronouncements of Hitler-like nihilism I had found in the Schopenhauer-Bergk correspondence.

I was frustrated at every turn. As hard as I looked for inconsistencies and contradictions, I could find none. Wherever Bergk and Clarus contradicted each other—and instances were few and extremely minor—the mistakes could just as well have been Dr. Clarus's. All my efforts to prove the documents falsifications only convinced me of their authenticity. I fared even worse in trying to demonstrate to myself that the brutal nihilism pervading the Schopenhauer letters, as well as some of Goethe's pronouncements, were not actually theirs but the sinister outgrowth of grandfather Bergk's half-demented brain. My search only proved to me that in both cases this nihilism was like the soil feeding roots which eventually branched out into whatever either man thought, said, or wrote.

To be sure, the great Olympian never spoke of it to the public. Instead, he kept his nihilism secret, anxious not to expose his Achilles' heel to the judgemental German public. But the story of his *Walpurgissack* poems proved to be anything but someone else's concoction.

Goethe, in terms nearly identical with those recorded by Dr. Bergk, spoke of them to Johannes Falk, at the same time venting his spleen on the Germans: about how the posthumous opening of his *Walpurgissack* would teach his Philistine readers to really hate him, with a hatred that would last some fifty or perhaps even hundred years. For hatred, he added, at least showed true character, something his countrymen would have to learn before they could once again hope to become a real people. So here I was, over a hundred years later: one of his Philistine German readers and, what's more, one totally loathe to embrace his gospel of hatred.

And how I shuddered to think of Germany's Führer when I read Goethe speak of the demonic character in the final book of his *Dichtung und Wahrheit*.

> They are not always the best men, neither in talent nor spirit, and they rarely display goodness of heart; but they emanate a tremendous force and exert an incredible power over all creatures, even over the elements; and who can say how far their impact might reach. All ethical forces combined will not prevail against them; in vain, if the more enlightened part of mankind will try to render them suspect for being dupes or seducers: the multitude will be attracted by them. Rarely or never do they find their equals in their own time, and nothing will prevail against them but the world itself, against which they have declared war.

Was not the same man who wrote these lines one of Napoleon's most fervent admirers, and loyal to him long after Bonaparte's battles had turned mere slaughterbanks for hundreds of thousands of people? *"Voilà un homme,"* Napoleon said to Goethe when he visited him after Jena and Auerstedt.

Yet my biggest surprise was to find that the actual contents of Goethe's legendary *Walpurgissack* had long been published. I went to look for them on the very first day I arrived in Paris. That was in the early morning of March 4th, after sitting up all night on the train. I left my two suitcases at the *Consigne* of the *Gare de Lyon* and with dizzy steps made my way to the *Bibliotheque Nationale*. Yes, there they were, in Georg Witkowski's 1906 *Faust* edition.

> SATAN *rechts gewendet.*
> Euch gibt es zwei Dinge,
> So herrlich und gross:
> Das glänzende Gold
> Und der weibliche Schoss
> Das eine verschaffet,
> Der andre verschlingt—
> Drum glücklich, wer beide
> Zusammen erringt!
> EINE STIMME.
> Was sagt der Herr denn?—
> Entfernt von dem Orte,
> Vernahm ich nicht deutlich
> Die köstlichen Worte.
> Mir bleibet noch dunkel
> Die herrliche Spur,
> Nicht seh' ich das Leben
> Der tiefen Natur.
> SATAN *links gewendet.*
> Für Euch sind zwei Dinge
> Von köstlichem Glanz:
> Das leuchtende Gold
> Und ein glänzender Schwanz—
> Drum wisst euch, ihr Weiber,
> Am Gold zu ergötzen
> Und mehr als das Gold
> Noch die Schwänze zu schätzen!*

---

* SATAN turning to the right
There's two things all yearn for,

How much Schopenhauer would have liked it: the genitals as the hermetic point of human existence, money and power as the quintessence of life! Here already was the cynical bravado with which Schopenhauer shocked his contemporaries and with which Hitler would drive his followers into frenzies of uproarious contempt for human values:

> MÄDCHEN.
> *Ach nein! der Herr dort spricht so gar kurios*
> *Von Gold und Schwanz, von Gold und Schoss,*
> *Und alles freut sich, wie es scheint.*
> *Doch das versteh'n wohl nur die Grossen?*

High, low, and common,
The resplendent gold,
And the cunt of a woman,
Productive's the one and
Voracious the other,
Happy the man
Who enjoys them together.

A VOICE
I wish I'd been closer
And heard every word,
That came pouring forth
From the lips of our Lord.
For closed to me yet
Is the secret way
To where Nature's forces
Forever hold sway.

SATAN turning to the left.
There are two things, you women,
That lead you to bliss,
The resplendent gold,
And a thick, shiny penis.
Gold gives you pleasures
You won't ever mock,
But your greatest joy
Is a long, juicy cock.

MEPHISTOPHELES.
Nein, liebes Kind, nur nicht geweint!
Denn willst du wissen, was der Teufel meint,
*So greife nur dem Nachbar in die Hosen!**

So I'd been wrong! The Woyzeck Papers were definitely not falsifications; particularly Schopenhauer's letters were not. All the facts of his life discussed in them tallied exactly with what's known from other sources: his row with Hegel, his failure as a university teacher, his escape to Italy, his insensitivity towards his mother and sister, his hardheartedness towards the Marquet—all of it could be verified, often down to the smallest details. If grandfather Bergk had indeed "invented" the letters, he, if anything, had made things all too easy for himself by often just paraphrasing his sources. But even such plagiarism could be explained in terms of the historical facts. This became clear to me when, a few days later, I came across an edition of Schopenhauer's notebooks. Obviously, the philosopher had used his journals like a quarry, often lifting whole blocks from them to include in his works. What wonder then that his letters to Bergk served him as similar quarries, or that he might include in them arguments and ideas he had already worked out elsewhere.

Hence my hope that I might rid myself of the Woyzeck Papers by proving them forgeries proved null and void. There was no way around it. As much as I

---

*YOUNG GIRL
Alas! the Lord speaks so curiously,
Talks for ever of gold, cunt, and penis.
But the adults react very cheerfully,
If only I knew what he means.

MEPHISTOPHELES
Don't despair, my dear child, do not cry!
To find out what the devil preaches,
Slip your hand down your neighbour's breeches.

loathed their ideological bias, I could not deny their importance, and it would have meant a betrayal of any code of literary ethics, let alone of my commitment to Klaus, to destroy or conceal them.

How I tormented my brain trying to think of ways to safely unleash them upon the world! Perhaps just send them out to a University Press without commentary and have them edited by some scholarly pedant who would lace them with footnotes. But as every morning I rushed to the Hotel Lutetia to hear the latest rumours on possibilities of emigration or as I eagerly read *Le Monde* for news of the German approach, such plans struck me as increasingly wrong-headed. On April 9th, the Germans invaded Denmark and Norway. On May 10th, Nietzsche's twentieth-century barbarians over-ran Luxemburg and invaded the Netherlands and Belgium. By May 13th, they had outflanked the Maginot Line, their armoured columns racing towards the British Channel, cutting off Flanders and forcing the Allies to make their evacuation from Dunkirk. By the end of the month we were expecting to hear the first artillery barrages outside Paris. Soon they'd sing their *"Deutschland, Deutschland über alles,"* as they'd march down the *Champs Élysées* to the *Arc de Triomphe*. Would my last act, before being shot or imprisoned, be to spread their deadly doctrine to the rest of the world without commentary or warning? Let the manuscript perish instead!

But for reasons I still can't explain, the opposite happened. Instead of ridding myself of this burden, I once again risked my life by hanging on to the manuscript. That's when, though only temporarily, I ran into problems with my papers trying to follow my parents who had already managed to escape to America. Earlier that year, President Roosevelt had decided to insist on his country's annual immigration quota. When I went to the Embassy to pick up my visa, I was told that the allowable quota had been filled for 1940. No further visas would be issued before 1941.

In my preoccupation with Woyzeck I had almost forgotten the taste of panic. But I quickly relearned. Friends advised me to get a visa for Bolivia instead. That would be expensive, but it was the only sure chance of getting out in time. I took their advice and sewed the Woyzeck Papers back into the lining of my suitcase.

When I arrived at the Bolivian tourist office the next morning, I found a line-up of some two hundred frantic, exhausted applicants. Most of them had been waiting for several days, camping on the sidewalk outside the building. I spent one night there myself. The following morning, the Bolivians announced that the price per visa had gone up to one thousand five hundred dollars, which, after some verbal protest and cursing, foreshortened the line-up by more than three quarters.

Money was not a problem: my father had left me an ample amount with the *Crédit Lyonnais* on *Boulevard St. Michel*. But later that afternoon, when I reached the visa counter, something unexpected happened. I was already counting my one-hundred-dollar bills on the table and was chatting with the official in my rudimentary Spanish, when the man said: *"Conoce usted las restricciones. Ningunas maletas o bolsas. Solamente la ropa que lleva en el cuerpo."*

When I stopped counting the dollar bills, he added: *"El barco estara muy lleno, y el capitan permitirá ningunas excepciones."*

I continued to hesitate, paralysed with indecision. Then he said, with growing impatience, in his broken French: *"M'avez vous entendu? Pas de bagages! Rien du tout! Mais si vous n'en voulez pas, prenez votre argent, et laissez passer les gens. Vous voyez bien qu'ils sont pressés!"*

So I made a totally irrational decision: no, I wouldn't be going without the Woyzeck Papers. Why not? The question has haunted me ever since.

The manuscript, curiously enough, served as my lucky star on that occasion. For most of the visas sold at such extortionist prices were finally declared invalid falsifications by corrupt officials. Hence, the emigrants were shipped back to Nazi-occupied France or left floating on the ocean until their boats, perhaps hit by a storm, perhaps by a British or German torpedo, vanished forever. Then, due to the intervention on my behalf by an influential friend of my father's, I was suddenly granted my U.S. immigration visa and sailed for New York just a week before the Nazis arrived in Paris.

Luckily for myself, I was far too busy to give much thought to the Woyzeck Papers during my first few years in a small Mid-Western University town of the United States—busy getting nationalized as a political refugee and busy building a new life. I opted for an academic career teaching German literature and language. By the mid-fifties I had completed my education, taken my Ph.D. (on the political involvement of the *Junge Deutschland* poets), secured tenure at the associate professor level, and successfully skirted the pitfalls of the McCarthy era. That's mainly, I think, because I'd never joined the Communist or any other political party. So the McCarthyites couldn't nail me.

However, as I grew more settled in the late fifties, the old obsession returned. And for good reason.

What further excuse did I have for not bringing out the Woyzeck Papers? All I'd have to do in order to appease my troubled conscience was to add an introduction stating my basic dissent from the philosophy they projected. And I did try, writing one preface after another. Modern philosophy, I argued, has to start where Nietzsche and Schopenhauer left off: it should go in search of means for improving man's social condition. The Schopenhauerian system, even if one ignored its more sinister implications, I wrote, is narcissistically self-defeating. Or as Georg Lukacs, my long-time mentor put it, it resembles a four-star hotel built on an abyss of nothingness and absurdity, an abyss whose day-to-day contemplation, interspersed by the voluptuous consumption of meals and art works, serves to enhance these refined, luxurious comforts.

However, nothing worked. Whatever I wrote sounded petty, doctrinaire, and self-righteous. What's worse, whenever I thought I'd come up with a new idea, I found dangling from its roots some major fact, problem, or memory from my life. As hard as I tried, I could not be objective. So I decided to write a separate essay instead. It was to carry the title "Schopenhauerian Echoes in Hitler's *Mein Kampf* and his other Recorded Pronouncements." I found enough materials to fill a small volume! Against people who claimed that Hitler's nihilism derived from pseudo-Darwinians like Neville Chamberlain, I argued that it came straight from the much older source of *The World as Will and Idea*. For life's ultimate nothingness, which was a quasi-religious core concept to both Hitler and Schopenhauer, was a strictly secondary concern to the Darwinians. Then I came across a biographical fact that seemed to clinch my argument once and for all. Hitler had bragged about it himself: during the four years that he'd fought in World War One, he had been reading Schopenhauer like his wartime bible, carrying the philosopher's works in his backpack wherever he went.

Yet, as the essay took shape, the old problem reappeared in different form. How could I include it with the Woyzeck Papers without explaining why. And that simply meant a new kind of preface. I was back to square one. The problem seemed insoluble.

I talked about it at parties, luncheons, and meetings; I discussed it with colleagues, secretaries, friends, and enemies; spoke of it with my stationer, mailman, and midnight cleaning lady at the college—none of it proved to any avail. As soon as I'd start, people changed the subject, cracked jokes, or simply backed away when they heard me mention Woyzeck, Schopenhauer, or Hitler. Could I blame them? People at parties wanted to have fun, at luncheons relax, at meetings go about their business. Why, here in America's Mid-West, so many thousands of miles away from the crime, should they concern themselves with an obsolete past that would best be forgotten? I began to feel like a dinosaur stampeding into their peaceful lives with my memories of a bygone, monstrous era.

It finally came to the point where our new chairman felt compelled to take me aside just shortly after he'd taken office. I should be aware, he said, that both colleagues and secretaries had remarked to him that I seemed "over-preoccupied" with this Woyzeck business, that it might "turn into something worse than a mere obsession," that everyone was worried that "I might come to grief over it." So perhaps I should seek the advice of some confidant (i.e., shrink). Or would I like an early sabbatical? I thanked him, declining the offer.

Instead, I decided to abandon the Woyzeck project altogether. I put the papers into the bottom drawer of the huge filing cabinet in my office where they collected dust for nearly two decades. As a result, my collegial relations improved dramatically and my scholarly work grew more prolific. Yet I finally did resume my long neglected task.

Primarily, I think, that was because of a gradual disillusionment with the Marxist Socialism I had made my life's philosophy. For decades I'd held on to that creed after first imbibing it from Carl. Of course, I had been distressed by the Stalinist purges and similar crackdowns of the workers' uprisings in East Germany and Hungary in '53 and '56; and even more so by the building of the Berlin Wall in '61.

But as an atheist with a remaining deep need for something to believe in, I dreamt up argument after argument of self-delusion. As least, that's how it strikes me now. What other choices, I argued, did the DDR rulers have? With its industrial installations dismantled by the Russians, who had had their own destroyed by the Nazis, East Germany was in no position to compete with its much larger Western counterpart, which had American money pumped into its speedy economic recovery by the billions. To claim that the hundreds of thousands who left the DDR before the Wall went up "chose freedom with their feet," was a simplistic distortion of the facts. The most one could say in favour of these so-called "refugees" was that they had abandoned the Socialist experiment in order to rejoin the Capitalist free-for-all, hoping to be among the strong and ruthless who would acquire wealth and power at the expense of their downtrodden, weaker brethren. I used to apply the same formula to Capitalist global politics. Here, the exploitation of innumerable underdeveloped nations provided a mere handful of industrialized ones with the wealth that I half-guiltily enjoyed in the U.S.A.

Events seemed to bear out these speculations. After the building of the Wall, East Germany, as I'd predicted, began to enjoy its belated economic miracle. Soon, the much-hoped-for liberalization of its interior politics would ensue! But following the suppression of Dubcek's 1968 Prague Spring Experiment, doubts began to creep into my arguments. To my dismay, I found that East German *Volksarmee* units had participated in the bloody crackdown. There were renewed waves of gratuitous repression. Unlike former dissidents such as Wolfgang Harich, the more recent opponents of the regime were no longer ready to recant their evil ways. Ours, as one wrote, "is a state machine the likes of which Marx and Engels wanted the proletarian revolution to smash." The nimbus of infallibility which the Party used to have for persons like myself was broken.

On the other hand, what was all the protesting

good for? The Party found ever more ingenious means to suppress, demoralize, and expel the critics of its growing corruption until, with its Marxist reformers silenced, the most powerful protests increasingly came from outside its ranks. The novelist Stefan Heym best expressed my dismay at this dilemma saying that "in East Germany today, the priests talk like revolutionaries while the functionaries talk like priests." Safely ensconced behind the Iron Curtain and protected by a bristling array of nuclear weapons, the Communist system, though corrupt to the bone, seemed impervious to all genuine reform. And there was no end in sight. The Marxist experiment had failed. Instead of engendering the Socialist paradise on earth Carl and I had dreamt of, it had created a mere cluster of Orwellian dictatorships.

These disillusioning thoughts received a crushing confirmation when I learnt of Carl's tragic fate. My informant wants to remain anonymous for obvious reasons. As a former member of Ulbricht's inner circle, he had, since the building of the Wall, held a senior position in the border guard department of the DDR State Security, then, making use of his special knowledge, he had managed to escape through the Iron Curtain. Even several years after the fact, as we were talking in my University's Faculty Club, he voiced his fear of secret DDR agents who, so he'd been warned more than once, would finish him off for his treachery at some unexpected moment. At the same time, he made no secret of his continuing to maintain multiple contacts with former DDR affiliates through unspecified channels.

Yet the reason he'd come to see me, I was assured, was curiosity: the wish to meet the author of some Georg Lukacs-inspired essays published in the sixties. He'd once been a Lukacs-fan himself, he told me. When I mentioned our Woyzeck Circle during the pre-war Nazi period, the conversation switched to Carl. My informant had never personally met him. But along with other official observers he had attended the show trials involving my friend, Janka, Harich and several others. These men had been accused of attempting to overthrow Ulbricht, and of trying to bring Lukacs from Hungary to East Germany as the spiritual head of their counter-revolutionary coup. Ironical, wasn't it? The same Georg Lukacs we'd both admired.

The whole thing, of course, was a frame-up. Janka and Kuhlmann had acted under orders from cultural minister Johannes Becher and of writer Anna Seghers, who had wished to rescue their Hungarian friend from the turmoil following the Hungarian revolt. But then Ulbricht had personally forbidden the rescue action and decided to use it as one of the arguments for convicting the would-be rescuers of attempted subversion. Becher and Seghers had to attend the trial, but never once spoke up to reveal the truth.

"Were Janka and Kuhlmann really trying to overthrow Ulbricht?" I asked.

"Not really. What they did was talk." Once in a while my informant almost imperceptibly picked his oversized nostrils, then swivelled his head around to briefly scan the other people in the club. "They talked about the need for inner reform."

"A kind of Woyzeck Circle?"

"Yes, I guess. Only that Ulbricht knew all along what they were doing. One in their group was a spy, and most of the places where they met were bugged."

"By the DDR Gestapo?"

"Yes, by the Stasi. They are consummate professionals. By comparison, the Nazis were mere amateurs."

What does the man want, I wondered. He seemed to be saying these things with a real sense of satisfaction, so that for a moment of revulsion I was about to break off our conversation. But my curiosity prevailed.

"Did the Stasi use torture?" I wondered.

"Back then, in the late fifties, things could still be

quite rough. Prison cells were either over-heated or too cold. Though they used little systematic torture like the Gestapo. But if you showed too much resistance, you might find yourself in a cell big enough to lie in, but not to stand, with water right up to your belly, as you were crouching on the floor."

"So Carl was innocent?"

"No one was ever deemed innocent in those days. He was an ingenue, your friend. An idealist. I heard about him once again after he'd been released from jail. His faith in the Party seemed unbroken. In spite of all the obviously unjust punishment it had inflicted upon him."

"'The Party is always right,' we'd say, though ironically, of course. At least most of us. But not Kuhlmann or Janka. Both of them had been expelled from the SED, and both, after their release, eagerly tried to rejoin it. So they were finally readmitted. Unfortunately, your friend couldn't leave well enough alone and again got into trouble. I don't know the details. But they finally caught him at the Iron Curtain trying to escape and sentenced him again. This time for twelve years at Bautzen. I haven't heard of him since."

During the weeks following that meeting, as I sadly reminisced about Carl, Klaus, and our Woyzeck Circle, something happened to turn my passive disillusionment with life into utter anguish and rage. Though a bachelor by conviction, I finally married—a woman much younger than myself. Three years later we were blessed with a child, a little boy, whom we named Klaus, in memory of my deceased friend. The christening proved a bad omen, for at barely three years of age, little Klaus died. I can't possibly describe it, save that it happened in the middle of nowhere, some fifty miles from the nearest hospital while I was desperately trying to fix a flat. We were on our way to some conference I'd decided to turn into a family outing. Glimpses of the long-drawn-out agony of Klaus's death flash through my brain while I am writing this; and once again, now as then, I hear a voice as if coming from some long distant past, a voice I'd made every effort to forget, a voice that seemed to have cast its evil spell on my life ever since that fatal Christmas visit in Kattowitz; the voice of Arthur Schopenhauer saying:

"Have you ever seen a child with the croup, its little chest choking for breath, staring at you with uncomprehending and terrified eyes, until it dies under horrid convulsions? There you have them, the ultimate joys of sex!"

From that moment I started damning life just like Woyzeck, uttering curses, not loud, but deep. And I went back to work on his papers, unperturbed now by what people might say, or by any ideological concerns, worked on them with all the fury of my saddened, anguished, and angry heart.

HANS MARTENS' STORY
Woyzeck's Life Since 1807 Reconstructed

To start with, I set myself two separate tasks, one of which was to see if the remainder of the Woyzeck Papers, which I hadn't managed to transcribe during my abortive '39 Christmas visit with the von Bergks', had or hadn't perished in the war. In other words, what had happened to Klaus and his family? I wrote to the two *Innenministerien* of the bilateral German governments in Bonn and Pankow asking that question. Bonn wrote back that Klaus had been reported missing near Trondheim, Norway, but that nothing was known of the whereabouts of his wife and children. However, given the fact that his widow Gerda came from an old Salzwedel family, there was every likelihood that she and her children would have fled there in '45. Why didn't I write to the municipal authorities of that town? I did.

In the meantime, I set about my second major task: the reconstruction of Woyzeck's life since 1807, the end point of his autobiography as I had it in my papers. From skimming through the remaining Woyzeck documents in '39, I knew that, apart from some curiously damaged pages which seemed to represent fragments of a later version of Woyzeck's *Life*, the earlier one did indeed stop in mid-sentence exactly at the point where I'd ceased transcribing it.

At first, I decided to follow my imagination, taking my dead friend's novella as a model. I'd read that

Jung, in just looking at someone, often divined that person's whole life and then started talking about it to the latter's amazement. And surely there were poets who had even deeper intuitions than the psychologist. Who, if ever glanced at by a Shakespeare or Büchner, would not shudder to think how his life lay exposed to their eyes more clearly than he'd ever beheld it himself? Perhaps I too could muster such insight by immersing myself in the known facts of Woyzeck's life.

What, for instance, was easier to imagine than the reason for which he had broken off his autobiography so abruptly; picture Woyzeck in his cell on that "blustering rainy day" in the autumn of 1822 when he was told the date of the execution! Imagine him busy recalling Anklam and about to complete the last sentence. Then there's a knock on the door; in comes Staffmaster Richter flanked by two beadles.

"Would he, Johann Christian Woyzeck, please rise and stand to attention!"

"Would he also put down his pen please!" Then Richter mumbles something about having to bring him sad tidings. As images of his beheading are beginning to flash through his brain, Woyzeck already knows what he'll hear.

"In the name of our just King, Friedrich August I of Sachsen, the Criminal Court of this land, after careful deliberations, has confirmed his sentence of death and set the date for the execution. It will take place on the thirteenth of this coming month of November."

But was this really what happened on the said "blustering rainy day" which Klaus evokes in his novella? A little searching on my part showed that there probably never was such a day. Instead, it became apparent that Klaus, while adhering to *some* facts, mixed others with a good deal of fiction. Thus I found a piece entitled "Punishment Methods in Ancient Leipzig" published by a certain Dr. Weiß in 1909 in the *German Solicitors' Journal* which Klaus seems to have used for his account of Woyzeck's execution. Weiß never once mentions Woyzeck, but instead deals largely with Woyzeck's predecessor in crime, the notorious Philipp Jonas Göring.

A more questionable instance of Klaus's trying to delude the reader into accepting as fact what is really fiction is his account of Woyzeck's dissection. In it, Klaus quotes the official dissection report which a certain Herr Schmitz published in Langermann's *Magazin für psychische Heilkunde*. Some digging revealed that there never was such a journal. A *Magazin für die psychische Heilkunde* which had appeared much earlier, during 1805-6, contains no dissection reports whatsoever. Could it be that Schmitz's report was a fabrication? Or was it possible that Klaus, after using it, had wished to obscure its whereabouts? Just in case it did exist, I went through all relevant journals of and around 1824. My search proved fruitful, but hardly in the way I'd expected. The dissection report I found, though by Herrn Schmitz, is not about Woyzeck, but about two other murderers: one decapitated in Köln, the other in Koblenz. It's in the third 1825 issue of F. Nasse's *Zeitschrift für Anthropologie*.

What's more, Klaus by no means limited himself to such semi-authentic sources. Everything served him, even pure fiction, as long as poetic fantasy suited the facts. With a man of his voracious reading one can never be sure, of course, if what appears to be plagiarism might not be unconscious regurgitation. Where one suspects the author of having copied word for word, with someone else's book open in front of him, a fleeting memory of the same words might have guided his hand unawares. Who anyway, after spending most of his time reading books, can be sure of ever writing a truly original sentence? Even Shakespeare borrowed freely from others, though in most cases we shall never know whether he did so consciously, unconsciously, or perhaps both.

The chances of ever disentangling such niceties in

Klaus's novella, were compounded by further facts. Let me give one example. When back in 1939 I copied his story I didn't realize that his evocation of hell in the chapter entitled "Childhood Memories" might owe a debt, and, if so, a large one, to Joyce's *Portrait of the Artist*. Now, after a lifetime of rereading the great works of world literature this possible indebtedness could hardly escape me. So I checked and indeed found a German translation of Joyce's work which Klaus may have drawn upon. But who knows?

From such labyrinthine complexities, my old scholar's brain returned with a sigh of relief to the remaining authentic documents. Henceforth, I decided, I would deal with nothing but the facts, verifying every bit of information about Woyzeck's life, like his participation in the Stralsund campaign and his final return to Leipzig, in the available chronicles, histories, and general accounts of the time. My archeological dissections of Klaus's novella, prompted as they had been by my obsessive concern for the truth, had left me with a deep distrust for fiction.

Who anyway, I decided, does not, in reading most fiction, feel put upon, his imagination straightjacketed by the predictable fantasies of some inferior brain, a brain with its narrow obsessions, persuasions, or, worse, convictions? And if I *were* to invent Woyzeck's life during 1807-18 from the few "facts" that we have? Would I not do precisely that, i.e. impose myself on those readers—those alone worth writing for—whose imagination may be deeper than mine? More alluring to me was a different venture: to unearth the perhaps actual, perhaps merely putative circumstances of the said "facts", thus to hint at what might have been rather than to claim what was (but just as likely was not); in other words, to suggest stories which won't be told but which the reader might tell himself, non-stories befitting Woyzeck himself as he emerges, or rather fails to emerge, from the papers I'd transcribed in '39. Woyzeck the non-person, prototypical for our age, the first instance of the man without qualities—modern man, analysed, tested, diagnosed, labelled, processed, and sentenced—man whose sense of himself comes from the stories he tells, stories he claims are his own, but which in fact are mere echoes of stories which—picaresque, realist, or romantic—have been told over and over again, perhaps spontaneously at first, but then codified by the poets, and in the end regurgitated by millions of readers or even by those who don't read, but who nonetheless follow them after having absorbed them from others. And who would want me to tell another such story?

So I decided to stick to the facts as Dr. Clarus had gleaned them from Woyzeck's lips. Here's what the first report tells us about his life during 1807-18: captured outside Stralsund by the Swedes on April 7, 1807; deported to Stockholm; joins the Engelbrecht regiment; takes part in the Swedish campaign against Russia in Finland; suffers famine and spends ten days in a hospital with a disease he can't remember; has a prolonged bout of scabies and receives treatment; his regiment is transferred back to Stralsund where it's disarmed by the French; so as to escape them he enlists with the Mecklenburgh forces; stands with them outside Ratzeburg and Hamburg; deserts back to the Swedes because he feels homesick for his old comrades; his Engelbrecht regiment, with the handing over of Swedish Pomerania, joins the Prussians; in 1818, he receives a discharge at his own request (not as an invalid) and returns to Leipzig.

But how reliable are these "facts"? Anklam, where Woyzeck was captured, can hardly be said to be "outside" ("*vor*") Stralsund, as Clarus writes: it's a good thirty miles from that city. Yet what Woyzeck tells us about this event in his *Life* is borne out by all main accounts of the Stralsund campaign. Or how accurate is it to speak of a war begun by the Russian invasion of

Swedish Finland in terms of the "Swedes' campaigns 'gainst the Russians"? Is this what Woyzeck told Clarus? Or did Clarus misquote him?

More serious doubts about the veracity of the said facts arise when we compare Clarus's first and second reports. While broadly restating most of the same events, the latter adds some important new data while also differing on a major point. In 1821, Woyzeck argued that he deserted back to the Swedes because he wished to return to his comrades. Now, many months later, he gives a rather more powerful reason for this decision. Back in Stralsund, he'd had a relationship with an unmarried female who had borne him a child; now, while he serves with the Mecklenburghers, this Wienbergin is reported to him as sleeping with others. Along with such new information goes a whole new self-image. Wracked by jealousy as well as mocked by his comrades, Woyzeck, before he runs back to his woman, tries to take his own life. What prevents him is a fluke. Here's what he told Clarus.

They're outside Lübeck besieging the French. Woyzeck, probably in his field tent, has loaded his gun, attached a string to both his foot and the trigger, has turned the muzzle towards his head, and is about to blow out his brains. Why all this? From "an attack of despair," Clarus writes (*"in einem Anfall von Unmuth"*). But right at this crucial moment, his troops sound alarm: the French have made a sortie. Like the trained soldier robot he's become, Woyzeck obediently picks up his gun and joins the general fray.

Not content with volunteering such striking new data, the new Woyzeck has also begun to analyse his own case. Come to think of it, the first symptoms of his mental disturbances, he tells Clarus, stem from the same fit of jealousy and despair. As much as he tried, he could not control it. As his comrades stood jeering at him, he'd suddenly fall silent and do everything wrong even though he tried to maintain his hold on things. It was as if his thoughts had abandoned him, for sometimes up to half an hour. Later in Stettin such black-outs began to go hand in hand with a hatred of certain people. In fact, he'd become embittered with almost everyone and wanted to get away. He also linked these facts to some frightening dreams he'd had about Freemasons. One afternoon, he and a friend heard footsteps in front of their room, but found no one outside; it's a ghost, he concluded, for he'd dreamt of one a few days earlier. This unrest continued after his transfer to Schweidnitz and Graudenz. After a dream had revealed to him the secret sign used by Freemasons, he decided that they were haunting him. One evening in the graveyard, a huge figure wearing a blue frock-coat and small triangular hat bade him "Good Morning" in a gruff voice.

I have deliberately colloquialized Clarus's red-tape prose so as to suggest how, through its hypotactical convolutions, we hear Woyzeck's new voice—pleading, insisting, rambling on, volunteering its information, and trying to both come to terms with and understand his own words—and through Woyzeck's voice yet another, Dr. Bergk's, the pre-Freudian analyst: a voice urging Woyzeck to unearth his story, and to find, through it, what will explain him to both Bergk and himself.

Poor, maligned Dr. Clarus who can make neither heads nor tails of Woyzeck's loquacity. Obviously, he detests what he hears. But the more he's offended, the more impartial he'll be. Yes, he will be objective, will stick to the facts! Woyzeck knows that he might save his life by proving his madness. Hence he exaggerates, Clarus concludes, which is natural, especially for someone of his poor education. But Woyzeck never once, he adds, lied to him or tried to deceive him. But is this really so? Didn't he tell an untruth in declaring that he deserted so he could rejoin his friends? Or might he have lied in claiming that he did so because of the Wienbergin and their daughter? Perhaps he did, but it's more likely that he didn't.

Though for the wrong reasons, Clarus is no doubt right in refusing to interpret such contradictions as lies. For if there is lying, it comes not from Woyzeck, but from the two types of stories he tells us: the first, that of the picaresque hero—vulnerable but reckless, downtrodden but resilient, desperate but proud; the other that of psychoanalyzed modern man—man without a soul, but in frantic search for an identity which he hopes to find in the stories he borrows from others.

But I ought to return to the facts. There's only one date in what Woyzeck told Clarus about his life during 1807-18: April 7, 1807. Yet others can be reconstructed from history. These were date-ridden times counted in battles and pacts, times when most people were overwhelmed by events—until Napoleon, who shaped them, was buried by the avalanche he'd set in motion and could control no longer. Woyzeck, more than most, was the plaything of these events.

Even when Central Europe enjoyed relative peace after Tilsit, he was involved in a war, a war of attrition, retreat and defeat for his party, in which we can see him, famished, frozen, and sick, on the run from the victorious Russian invaders under the arctic circle, see him stumbling through snowdrifts and shrouded in the almost perpetual darkness of winter, or in summer imagine him wading through eerie swamps, even at night steeped in the violet light spread by the sun just slightly below the horizon. It was a savage war fought in the anonymity of a far-away Northern country, where towns and villages seemed like oases in vast expanses of uninhabited wasteland. According to one source, there was mutilating of the wounded, flogging innocent peasants to death, hanging them head down over a slow fire, or tying them to wild horses. Would Woyzeck and his Engelbrecht regiment during their legendary retreat "beneath the Pole" have witnessed, suffered, or committed such horrors? But I'm digressing again.

April 7, 1807: Woyzeck is taken prisoner "outside" Stralsund. His own account more or less sums up what precedes this event. On January 28, Bonaparte's regiments under Marshal Mortier cross the frozen Peene and entrench themselves before the town. But about a month later, Mortier receives orders from Bonaparte to move three of his French regiments further East. Napoleon's own testimony suggests what happened as a result. "Our provisional regiments, consisting of untrained recruits," he explains, "bring [Mortier] little help."

Taking advantage of Mortier's departure, some 5000 Swedes under General Essen make a sortie from Stralsund in early April, force the besiegers from their redoubts, and chase them all the way across the Peene. They also take several hundred prisoners, among them our hero. After being taken to Stockholm and there made to enlist with the Swedes, Woyzeck remains with them for just under five years until his recapture by the French on January 27, 1812, in Stralsund. He then joins the Mecklenburgh forces, and stays with them until early 1814, when he goes back to Stralsund. Here he remains until October, 1815, when Swedish Pomerania is handed over to Prussia. Hence he ends up with an army which, as we know from his *Life*, he'd tried to avoid like the plague. He remains with them for three years, first in Stettin, then in Schweidnitz and Graudenz, and finally goes back to Leipzig.

We also know that his Engelbrecht regiment left Stockholm for Finland soon after February 21, 1808. For that's when the Russians invaded that country. Czar Alexander I had chosen the opportune moment. After suffering defeat at Friedland, he had made peace with Napoleon at Tilsit. Meanwhile, Sweden, the longtime ruler of Finland, maintained its hostile attitude towards France and its Continental blockade against England.

Hence Alexander would have Bonaparte's tacit, if not active, support in taking Finland from the Swedes.

How history repeats itself! Remember 1939! Germany, after signing its non-aggression pact with Russia, invades Poland on September 1. Kattowitz falls on the fifth, and by the middle of the month, German troops are besieging Warsaw and Lemberg. Then on the seventeenth, the Russians, both frightened and animated by Hitler's *Blitzkrieg*, cross Poland's Eastern borders. Several days later Stalin concludes his Tilsit with the prospective new emperor of Central Europe; Molotov and von Rippentrop sign a treaty dividing Poland (in 1807, the main victim was Prussia), making a joint front against the rest of Europe. Then, on November 30, Stalin sends his troops across the Karelian Isthmus into Finland. Like Czar Alexander before him, he's protected by his brand new alliance with Europe's strongman.

Where did I stop? Woyzeck's departure for Finland after February 21, 1808. We also know that he would have returned to Stockholm not much later than September 17, 1809, the day when Sweden, after losing the war, signed the treaty of Fredrikshamn. Other than that we know nothing except that he suffered severe starvation, probably during one of the Swedes' slow rearguard battle retreats, early in 1808 and once again, after their summer counter-offensive, during the winter of 1808-9. They were chased north across Finland, around the Bothnian Bay, and finally deep down south into Sweden as far as Umeå, the soldiers, as one witness writes, often losing "their way in the midst of the frightful masses of ice and snow, confusedly heaped together by the storms of the winter. They appeared bewildered by the desolate appearance of everything around them, and were unable to find the stakes placed at distances, in the manner of landmarks, to direct the march of the troops, by the officers who had been sent beforehand to reconnoitre; and before long they had to depend upon the compass as their only sure guide. The sledges were continually stopped by wide chasms, either requiring to be crossed like rivers, or rendering so great a détour necessary, that there was the greatest danger of their being entirely lost in those trackless wastes. The horses stumbled and lamed themselves on the ice; the infantry was exhausted with the effort of walking."*

Tavastehus, Luleå, Oulu. Which of these places did Woyzeck pass through or fight at? To my ears, they came to sound like magic formulas: Kemi, Tornio, Haparanda. There is an old German saying: "See Naples and die." For me that turned into: "See Haparanda and die." Or Stralsund, Graudenz, Stettin, Schweidnitz, Breslau, Posen, Grabow—all the sites Woyzeck knew during his journeyman's travels and as a soldier. I finally decided to chase Woyzeck's shadow all over Europe. How hard I tried to get into Eastern Germany and Poland! I wrote to Warsaw and once again to Pankow pleading my pro-leftist, anti-fascist activities during World War Two. There was no reply from Warsaw, while Pankow told me point blank that the DDR *Staatssicherheit* was aware of an essay of mine entitled "Ideology leads to Genocide," which argued that Stalin's purges were the direct precedent to Hitler's holocaust. Of course, they refused me the entry visa.

But I finally did go to Western Germany and Scandinavia—visited Grabow where Woyzeck joined Napoleon's army; stopped at Lübeck, Ratzeburg, Hamburg; pored over city maps at the *Stadsmuseum* in Stockholm to locate the area around *Ladugårdsgärdet*

---

* Evidently, Hans Martens, in recreating Woyzeck's life from the known facts, availed himself of some of the same tricks he criticized in Klaus von Bergk. The eye-witness he quotes was neither Swedish nor Finnish, but Russian. See the *Narrative of the Conquest of Finland by the Russians in the Years 1808-9. From an Unpublished Work by a Russian Officer of Rank.* Edited by Gen. Monteith, K.L.S. F.R.S. Madras Engineers. London: Lionel Both, 1854, p. 197.

where Woyzeck was stationed. I even taught myself Swedish to be able to study accounts of the Swedish-Russian war like Gustaf Adolf Montgomery's *Historia öfver Kriget emellan Sverige och Ryssland, åren 1808-1809.* * I read this book while travelling north to the Arctic Circle from Helsinki, from time to time peering outside my railway compartment into the gloomy landscape, getting lost in a daze until once in a while one of those vast, torrential rivers spanned by our narrow spiderweb railway bridge would bring everything into sudden sharp focus. And everywhere, like a phantom army, I could see Woyzeck and his friends wading through swamps, fording rivers, and dragging along their wounded—all their starved, cold and anguished bodies that have long since decayed in the earth. I even stopped overnight at Nederkalix to see the mass graves from that war. Did I hope, as I stood there, that Woyzeck's dead comrades would rise to tell me about the man who'd sent me tracking through these faraway northern regions? Of course, nothing happened, though I did get soaked after forgetting my umbrella at the hotel in Helsinki.

Late in 1809, then, Woyzeck is back in Stockholm, and shortly after January 6, 1810 in Stralsund where he is to stay until January, 1812. Would he've been aware of the forces that shaped his life, making him one of millions of movable and disposable pawns in the arena of international politics as Bonaparte's rule neared its end? Would he have known what happened on said January 6, 1810? Humiliated by Napoleon's ally, Russia, Sweden had finally joined the Continental blockade against England. In return, it was allowed to reoccupy Swedish Pomerania. So Woyzeck's Engelbrecht regiment was shipped from Stockholm to Stralsund.

But the new alliance was short-lived. To enforce his blockade, Napoleon had pirate boats harass Swedish

---

* Swedish, *History of the War Between Sweden and Russia During 1808-1809.*

vessels, causing Sweden to send out its warships. At first they simply gave chase to the pirates, but then brought up one of them, the *"Mercure."* News of the incident quickly reached Napoleon in Paris and Marshal Davout soon thereafter reconquered Stralsund and levelled its fortifications. Two Swedish regiments were disarmed and the soldiers deported to France. To escape the same fate, Woyzeck, as we know, joined the Mecklenburgh troops, having to leave behind mistress, daughter and friends. For the first time he'd come close to realizing his dream: with the support of his officers, Wutzig (as he called himself there) was about to get married, perhaps even leave the army and settle down.

But Napoleon's politics sent him back to the wars. The emperor was about to embark on a gamble that would eventually cause his downfall. We don't know what exactly happened to Woyzeck during that time. Clarus's phrase that "after the war in Russia he deserted back to the Swedes" suggests his participation in that campaign. This is also borne out by the fact that most of Mecklenburgh's troops joined the *Grande Armée* on their march into Russia. Was Woyzeck, steeled by his war experiences in Finland, one of the few who survived that ordeal? Did he fight in the battle of Borodino or watch the burning of Moscow? Did he finally make his escape across the Berezina? As a soldier who had had to cross some of the great northern rivers, he may have fared like the following witness of that occasion.

To a distance of more than two hundred yards the bridge was ringed by a half-circle of dead or dying horses and several layers of prostrate men. You could not afford a single false step, because once you were down, the man behind stepped on your stomach . . . So however much you were pushed from behind, you had to choose your next stepping-place, as far as possible on the middle of the dying, so that the legs of men who were still moving did not break your own. We were pushed and pulled as in any crowd which is gripped by terror. . . . I had been struggling for two hours and was exhausted . . . if the struggle had lasted another quarter of an hour I should have collapsed. Despite the cold, sweat covered my face . . . I was now only two paces from the bridge. . . . I grasped one of the trestles. . . . The final obstacle was a frenzied horse on the ground . . . [Then] a violent shove shot me over the horse, which in an instant was covered by a dozen people trampling on its head and belly. As for me, I found myself propelled between the horse and the bridge. I was safe. The bridge came up to just above my waist. I mustered my remaining strength and managed to climb up.

A survivor of that campaign or simply one left behind while it happened? Whatever the case, Woyzeck certainly fought in the following skirmishes around Ratzeburg, Lübeck, and Hamburg. After all, he himself told Clarus that he stood outside these cities with the Mecklenburgh troops. But why not inside? The changing tides of war. Von Tettenborn's forces, that Woyzeck had joined in Hamburg, were once again chased from that town by Davout. They then shared in the long, drawn out effort of reconquering Northern Germany from the French and their allies. Until October 1813, that amounted to little more than a cat and mouse game. For most of that time, Woyzeck's Mecklenburghers camped north of the Ratzeburg-Gadebush road, now as part of von Vegesack's fourth Swedish division under the North Army head command of Sweden's new crown prince, Karl Johann, former count Bernadotte, one of Bonaparte's marshals.

Things only started to heat up after Napoleon's defeat in the great battle of Leipzig. Marshal Davout, so

Karl Johann decreed after leaving that battlefield, was to be locked up in Hamburg. He himself would lead part of the North Army to storm Lübeck which Davout, after vacating and burning the Ratzeburg stronghold, had left in the hands of his Danish allies. And with Karl Johann went our hero. Hence Woyzeck's wartime career ended roughly where it began. Yet at the same time how differently!

Then, Woyzeck entered Lübeck in the wake of Bernadotte's victorious French forces. Now he is part of an army led by the same Bernadotte but out to reconquer the city from Bonaparte's allies. Then, he went looting and raping inside Lübeck. Now he sits outside its walls, distraught by jealousy over his mistress's infidelity back in Stralsund, ready to blow his brains out, and no doubt unaware of what's happening around him. "Still wars and lechery! Nothing else holds fashion," as Thersites puts it.

But this time the storming of Lübeck is averted at the last minute. The day is December 5th. By 1:00 A.M. the besieging forces, some 30,000 strong, are filling the plain before Lübeck. Their right wing has moved within shooting range of its fortifications. During the night, a bridge has been thrown across the Wakenitz and a Swedish guards regiment, after crossing that river, is chasing the Danish militia men from their ramparts. Renewed negotiations towards peaceful surrender have broken down that same morning. Karl Johann's army, including our jealous, heartbroken Woyzeck, are making ready to storm the city.

Only a technicality holds them up now. The scaling ladders, ordered two days earlier, fail to arrive. Minutes and hours pass under growing suspense. Ten o'clock. Midday. One o'clock. Two o'clock. Even by three o'clock none of the expected ladders have come into sight, and night is approaching. Meanwhile, talks are resumed. And this time successfully. A surrender treaty is signed just shortly past four o'clock as darkness is about to descend upon Lübeck. At five, the besiegers are to be handed the keys for the *Möllner* Gate. By ten the defending troops are to vacate the city; their pursuit is not to be taken up before daybreak.

Shortly before midnight, crown prince Karl Johann marches into Lübeck at the head of his army, and its citizens greet as their triumphant liberator the same man who, seven years earlier, had his victorious Napoleonic soldiers loot their houses and rape their daughters. Church bells all over Lübeck are ringing; people's jubilations are said to have been "indescribable." "Thus the arm of justice strikes down what violence tried to erect," proclaims Karl Johann's twenty-second bulletin. Napoleon had always distrusted Bernadotte's penchant for self-righteous platitudes.

It's shortly afterwards that our hero must have deserted from his battalion and walked to Stralsund. Of course, he'd have known what he risked. Desertion in the midst of war could mean death or worse. What may have helped Woyzeck avoid this was the perplexing nature of his case. Unlike the hundreds of thousands who, during the Napoleonic wars, are known to have deserted in order to avoid death and mutilation, he did not run to elude the horrors of battle. As someone who'd just tried to blow out his brains, he was more likely to have searched out such destruction. Instead, the only battle he was concerned with raged in his heart, and like a man gone mad he did not care which way it went with death meted out either to himself or someone else.

There is a letter the Wienbergin wrote to Dr. Bergk about what happened when Woyzeck returned to Stralsund. For understandable reasons—her daughter's father had been gone for nearly two years—she was now living with someone else, someone called Eric. She describes Eric as "easy-going." What Eric's surprise must have been to suddenly see this hirsute, manic-eyed, filthy infantryman in his tattered uniform appear on their doorstep. What even greater surprise when, after a brief altercation, Eric found himself locked in an asphyxiating grip that bespoke both warlike skill and unusual strength. Once again, how amazed Eric must have been when he realized that this man, after nearly strangling him to death, left without saying another word, leaving behind a bag full of gifts for the Wienbergin and her daughter. But most perplexing to Eric was to find that he had to yield his place to the stranger. Especially after his mistress had protested that things were over between her and this Wutzig.

Even after he realized that the man was Marie's father, Eric had every reason to doubt that the Wienbergin had made the right decision. Every so often she would come running to him to pour her heart out about this terrible Wutzig. How he'd frighten her with his tales of rape, murder, and torture; or depress her with his constant harangues against God and the world; or worst, terrify her with threats of killing her, Marie and himself; or how he'd subject her to some strange sexual rituals he must have learnt in the war. How could the Wienbergin run back to this man again and again, Eric wondered.

But I am digressing again instead of sticking to the facts. Or more accurately, I may be telling stories from memory without being able to verify what I seem to remember. For there were several items in Klaus's metal box which I read through in '39 but didn't manage to transcribe. Particularly, there was a letter from the Wienbergin to Adam Bergk in which she dwells on the specifics of her relationship with Woyzeck, especially on his violence. Our pre-Freudian analyst Dr. Bergk, in his lost letter to her, must have been probing for the missing link in Woyzeck's life story towards that "intelligible, consistent, and unbroken case history" which would explain all of Woyzeck's troubles. Yet as much as I racked my brain, I couldn't remember.

But then something happened which not only solved that problem, but also put an end to my efforts of reconstructing Woyzeck's life.

HANS MARTENS' STORY
A Visit With Gerda

Upon my return to the States, there was a letter from Klaus's widow. A former school friend of hers, now working for the Salzwedel *Rat der Stadt*, had seen mine before it was passed on to the *Staatssicherheit* on the *Braunschweiger Straße*, no doubt to add to my growing dossier. This certain Klara, who remembered me as a friend of Klaus and Carl, had told Gerda about it and passed on my address.

After a short deliberation, I flew to Frankfurt hoping that the *Ständige Vertretung der DDR* in Bonn would allow me to do what the Pankow regime had so far denied me. I was right. Within three days of my arrival I sat facing Gerda in the cramped, malodorous living room of a dilapidated farm in Dahrendorf, a tiny village near Salzwedel about one kilometre inside the Iron Curtain. I'd been given a special day pass to enter this so-called *Sperrgebiet* or "off limits area." Gerda knew what I'd come for and almost instantly handed me the box with the Woyzeck Papers. Honouring a promise she'd made Klaus before he left for the Norwegian front, she had saved them from sure destruction by taking them with her when she, Dietrich, and Peter fled from Kattowitz in '45.

We were looking at an oval, gold-framed picture of Klaus as a *Wehrmachts* officer. He was smiling at us, looking so handsome, aristocratic and Aryan.

"Yes, that's his last photograph taken just before he left for Norway. I had two more letters from him, then a notice from the *Reichs Kriegs Ministerium* that reported him missing in action near Trondheim. To disappear in that way was rare at that stage of the war. So who knows? I tried to find out, of course, but in vain."

"But why did he end up in the *Wehrmacht* at all? One would think they'd have wished to keep him working for German science rather than have him killed at the front," I wondered. Gerda nodded, yet remained silent.

Crossing over into East Germany and spending the night in Salzwedel, had somehow put me in a time warp. Everything here—the houses, farms, cobble-stone roads, and old fashioned clothes—made me feel as if I were watching some pre-war German movie. This was the time for fertilizing the fields and the farmers used cow dung, its pungent smell penetrating into the room. Even Gerda looked to me as she'd stepped out of a family album, still so handsome with her wavy blond hair combed neatly close to her well-formed head, sitting erect and self-composed in her frayed old armchair.

"Klaus joined the *Wehrmacht* about four months after your departure. One day, the same Gestapo men had come back to our house, this time while Klaus was home. 'We'd like to have a private word with your husband,' they said to me. So Klaus took them into his study, the same one that you had worked in. When they returned, Klaus was ashen-faced. He'd been ordered to attend an interrogation at the SD headquarters the next day.

"*Gnädige Frau,*' said one of them, briefly turning to me at the door as they were leaving: 'you should teach your husband to choose his friends more carefully in the future. *Heil Hitler!*'"

Then Gerda fell silent again, looking through the window at the farmers working in the summery fields.

"By God, what happened?" I burst out, my heart missing a beat.

"They had caught one of your associates in Berlin," she went on. "Like yourself, the man had been gathering information for BBC London. His name was Peter."

"Yes, Peter Kindler."

"After being taken to the Prinz Albrecht Straße, he confessed, telling them that you had stayed with us over Christmas. He was shipped to the SD headquarters in Kattowitz for further interrogations in Klaus's presence. But perhaps you don't want to hear," Gerda said.

"No, I have to know," I replied, from then on listening to her words the way someone asleep is compelled to witness a nightmare.

"That evening," Gerda went on, "Klaus returned from the *Hauptquartier*, I remember as the most dreadful of my life. He seemed beside himself, merely mumbling and cursing, 'Those damned swine. Those filthy, dirty swine.' Again and again, 'Those swine. Those rotten swine.' Then he broke down sobbing, so loudly that Dietrich, our eldest, woke up and came running from the children's bedroom, asking 'What's wrong with *Vati*? Why's *Vati* crying?' Then he began crying himself, with that instant and deep perception children have of things horrendous. So Klaus took him in his arms, trying to quieten his sobs. 'Don't worry, my son,' he said to Dietrich, 'I'd rather die before they ever touch one hair on your head. I swear it.' 'Who's they?' Dietrich asked, once again turning to me. So I took him back to his bedroom saying, '*Vati's* just tired and needs a rest. We'll tell you tomorrow.'

"Later that night, after we'd gone to sleep, Klaus was still sobbing and cursing, sitting up in bed, sometimes covering his face, and repeating: 'Those damned, rotten bastards! Those filthy, devilish swine!' Finally I said to him: 'Stop Klaus, you can't go on like this. You have to tell me. Please, Klaus, tell me. At least try!' So he did, beginning: 'We're sitting facing each other, the man at the other end of a long table. They'd turned down the lights, so I could just see his contours, the Gestapo men asking him questions, to which he replied in what seemed to me like a broken, whimpering voice. But at a certain point, when they asked him about your visit with us, he started faltering, then asked me to forgive him. Right at that moment, they put the spotlight on him, and I noticed what they'd done to him. What I looked at was not a face any more. . . .' That's when Klaus again broke down sobbing, his whole body thrown into convulsions. In fact, that's all I ever got out of him about that.

"Two weeks later, Klaus signed up as a volunteer for the front. Given his previous career as a student duellist, there was no problem with that. Also, everyone knew that since he still refused to join the SS, there was little else he could do, or he'd soon run into trouble.

"For the last two weeks he was with us, life was happy once more, at least on the surface. He now constantly wore his new uniform, while going to work for his last days at *IG-Farben*, and even at night during dinner. It's amazing how well he kept up the charade, mainly for our two boys, of course. And how much they admired their daddy! *'Vati's* going to fight for German blood and soil,' said our eldest, who'd just entered *Kindergarten*. 'Yes, my son, and after we've won the war, I'll come back, and we'll all go to some new, distant land, and be happy there.'"

"How about your two sons," I asked Gerda after a moment of silence.

"One's alive," she answered, "our youngest, and doing well."

"What happened to Dietrich?"

"He's missing. Like his father."

"Missing?"

"Yes, during our flight from Silesia, just ahead of

the Russian army.

"We'd safely made it to Berlin, where we were supposed to spend the night at my aunt's. I still remember him standing there, about four metres from me, in the crowded subway, with his curly hair, the head of his teddy bear sticking out of his rucksack. He'd insisted on taking it with him instead of more important things like clothes. He was talking to some war nurses who had made funny signs at him—he'd always been very outgoing. So he'd pushed through the crowd to get closer to them. Then I suddenly realized that we had to get off, at *Bahnhof Friedrichstraße*. So I called him to come and got off with Peter. But before Dietrich managed to push his way through the crowd inside the subway, the automatic doors closed on him. I last saw him banging his fists against the glass screaming 'Let me out! Let me out!' as the cars started moving.

"Peter and I immediately got onto the next train to see if the nurses had gotten off with Dietrich at the next station, but they hadn't, so we returned to *Bahnhof Friedrichstraße* to see if they or anyone else would bring him back there. What else could I do? There was no one to turn to for help. Just the late rush hour stampede of people wanting to get home to their air-raid shelters before the next bombing attack. Then the sirens began howling and two SS men blocked the subway exit ordering everyone to stay where we were until the raid was over. It was one of the worst of the war, so perhaps Dietrich perished in it."

"And Peter?"

"He's with the ministry of foreign affairs in Pankow. He had a falling out with me when he was fifteen that lasted until five years ago. That's after he'd become politically active in the *Freie Deutsche Jugend*. He started haranguing me because of Klaus's involvement with *IG-Farben*. Who could blame him! That's what they are taught. And for good reason. He even changed his name. So as far as I know, the von Bergks are extinct now. More recently he's somewhat mellowed, and since I remarried he's even coming to see me again. About twice a year. He and Wilfried, my husband, get on splendidly. By the way, Wilfried should be home from work any minute."

A little later someone let himself in through the front door. When Wilfried failed to appear, Gerda went to the kitchen, where there was a rattling of cutlery, plates and cups. I could hear them whisper for a few minutes, with only Wilfried once raising his voice to an audible, "No, I won't. I warned you!" followed by Gerda's soothing, but incomprehensible whispers. Then to my surprise, both appeared in the living room.

The man who I'd feared would refuse to meet me, rushed forward to shake my hand. After barely exchanging the usual formalities, he said: "I'm sorry but I won't be able to talk to you as I'd like to. My wife and I talked about you a few weeks ago, when she was told about your letter, didn't we, Gerda? But there's a collective's meeting I have to go to. At a local inn. A semi-official affair."

And before I could mumble, "I understand," he added: "And I'm afraid I'll have to deprive you of Gerda's company. You won't mind, Gerda, will you? The wives of the other comrades will be there. I am sorry. But as they say, duty calls."

Not a word about Goethe, Schopenhauer or Woyzeck. Was he unaware of why I'd come here? At the same time, there was nothing defensive about him. Just a certain nervous intensity and perhaps absent-mindedness. Then I suddenly thought to myself, how would a plant manager from, say, Kansas City, react if his wife were interviewed by some foreign professor who was bringing out certain papers about a murder case of over hundred and sixty years ago, even if those papers once belonged to his wife's first husband or involved some former celebrities?

"Why don't you call on us if you happen to pass through here again," Wilfried continued. "Perhaps we'll find time to get together then. We'd certainly like to hear you tell us about your country, wouldn't we Gerda?" Then he once again shook my hand so firmly it threatened to crush my bones. But now he looked at me with a broad open smile from which all former nervousness had disappeared. Still, how incongruous they seemed, Wilfried and his Gerda—he, so drab-looking in his shabby clothes, but full of obvious pride in his role in society; she, elegant, aloof, and clearly older than he, and responding to every one of his "won't we" or "don't we, Gerda" with an attentive smile. Did anything in this man ever remind her of Klaus, I wondered.

Then I said *"Auf Wiedersehen"* and drove off to Salzwedel's *Hotel Union* to immerse myself in the papers I hadn't seen for almost fifty years. Gerda had given me the entire box with the request that I return it to Klara once I'd copied what I needed. The first piece that caught my eye after settling down in the *Bierstube* was a letter to Dr. Bergk in Leipzig from the Wienbergin in Stralsund, the only one of Woyzeck's mistresses who is known to have borne him a child. It was the piece I'd been wracking my brains about in the States.

"He wasn't a tall man," the Wienbergin wrote. *"But he was stocky and strong, particularly his hands, like a bear's, full of hair. And his eyes, so green, just like water, though scary. He seldom looked you straight in the eyes, and it made me flinch when he did. But he could be so kind, always telling me how much he loved us, me, and Marie, our daughter. He'd say: 'You're all that I have in the world.' At the same time he'd go on and on about how life otherwise was without justice or purpose. Until I'd say to him: 'Stop Johann. You're just making yourself feel miserable. And me, too.' I'd never thought life was that awful before I met him.*

But I'm sure he loved us. Loved us so much I some-

times felt sorry for him. Then when the French captured Stralsund, he had to go with the Mecklenburgh troops. So after a few months I started living with Eric. I remember the day, just about two years later, when Johann suddenly turned up again on our doorstep. Poor Eric! He's such a peaceful man. Johann almost killed him: strangled him till he went blue in the face but finally let him go at the last moment. When he'd calmed down a bit I told him that things were over between us. What did he expect? He'd been gone for a long time, and for all I knew he might have been dead. He listened silently, staring at me, then took a bag he'd dropped at the door, put it in front of me, turned round and left, still without saying a word. The bag was full of presents.

So I finally took him back in, mainly for Marie's sake. But things never went back to normal. Johann had never been easy-going like Eric. He was always brooding on something, trying 'to make sense of things,' as he put it, or cursing life. But now he'd often sit silent, just staring at something, until I'd shake him, screaming: 'What's happening Johann? Wake up!' But he wasn't asleep at all. He would just turn on me quietly, as if nothing had happened, and stare at me, when I suddenly realized I didn't know that face. He was like someone I'd met in a dream, not in real life. And I got scared.

And then his rages. Johann always had been jealous, but not like this. And I was faithful to him, at least at first, though I still kept seeing Eric, as a friend. But Johann did not trust me, and would start cursing me for no reason. Just as he'd curse everyone else: officers, captains, and comrades. Or the world, Christ, and God. And more than once when he beat me, he threatened to kill us all: first me, then Marie, and himself.

And I realized that he meant it. Shortly afterwards he was caught stealing something and locked up for six months, so we were safe. By my God, he was a chastened man when he got out, and so confused. It's the Freemasons, he'd say. They were hounding him and wanted to kill him. But he vowed to me he'd never again beat or threaten me and Marie, or curse life and God. As he told me that, he was crying and shaking all over.

I am glad to hear that you saved him from execution. I think he's a good man at heart, just so sad and confused.

So we took him back in with us, me and Marie, and for a few months we were quite happy, though because of the theft Johann's officers would not let him marry me, and he was angry at that. So he asked for his discharge, but was turned down again, because of the theft and because he had deserted from his battalion in the middle of war and gone back to Stralsund. Then in June of 1815 he was transferred. I still remember the day. There was lots of rejoicing in town. For Stralsund would be German again. But poor Johann looked like death. As part of the treaty, his Swedish battalion was to turn Prussian. 'That's the end,' he said. 'Those damn Prussians will never let me out. Not with my record. And if I desert again, they'll just kill me running the gauntlet.' Then he walked around like one distracted, aimlessly picking up things here and there, then putting them down again, looking miserable and crying, and once in a while hugging Marie, sometimes so hard I was afraid he might choke her. That's the last of him I remember. I never saw him or heard of him till you wrote me."

Thus writes the Wienbergin in her undated letter of 1824. Woyzeck, one day before his decapitation, decreed that most of the alms he'd gathered during his final days should be given to her, Marie, and Marie's teacher.

While reading the letter, I noticed two men at a table near the entrance of the *Bierstube*, who were watching me. Suspecting that they might be *Stasi* agents, I paid, left, and, after locking myself up in my room, started copying the rest of the Woyzeck Papers.

THE BERGK-SCHOPENHAUER
CORRESPONDENCE
Part Two

November 20, 1822

Dear Adam:

Thank you for sending me Woyzeck's *Life*. What's so unique about it is that most autobiographies make life appear in the distorting mirror of the author's mind. In his, life more or less tells its own story. It's like a chapter in the long history of the pathology of the human spirit, as where he talks about his delight in shooting the Swedes at Stralsund; whoever watches himself honestly will observe how much we delight in other men's suffering. But it obviously needs an uneducated person like him to admit to such facts. Of course, our Philistine German readers will have to make him a "case" by applying to him all their ill-conceived psychological jargon; they'll treat him as an "abnormal" person who has nothing to do with *their* lives. But in truth we are all of us Woyzecks at heart. If we assume a global catastrophe with just two survivors, I am sure, the stronger wouldn't hesitate for a second to kill the weaker, even if only to grease his boots with the dead man's fat. *Homo homini lupus**, although *sub specie aeternitatis*** the tor-

---

* Latin, "Man is like a wolf to his fellow man."
** Latin, "From the perspective of eternity."

mentor and the tormented are one. Who, after reading this *Life*, can doubt that Woyzeck is more the tormented than the tormentor? I am curious to know what Goethe will say about it; also let me know as soon as you can if this saga is to continue.

Yours
Arthur

[Undated]

Dear Arthur:

I hope you don't count me among the Philistine German readers! To print Woyzeck's *Life* in Nasse's journal will no doubt play into their hands. But what choice do I have? Even with all its most shocking passages rendered in my clumsy Latin, we'd never get past the censor in trying to publish it as a pamphlet or in my *Museum*— already when Baumgärtner and myself brought out its first series we were attacked for our emphasis on the obscene and abnormal*; and now that the journal has

---

* As the editors stated in the programmatic "Preface" to the first issue of the original *Museum des Wundervollen*, their journal was to record everything that arouses "admiration and amazement." "Man shall be presented in his dignity and baseness, in his greatness and impotence; nature in her . . . creativeness and urge towards destruction. . . . The maladies of the human mind, all kinds of derangement, e.g. madness, foolishness, raging mania, *idées fixes*, etc.; moreover the natural conditions of man, such as dreaming, sleeping and so forth; finally notable aberrations of his ideas, strange modes of thinking, admirable or ludicrous ways of behaviour . . . un-natural physical excesses, e.g. gluttony etc. . . . will be de-scribed, and nothing shall be ignored which can contribute to the dissemination and advancement of the science of psychology and anthropology." (Pp. VIII-X).

entered its second, Schopenhauerian phase, the storms of protest rage even more loudly. I can't wait to hear how they'll scream after reading the following "true" account of a "Marital Quarrel" (to appear in the next issue)* which just reached me from a correspondent in London. Might the story be true?

A few years ago, a husband and wife got drunk together and thereupon had a quarrel in the park of the Duke of Dorset at Knovies; abuse led to violence, and the husband beat up his wife so badly that when he emerged from his fury he found her lying motionless on the ground. In his despair he hung himself from the nearest branch with a rope which he carried around his body.

Soon the wife came to again and, seeing her husband hang from the tree, dragged herself to him as best she could and with all her remaining strength started pulling him by his legs, all the while telling him with a cooing voice: "Yes, my dear friend, your wish shall be fulfilled!" Yet she exerted herself so much that the rope broke in two and the hanged man fell to the ground.

After barely fifteen minutes, the husband's consciousness returned with his fury, and when the wife confessed what kind of service she was about to render him, he pounced upon her again, wound the rope round her neck, and hung her on the tree in such a way that she soon gave up her spirit.

But to the main event. Due to my last minute intervention, Woyzeck's execution has been suspended and the trial reopened. Woyzeck is back in his cell at the *Grimmaische* prison; already the scaffold has disappeared

---

* Cf. *Neues Museum des Wundervollen*, ed. J.A. Bergk, I, 5, 1823, pp. 395-6.

from the *Marktplatz*. So the Woyzeck saga is to continue.

Shortly before this little triumph, I had a curious showdown with Woyzeck's shepherd, the Reverend Grobmann (I've mentioned him to you). To everyone's amazement, the condemned man refused to receive further visits from him. Thereupon Grobmann wrote to judge Deutrich, blamed me for Woyzeck's refusal to see him, called me his Mephistophelian mentor, and asked that I be barred further access to Woyzeck. "It's enough of an outrage to public morality," writes he, "that Dr. Bergk is allowed to corrupt young and old with his filthy *Museum* and his other heretical writings. Should he now be permitted to spoil a soul on the brink of eternal life or damnation?" The conflict remains unresolved, but given recent events the Court has so far ignored the request.

Now that there is hope for him, Woyzeck's attitude towards me has undergone drastic changes. Instead of talking with his usual tight-lipped defiance, he reveals himself with an eagerness which, to be frank, often makes me shrink with disgust. But, of course, that's exactly what I asked him to do, urging him to hide nothing that might strike him as shameful or revolting. I let him ramble on, amazed (and often aghast) at the seemingly unending flow of sordid and obscene anecdotes flowing from his lips. Just this last Monday I noticed, to my considerable dread, that the person talking to me (or rather to himself) was no longer the Woyzeck I knew but some other strange self that had taken possession of the same body: like someone who's stepped into this world from beyond the threshold of trance, dream, and nightmare. For that's how he talks now, as if he were deeply immersed in a waking dream which suspends all normal coherence, pays no heed to chronology, and eschews all familiar responses and feelings. Who is the true Woyzeck, this somnambulistic *Doppeltgänger* or the man who murdered the Woostin? Perhaps he will finally tell us himself, for which purpose

I'll ask him to rewrite his life, if possible, in the same somnambulant fashion. Sometimes I've qualms about what I am doing, so let me know soon if you approve of your Apostle's latest manoeuvres.

Your friend
Adam

[Undated]

Dear Adam:

Did I ever tell you about the two melancholics at Berlin's *Charité* I used to visit as a student? Both were aware of their plight, but nonetheless unable to extricate themselves from it. Even then I thought that to let them just ramble on, as you put it, might eventually reveal what the blackguard methods and straight-jacket jargon of the attendant doctors obscured. They called me their Buddhist: I still remember the poem one of them wrote me:

> *Dem Edlen, welcher hold erscheint*
> *Auch dem, der in der Zelle weint,*
> *Der leidende Menschenfreund.**

So I certainly don't disapprove of your present experiment with Woyzeck. No doubt we should all do just that, *viz.* tell our life story in associative or, what you call, somnambulistic fashion, because the motives for most of our acts are involuntary and therefore inaccessible to logical thought. For a man to claim "I am free to do what I wish" is as if water were to say "I can make big waves" (yes: when there's a storm on the high sea!), "I can plunge down a cliff" (indeed: when there is a

---

* German, "To the noble soul, who wishes us well, / To the man, who weeps in our cell / To the suffering friend of mankind."

waterfall), or "I can disappear into the air" (yes: at 100 degrees above zero). Not only is the Intellect the Will's servant, it serves a master whom it knows only by hearsay, a master who constantly hoodwinks, misleads, and deludes it. Hence we never quite trust our resolutions; always there remains some Hamlet-like doubt that we may not be in complete earnest about this decision or shall not have the firmness to carry it through. It requires the act to convince us of the genuineness of our resolution.

For the Intellect is forever barred from the Will's workshop; whatever glimpses it can catch of its operations have to be gathered by stealth and indirection. It will have to catch the Will's resolutions *in statu nascendi** or try to spy on them as on those of some devious, hostile stranger. Let's take someone who's put aside some long-cherished plan because he doubts its feasibility; when news arrives that this feasibility is a good as a fact; only now, in his joy, does he learn how committed he has been to his plan throughout, and at once he'll proceed to its execution. Or take someone else who finds that some mutually contracted obligation begins to show drawbacks; yet he still tries to assure himself that what he has done by entering this obligation is what he wanted to do and what he would do again; when the contact is unexpectedly broken by the other party; only then does he realize, in a sudden outburst of joy, how much he wished all along not to have entered that obligation.

I sometimes let my *Doppeltgänger* talk to me in a secret book entitled *To Myself*. It's my *Walpurgissack*, so to speak, which, like Goethe, I keep hidden from the world. For readers will have trouble enough digesting my published works. How could I unleash upon people who shrink in dismay at reading Rousseau and your *Museum* thoughts from the innermost hell of man's mind? The conflagration would be too sudden and consume

---

* Latin, "In the process of being born."

everything before it; the changes my actual writings will work upon mankind over time are enough. As their result, the next century will accept as mere facts about human nature what most of us now would not even dare entertain in thought. For there is no doubt in my mind that a true humanity must be founded upon precisely such knowledge.

Yours
Arthur,

Leipzig, January 13, 1823

Dear Arthur:

How I'd like to test on Woyzeck what you write about the hidden motives for our actions! But the chances for that have suddenly turned very slim. Clarus has been appointed to conduct the re-examination, a venture whose outcome is easy enough to predict.

I have already sat in on one of his new sessions. While feigning interest in the latter's ghosts, Clarus tries everything to explain them away. Meanwhile, Woyzeck has started to talk in ways that dispel all doubts about his veracity: slowly, seriously, weighing each word, correcting himself, and even apologizing for his mistakes. Thus he first told us that the voices around him were screaming, but, after searching his memory, he added "and yet they seemed low, as if they came from a distance." Hence one has little cause for assuming that he exaggerates or invents. On the contrary, he acts as if in telling us what he does, he's fulfilling some mission; as if his private visions and dreams are merely part of a larger body of wisdom; or as if the most seemingly insignificant detail might, like the hieroglyph of a magical script, harbour the deepest mystical meaning. For connections there are in whatever he tells us, although I am far from believing that I've found, or perhaps ever will find, the Ariadne's thread through the maze of his visitations. Often it seems to me as if Woyzeck is, in his own way, searching for that thread himself. So far I have no idea why he sees parallels here or draws conclusions there, but the scepticism one is inclined to feel towards such primitive exegeses once again is dispelled by his manner of communication. It's as if he were talking in some ventriloquist voice which, carefully weighing and testing each word, was trying to render in language what is communicated to him in mere images, signs, and symbols. Dr. Clarus assures me that he'll devote another full session to what he calls Woyzeck's "delusions." That will be on the 29th. I'll write you again after that.

Your devoted friend
Adam

January 30, 1823

Dear Adam:

Your saying that Woyzeck speaks in a ventriloquist voice probably is not a mere metaphor. Did you know that the *Septuaginta* calls its prophets, and even the witch of Endor, ventriloquists throughout. Saul does not see or speak to Samuel directly, but through the witch who describes to him what Samuel looks like. She is a *clairvoyante*, which means a person who sees and hears, not with her eyes and ears, but with her dream organ or *cerebrum abdominale*; the same applies to all visions, whether spectral, somnambulist or oneiric. I remember reading in Kieser's *Archiv* of several sleepwalkers who perceived through their epigastrium rather than through their senses—and not just their visions but also the real world. Karlsruhe's Auguste Müller, for instance, could hear even when people blocked her ears. It seems that Woyzeck's visions are primarily aural, so you might ask him how exactly he hears them; also try to find out how his dreams relate to his spectral visions.

In spite of the work now done in this field, subjects like Woyzeck are still hard to find, and we are badly in need of a new *Oneirocriticon** or *Interpretation of Dreams* which takes account of Mesmerist research. Schubert's *Symbolik des Traumes*** unfortunately has nothing to commend it but its title, for Schubert ignores the diverse demonic, alienating, yes, clownish transmogrifications and displacements through which the original dream finds its way into conscious awareness. We cannot simply draw up a dictionary of dreams, for, although the original visions may be common to all men, it depends on the dreamer's character, education, and background as to what allegorical trappings these visions will assume. But the more dreams we know about, the closer we'll come to retracing these labyrinthine transformations. Of course I am speaking of those theorematic dreams only, to which very few of us ever gain access. Even Goethe's large family could boast of one member only, the poet's grandfather, *Schultheiß* Textor, who had repeated clairvoyant dreams.*** So you are lucky to have found such a rare and communicative subject in Woyzeck.

In spite of the Marquet affair I am having a wonderful time here. With spring approaching, Italy once again proves its superiority over our country. Here, all things bestowed by nature—the sky, the earth, plants,

---

* Schopenhauer is no doubt alluding to Artemidorus's work of that title of which he had a copy in his library.

** *The Symbolism of Dreams* by Gotthilf Heinrich von Schubert, first published in 1814.

*** Schopenhauer's own note here refers to Goethe's *Dichtung und Wahrheit*, "Book I, towards the end."

trees, beasts, human faces—are as they should be; in Germany they are no better or worse than dire necessity lets them be. A cheerful and comfortable *logement*, much contact with strangers, mostly English, my habitual services to the muses—all of these make my life as pleasant as ever. I am at my most sociable in a long time, frequent the rich and at times even high-born, and hence am so much increasing my knowledge of people and life that I consider the time here very fruitfully spent. Seeing and experiencing is as necessary as reading and studying. Especially, I am learning about people of rank, how pathetic their lives are and how plagued by ennui, despite their desperate attempts to elude it.

Yours
Arthur

Leipzig, February 12, 1823

Dear Arthur:

I asked Woyzeck about how he heard his voices, and, without hesitation, he answered: "With my right ear, always."

"Are you deaf on the left?" Clarus wanted to know.

"No, not at all," Woyzeck replied.

"What, then, do you mean by 'with the right ear'"? Clarus insisted.

Clearly this fact didn't fit with how he'd like to explain Woyzeck's aural visions. Most of these, such as footsteps and tappings, Clarus explained to me after the earlier session, come from circulatory disorders. Given his penchant for the fantastic, Woyzeck mistakes subjective feelings for objective facts, so that the throbbing of blood in his head veins, for instance, becomes a ghost's footsteps in the attic.

"Yet there's a big step from hearing mere sounds to hearing whole phrases," I ventured to interject.

"Don't you remember him telling us how he'd talk, and even gesticulate to himself? In other words, he's quite used to hearing himself articulate his own thoughts. *Mutatis mutandis* he will sometimes hear words and phrases when he's merely conceiving a thought, and then falsely conclude that what he heard was a voice from outside."

I feigned agreement so I might see how far Clarus would take this strange logic.

"When feeling suicidal," he continued, "a voice tells him: 'Throw yourself into the water!' when homicidal, another voice shouts: 'Stab the Frau Woostin to death!' while his conscience retorts: 'No, you won't!' yet his evil thoughts triumph, whispering: 'You'll do it anyway!' He often heard two voices, Woyzeck once told me, one leading him into temptation, the other warning him against evil."

But why hear these voices on the right only? The question threatened to undermine Clarus's explanation.

"You'd better not lie!" he burst out when Woyzeck stayed silent. "If you do, it's easy enough to find out"— which was precisely what Clarus proceeded to do, first testing his right ear, then his left. When he couldn't find what he wanted, he began asking him questions about diverse ailments which Woyzeck had mentioned in different contexts. Had he not told him that often his heart cramped up, shook, or stopped altogether, and that from his heart these spasms shot up to his head making him hear strange noises like hissing, buzzing, and pattering? Did he always hear these in both ears, Clarus wanted to know? Woyzeck, of course, had no clue as to what any of this was about and looked much relieved when, after a moment's reflection, he recalled something to satisfy

Clarus.

"Once in Stralsund," he said, "I felt as if someone hit me here in the neck (pointing to his right shoulder) and then hissed into my ear, my right ear that is. That's the Freemasons taking revenge on me, I thought to myself."

"Revenge for what?" I asked him.

"For cracking their secret," he answered. "But that's a long story."

"Tell us!" Clarus commanded.

When in his twenties, Woyzeck began, he'd heard a great deal about the Freemasons; for instance, how with no more than a tiny needle they could kill a man, even though he were hundreds of miles away. Then once, in a dream, three fiery faces glared at him from the sky, and he thought to himself: that's the trinity, with the largest face, that of Christ, in the middle. Upon waking he thought that the number three also contained the Freemasons' secret, and that raising three fingers must be their code.

"Could he make that sign for us!" Clarus demanded.

"But it's a secret. I've never yet shown anyone," Woyzeck replied.

"Don't worry," I said, quickly touching my forehead with my right hand's thumb, middle finger, and index. "He won't betray secrets with us. Or will he, Herr Hofrath?"

"No, he won't," replied Clarus. (We both belong to the Leipzig Lodge.)

Staring at us in amazement, Woyzeck joined thumb, middle finger and index of his right hand and, after touching the fingertips of Clarus's left, slowly raised them to his forehead, then said: "Once in Stralsund, I kept watch at the door while they cross-examined a comrade. As I stood there facing the commander, who was asking the questions, I said to myself: Let's see if he's one of them, and made the sign. Afterwards, the commander had someone pour me a glass of wine while he looked at me sharply saying, 'He'd better confess what he knows.' But I had nothing to say and got scared. Then, six days later, during drill, he said to the colonel: 'Let me know right away when the fellow starts spitting blood!' barely looking at me. But I am sure they were talking about me. That's their revenge, I thought, and after drill I ran away into the woods, but in vain. Three times my heart shook, just like some liquid tossed in a bottle; then I was struck in the neck and heard the hissing in my right ear. So I fell to my prayers thinking: No, not this time, they can't kill me yet."

Do large dreams differ from small ones by being clairvoyant? If so, then many of Woyzeck's belong to this rubric. In turn one might argue, I guess, that spectral events foreseen in dreams are authenticated by such clairvoyance. Once again, such dream prophecies abound with Woyzeck. For instance, just six days before the young woman's voice at the Haases' called Woyzeck to her, he'd dreamt of a ghost who told him: 'I'll send you another,' upon which he answered: 'That doesn't scare me.' Years earlier, in Stettin, he'd dreamt of a ghost dressed in a hood like a monk. Then, six days later, he and a friend, sitting at home, heard footsteps out on the hallway. How did this person get in, since they'd locked the front door? Then the footsteps went up to the attic but never came back. Not until evening did they find courage enough to go up and check. There was nothing.

What also makes Woyzeck's visions appear so authentic is the bizarre recurrence of crucial symbols, emblems and numbers. For instance, one evening in Graudenz, he saw three fiery bands in the sky, much like the heavenly faces he'd seen in his dream. Then the bands vanished, but when he turned round, another band loomed at the other end of the sky. At the same time he heard the subterranean ringing of bells.

"They've changed their sign, I thought," Woyzeck told us, and then asked an old woman if she'd seen the bands too. No, she hadn't, she said, but lots of people had heard the bells. 'That's from a place where a long time ago a castle was swallowed up by the earth.' "

Rather than making them up, Woyzeck seems to dread these symbolic relations, almost as if he feared being enmeshed in a web at the centre of which threatened some horrid, devouring spider. At the same time he's convinced that it's God who's trying to speak to him though these visitations. A most strange contradiction!

Yours as ever in friendship,
Adam

April 30, 1823

Dear Adam:

From what you tell me I am quite convinced of the genuineness of Woyzeck's visions. But why contradiction? If he should ever confront that God he thinks is revealing himself through them, that's what he'll encounter: your "horrid, devouring spider." Of course, we speak metaphorically, and so does the visionary who wrote the *Bhagavad Gita*. He describes God as a cosmic monster, "The Destroyer of Worlds," "eating this entire universe" with his "blazing death-like faces and awful teeth." Although our limited minds can only picture this ultimate Will allegorically, Nature herself has placed hundreds of miniature replicas of it all around us. Have you heard of those mighty oaks that grow on the banks of the river Missouri? Every so often one of them has its trunk and branches so tightly laced, entwined, and fettered by a gigantic wild vine that it'll die as if smothered. There you have it, your "horrid, devouring spider!" Or is there a more accurate image of cosmic strife than the Australian bulldog-ant? When cut in two, this creature's head starts to wage battle with its own tail, the head attacking the tail with its teeth, the tail defending itself by stinging the head.

Sorry for being late in answering your letter. These last months have been rather unsettling—you no doubt guess why—and I am finally forced to return to Germany. But my mail will be forwarded. If I should pass through Leipzig on my way to Berlin I'd like to hold colloquy with Woyzeck's double. Has he begun to rewrite his life?

Yours
Arthur

Leipzig, May 10, 1823

Dear Arthur:

What comfort can come from such knowledge? Should I tell Woyzeck God is a horrid, devouring spider? Perhaps you are right, but I can't even find the heart to reveal his fate to him, for that now seems sealed. Dr. Clarus has sent in his new report which, as I feared, confirms the first.

Just the day before our last session, Woyzeck dreamt a prophetic dream: lying as if dead at the bottom of a dark and precipitous pit he could see and hear people, who were trying to rescue him, gathered around the pit's rim. He was all eager to tell us about it, saying that no doubt it meant his rescue. I asked him how the dream ended. Poor Woyzeck! He woke up before he was rescued.

The other day, he asked me about God and what I thought God was like, and I said: "God's simply the force that creates and destroys us, the force that's everywhere."

"But where will He take us after death?" Woyzeck wanted to know.

"He will make us come back to life," I replied.

"That's all right for the rich, but not for the poor like me," he protested.

Continuing my Schopenhauerian catechism, I explained that no one comes back in the same individual shape, but that in the long run, over millions and billions of reincarnations, we would go through all the ups and downs of existence. The rich would reappear as the poor, the powerful as the downtrodden, the tormentor as the tormented.

"I can't believe that!" said Woyzeck. "Why all that pain? Only Satan could have made such a world."

What should I have said? I remembered you telling me once that if God has created this world you would hate to be God; looking at the world's misery would break your heart. But I remained silent, then changed the subject. For should I have said: you must negate life! To someone with one foot in the grave? And if I had said so, how could I have explained it? By negating what we know is irrepressible and everlasting? Might we not just as well say yes and affirm what can't be helped? Gratuitously yet heroically? Say yes, in spite of the meaninglessness and cruelty of existence. But again how could I, leading the pampered life of my class, dare preach such affirmation to one whose downtrodden, wretched existence is soon to end on the scaffold? I've sadly followed you to the end of your bitter logic. But at that end what comfort? Can man live and die in such knowledge?

Even at the risk of losing my Apostolic see, I remain as ever

Your friend
Adam

P.S. Yes, Woyzeck has started to rewrite his life, and I'll send you some excerpts anon.

June 1, 1823

To Adam Apostate:

Après moi le déluge!* I'm here to tell the world, not to save it. I know I have cracked life's riddle. Should I have sealed my lips, keeping the solution a secret? Also, I'm not the first to have glimpsed the ultimate horror of life; most Buddhists and Hindus share the same vision and, like me, teach that life must be negated. Though I'm by no means a saint myself, a small Buddha graces my desk wherever I go.

Yes, and I know all too well that there will be Apostate followers of my doctrine, who, driven by their despair, will claim to affirm what I deny and tell people that life should be lived like a Dionysian dance on the brink of destruction. But mankind beware of those who, seduced by such thought, will claim to celebrate the eternal struggle of life.

Entranced by the calm regard of the lion and eagle, these future prophets of doom will make Nature say: "Look at me! All you see proves to you that, what seems cruel to man because he feels hurt by me, is mere necessity; and that there can be no other law in this world where stars compel planets to circle around them, where planets force moons into their orbits, and where suns explode in huge cataclysms ceding their places to new

---

* French, "May the deluge come after me!"

ones."

They will say: "Nature above all ignores what we call human, ignores the law by which the weak should be preserved at all costs, even at the expense of the strong. Man only, in his perverseness, decadent man, who has ceased to see clearly, will pay homage to such a notion. For in Nature, weakness meets with no mercy, but simply spells its own doom."

Who will be able to disprove these future apostles of cruelty, when they argue: "Man did not create this world in which we are no more than so many infinitesimally small microbes. So who are we to deny, let alone abrogate Nature's laws? Though we might deny them, we will not escape the results, namely that we, the propagators of weakness, will have to yield our place to the strong and ruthless."

Who will stand up to these evangelists of violence, when they conclude: "Look at history: a people's weakness arouses no pity in Nature; instead she exterminates what isn't strong, and she shows her true wisdom in such merciless cruelty. Throughout the ages, weakness, to her, has been the true evil. She does not judge by the so-called law man sets himself, but by the law she sets herself, the law of force and strength. Whoever disowns that law or does not have strength is simply unfit for life in her eyes."

Thus will they speak, and few will have imagination enough to believe that they'll ever enact what they preach. And yet their deeds will match their words, or be worse. They won't wage wars so as to conquer and rule, but endless war will be their mode of life; nor will they torture and burn for some holy purpose, for murder will be their very mission.

And they will point to Nature and make her say: "What seems cruel to man, is mere wisdom to me, and I want you to be the celebrants of my wisdom."

And future generations will blame me, shouting:

"It's his fault because he raised the veil of the truth more than is good for mankind."

But I answer: "That guilt come upon those who proclaim a divinely ordered unfolding of history. For though their words will be blown to the wind, the presumptions they've implanted in man will persist; and people will follow these future metaphysicians of murder who tell them: 'We hold destiny in our hands, and we kill because destiny wills us to do so.' "

Yours
Arthur.*

---

* The immediate reason for which Schopenhauer broke off his correspondence with Dr. A. Bergk at this point was no doubt the poor state of his health during much of 1823-4. Even Friedrich Osann, a much closer friend than Bergk, for a long time did not hear from the philosopher for the same cause—"a concatenation of illnesses," as Schopenhauer explained to Osann on May 21, 1824, from Munich, "which kept me here for the whole winter: haemorrhoids complicated by fistulas, gout, and nervous disorders succeeded each other rapidly. I recovered about a month ago, but my nerves are still so weak that even now I am barely able to answer your letter, my hands shake so much; I still crawl around feebly and fall asleep during the day; what's more I am now totally deaf in my right ear."

Apropos his court case in the matter of Caroline Louise Marquet, Schopenhauer, in 1826, was finally sentenced to pay the plaintiff a lump sum of three hundred Thaler for medical costs and support as well as an annual rent of sixty Thaler, which he did for some twenty years until the end of the Marquet's life. When finally in receipt of his dependent's death certificate, Schopenhauer noted in his diary: *"Obit anus, abit onus."* ("The donkey has died, the load has been lifted.")

Leipzig, June 3, 1823

Dear Arthur:

I won't wait for your next to send you the enclosed: Goethe's long awaited response to Woyzeck's *Life*. After hearing him talk about his *Walpurgissack* vision of life I am somewhat surprised by its strong moral tone; but perhaps that is due to his recent illness.

"Much honoured, dear Dr. Bergk: your thoughtful letter and its unexpected enclosure were much appreciated. However, a long, weary illness prevented me from responding to both more promptly. The affinities between your Johann Christian Woyzeck and my Johann Christoph Sachse run deep indeed, and they may reach even deeper than my protégé's autobiography makes apparent. Just two years before his death did this then nearly sixty-year-old man force himself on and severely maltreat a female of this town, the widow Johanna Maria Querndt; hence, he was sentenced to six weeks in gaol. Sachse himself pleaded a mind perturbed by passion, a plea I reiterated in my letter to Grand Duke Karl August, adding that during his many years' service in his highness's library, a task he had on the whole performed with diligence and some use to the public, he had nonetheless caused his superiors and colleagues much aggravation by his broodingly threatening stubbornness, stiff-necked arrogance and self-righteousness. His final decline (for this one may indeed call it) was equally curious. He set out on his life's career as a vagabond travelling on foot, and he concluded it as a vagabond driving a horse-drawn cart which he had bought with the royalties from his Life. I, no doubt, murdered him by getting it published: he just didn't know where to turn with his little money.

"I am sure you will know how to use your pen before, if ever, proceeding to publish Woyzeck's Life. Truthful it certainly is, but truthfulness is by no means the only responsibility we authors and editors have towards our readers. To

dwell in detail on everything that is ugly, repugnant, undignified, and obscene will help no one, especially when it is forced upon us until we know no longer where to turn, with the Satanic brood of all that's depraved leering at us from every corner. Equally, nothing that is advantageous to the conduct of anyone's life, as far as I know, has ever been won from too much introspection, which, on the contrary, breeds but self-torment and self-destruction. As it is, we have too much of all this already: from all sides we are invaded by the subjective, the morbid, the pseudo-pious, and the insane; our modern novelists insist on foisting upon us their literature of despair; Romantic poets spin out the feverish dreams of their hospital poetry ("Lazarettpoesie"), as if they were all ill themselves and the whole world a home for the sick.

"I am happy to know that in our dear Hofrath Rochlitz we have a mutual friend who shares these concerns.

"With my warmest good wishes to you and to him I am your obedient"
    Johann Wolfgang von Goethe

Weimar, the 15th April of 1823

I am also enclosing the first few pages that Woyzeck has written since his reprieve. Contrary to what Goethe suggests, I have followed my previous practise of transcribing Woyzeck's words as faithfully as I can, just correcting the odd mistake and rendering sexual details in Latin; otherwise everything's been left in its original order. This could prove essential, for Woyzeck's progressively incoherent ramblings might, if ever we find their subterranean logic, reveal to us what's somehow blocked out in his former relations. He should "explain" why he murdered the Woostin, I told him, and you'll see how in trying to do that he's gradually shedding his picaresque bragging. Instead, he seems to follow some daydream in which his *idée fixe* of being made fun of links the most incongruous facts. Since then he's begun to meander even more wildly, to the point where all normal—logical, chronological, even associative—links are often submerged altogether. I'll soon send you more of these effusions hoping that your exegetical talents will help me uncode them. For the time being, here's Woyzeck's account of the actual murder—no doubt the fullest we've had from him so far:

"I'm supposed to explain why I killed her. I already did, your honour. She deserved it. She lied to me. And when I found out about it and about Böttcher, and told her, she just jeered at me.

"I thought she'd stop lying to me but she didn't. She lied to me on the day that I killed her. She'd promised to meet me at the Funkenburg, so I went there, while she pranced around with that Böttcher. Then I met her at night, just by chance, on my way to the Krug. 'You said you would meet me,' I said. She just laughed and asked me to come with her.

"But when we got to her door, she said: 'You have to go home now, Johann!' Just like that, as if talking to a child. 'I don't know what you want from me. Go home, will you! You need a good wash. Have a look at yourself. You look like a hoodlum. Just fancy the landlord seeing you here again with me.'

"I don't know if she screamed, but her mouth was wide open with her eyes glaring at me. I was screaming myself. I can still feel my face like a grimacing mask and the strength in my arms like some monster's, as I pushed her up the corridor wall by her throat, then noticed my right hand with the blade in it stuck in her belly, then a sound as of laughter, her face grinning at me. I stabbed her again and again, to make sure she'd be dead, really dead, so she wouldn't come back jeering at me.

"I'd known her since I was fifteen when I was Knobloch's apprentice. She was his stepdaughter, around twenty-years-old at that time, and already married for five years. But then there was nothing between us. That started

much later, after I'd left the army and come back to Leipzig. Her husband had died. At first she just listened to my wild stories, always laughing and buying me Schnapps. I never thought of sleeping with her, her being much older than I am. But once we got drunk together, so drunk I could hardly stand up straight pissing.

"Then this fellow called Schindler, a retired drum major, said to her: 'The old whoremother found herself a new boyfriend!' And then turning to me: 'Tell us, my friend. How much is she paying you for it?'

"I just stood there, while she was cursing him, with everyone laughing at us. I was too drunk to start shaking, but instead got dizzy so I had so sit down, with everything spinning around me. When I saw clearly again, Schindler had turned his back, with people still laughing about us.

"I could have killed him now, I was so angry, and ran after him screaming: 'Swine, you'll pay for that!' Just like that without thinking, for he was much taller than I am.

"Schindler turned around slowly, and stood there, legs wide apart, with his hands on his hips, saying: 'Let's see it. What will he do about it?'

"So I hit him with my right boot, mediis in testiculis suis,* (pardon the foul language, your honour), a trick that a Swede taught me. He doubled up howling, while I gave him a few on his head with my fists.

"Everyone was on our side now, the Woostin screaming: 'Serves you right, Schweinehund, for insulting a lady!'

"She was ecstatic, thinking I'd done it for her, and dragged me to her place. I thought I'd be too drunk to do anything, but she got me going, by God. But next morning I just felt disgusted, waking up with a hangover and this snoring old woman beside me. But we kept at it somehow, me telling her stories, and she laughing a lot and buying me Schnapps before she'd take me to her place.

"I'm not a coward. I'm just afraid I might look scared. That's what makes me shake: that people might notice I do and

---

* Latin, "Right in the testicles."

make fun of me for it. I wasn't always like this and remember the first time it happened. I was with the Schindelin, after she told me we'd have to stop seeing each other—I've already written about that. We were supposed to get married, though we were living apart, she at Buschendorf's in Leipzig, I out in Barneck, at councillor Honig's.

"I still came in to see her from out there, almost every day, but all of a sudden she told me: 'We gotta stop seeing each other. I don't want to lose this place, and the landlord has told me he doesn't want you to come here no more.'

"That day though she still let me sleep with her. But when I got dressed she said to me: 'That's the last time, Johann, you can't come here again!'

"So next day I waylaid her in the hallway and grabbed her. She got angry, saying: 'Go away or I'll scream. Herr Engler has sworn he'll have you thrown out by his men if he ever sees you again.'

"I said: 'Why don't you come out to Barneck to join me—there's plenty of work there.' But looking into her eyes, I knew that she wouldn't. It was all lies anyway, what she told me.

"Then she said: 'You just have to face it: it's over between us. You have to go now.' That's when I started to shake, so bad that she noticed.

"'What's wrong with you Johann?' she said, looking at me. 'You're trembling all over.' So I just felt ashamed and walked off.

"Then I saw her again at the Fireball, dancing with someone, and started trembling again, walked away to calm down, then went back to the dance floor and gave her one in the face screaming: 'Listen, canaille, you are cheating on me!' then landed her a few more, so she ran to the town hall next day. But I had my revenge on her before they could get me. I just knocked on her door at Engler's that night. She never thought I'd dare come back there, and opened the door all naked with only her coat on.

"I grabbed her left tit and pulled her out in the hallway

shouting: 'Bitch, you must die!' and hit her with my big key.
She had a wound the size of a copper coin on her damn face.

   "Then I took off with my stepbrother. He knew nothing
about it. We walked all the way East to Berlin and Posen, then
back to Leipzig. That's the year when I joined the French after
Jena and Auerstedt."

[Undated]

Dear Arthur:

Woyzeck has burnt his papers and by doing so has left me
a confused and saddened man. He accomplished the
deed at about one o'clock in the morning, when most
people are deep in their dreams. It seems that he split the
manuscript into three even sheaves, shook each of them
to make them open up like fans, stacked them upright on
the cell floor using his Bible, inkwell, and chamber pot to
support this starlike structure, then set fire to its three
corners. The conflagration must have been voracious:
the Bible was half consumed by the flames before the
guards, at around two o'clock in the morning, retrieved
it from the wet ashes. Even then, in spite of what he'd
done, Woyzeck was treated with a strange awe. "The
mad poet has burnt his book," I heard one of the guards
say when I arrived.

   No doubt Woyzeck did what he did in revenge
for my hiding from him his true fate. The extent of his
anger about that can be measured by the carefulness with
which he went about this meticulously planned manoeuvre. In order to get back his papers he made me
believe that suddenly, thanks to a dream, he might be
able to decode his own writings by quickly rereading
them all in terms of the hidden meaning that I was after.

   I was suspicious at first: his deliberateness in

telling me so was in sharp contrast to the anguished, but hopeful confusion into which my experiment had plunged his mind over recent months. But in my inhuman eagerness to achieve what I hoped for, I finally fell into his trap, and took the entire manuscript of his recent writings to him early the following day. Then at two o'clock the next morning, I was called to his cell by Staffmaster Richter. All that was left of the manuscript were some twenty or so half illegible pages of which a transcript is enclosed with this letter. If nothing else, they show clearly how far Woyzeck had gone towards seeing the murderer in himself as an alien *Doppeltgänger*.

When I came in, Woyzeck was just about to be taken to another cell. Passing, he stared at me silently with wide open eyes that had no anger in them whatsoever. His revenge was complete. I was about to explain to him, but something in the same eyes, something so disillusioned, candid, and sad, made the words stick in my throat. What could I have said? Should I have argued: I had to lie to you because I thought that as long as you entertained hope you might yet reveal what could save your life in the end? Saying so, I would only have added an overt lie to the tacit one I was guilty of already. If anything, I should have said: I misused your soul for the sake of the advancement of mental science; I, Adam Bergk, who in his youthful idealism argued that any state interference with the mental health of a subject should be punished like theft and murder; I, Adam Bergk, who betrayed my deepest convictions for the sake of my vaulting ambition. But shame closed my mouth and it chokes my heart now as I sit here fingering the last, half-burnt pages of Woyzeck's manuscript with my treacherous hands.

Even given my hopes (no doubt vain) of perhaps being able to enter the innermost realms of man's mind, what right did I have to make that journey via the anguish of a condemned man? What could I say when pastor Grobmann, once again, started to argue precisely that point against me? Should I have pitted the "horrid, devouring spider" against his threats of eternal damnation? These at least leave the hope of salvation to the repentant sinner, whereas the cosmic spider leaves no hope at all. Hence, in my letter to judge Deutrich,* I simply expressed my compliance with Grobmann's request that the last few weeks of Woyzeck's life should be left, without further interference on my part, to the guidance of pastor Grobmann. But now I can see that in abandoning him to Grobmann's mind-destroying fire and brimstone oratory, this letter simply constitutes my last act of betrayal and treachery towards Woyzeck. Where do I turn in my heart's tribulation? Apostate that I am, do not abandon your long-term disciple to this misery by remaining silent.

> Yours as ever,
> Adam

Here the Bergk-Schopenhauer correspondence ends. The only other item, contained in a separate

---

* For unknown reasons, copies of the two letters by pastor Grobmann and Dr. Bergk to judge Deutrich somehow ended up among the Woyzeck Papers. The first of them, by the Reverend Grobmann, pastor of the *Thomas Kirche*, requests "in the name of the condemned man's eternal life" that Woyzeck be barred from receiving further visits from Dr. Bergk. The second, Dr. Bergk's reply, disagrees sharply with the pastor's line of argument, but offers to comply with his request as long as the *Königlich Sächsische Kriminalgericht* would maintain its previously granted permission that he be allowed to attend the dissection of Woyzeck's body.

"A letter like the present one," Grobmann writes, "does not afford the space to list all the dangers to the Christian community which result from the so-called research in animal magnetism and similar pseudo-disciplines which Dr. Bergk envelope, are the remains of Woyzeck's second *Life*. In transcribing them, I had to guess at the odd word or phrase made illegible or obliterated by Woyzeck's *auto-da-fé*.

"I hardly recognize him, with his face distorted into a horrid grimace, his mouth open, screaming, and the woman, too, screaming with horror, as he's screaming with hatred, his hard scrawny fingers clutching her throat, and the right hand as if he were hiding it, pushed into her belly. Then his right hand pulls out the bleeding sword blade, and jabs it back into her belly and breasts, again and again, mechanically, like some machine, and he is still screaming, his face still distorted. But suddenly there is silence, as her body slumps to the ground,

---

propagates under the cloak of his diverse pseudonyms. We know who hides behind Hainichen and Julius Frey [Dr. Bergk published several of his books under these pseudonyms], and we also know that this man who is afraid to profess his devilish doctrines in plain daylight, is a supporter of Arthur Schopenhauer whose *Die Welt als Wille and Vorstellung* reveals him to be the true Anti-Christ of our age. It is bad enough that such men should benefit from the enlightened tolerance of our authorities; but God beware that we allow them to meddle with matters of judicial or spiritual import. Should Dr. Bergk be permitted to misuse a condemned man, so urgently in need of religious admonition, as a guinea pig for his questionable experiments? From previous visits to the delinquent's cell, I have had ample occasion to deplore Woyzeck's recalcitrant attitudes and perverted opinions. Once when asked to pray to God, for instance, Woyzeck protested that he had recently talked to God in a dream; when requested to desist from the sexual fantasies and memories which his jottings record with truly abominable minuteness, the answer was that such filth is needed to establish his mental state and possible innocence. *Paradoxa diaboli et magisterii Bergk!* More recently this pedagogue from hell has caused his disciple to stage a midnight burning of the Bible in his prison cell. Should Woyzeck's mentor be permitted to take his victim right past the gates of Hell?"

while he can hear footsteps outside on the sidewalk. Then, I see him run up the Sandgasse *towards the* Roßplatz *where he stops; he wants to be dead like the Woostin whom he's left lying in her blood in the hallway. Once again, his mouth opens wide as if to scream, but he doesn't. He's about to plunge the bloody swordblade into his chest, but then sees people running towards him shouting 'Stop him!' He throws the sword blade away and once again starts to run, but now there are people everywhere around him, and he begins to cry, his mouth distorted like that of the twelve-year-old who's been beaten by*

A careful reading of the second letter makes clear that the Reverend's injurious diatribe may not have been communicated to Dr. Bergk verbatim at the time. It takes issue with the reasons for Grobmann's request but does so in a tone of urbane, though ironical, reason and tact. Bergk points out that "the Reverend Grobmann is in error for believing that a person's spiritual welfare should under all circumstances be left to the guidance of his religious shepherd. What if the person is a lunatic *(Narr)*, or, worse, if he or she be a victim of *melancholia religiosa*? A visit to any *Irrenhaus* could teach pastor Grobmann how frequently mental disease is caused by ill-advised clergymen, who, like wolves hiding in shepherds' garbs, drive their sheep into despair and madness by their horror tales of eternal damnation. In view of such facts it has long been argued by the foremost authorities in the field that the religious instruction provided in madhouses should be subject to the scrutiny and approval of the institution's medical superintendent. I would personally go on to claim that all religious instruction, whether in schools or churches, should be permanently surveyed by a rotating committee of psychological experts regarding the possibly deleterious impact on the mental health of the public." Such general arguments lead Dr. Bergk to his final *captatio benevolentiae* exempting Grobmann from the need for such yet to be instituted supervision. "For years now we have had reason to admire this doughty *(wacker)* pastor for his stalwart, yet liberally enlightened attitudes. Hence even a madman like Woyzeck will no doubt benefit from his religious care, and I have no objection to entrusting the murderer's final spiritual destiny to his understanding and caring guidance."

his father. He seems like someone else, yet I still feel the fear and despair in his heart, as I once again see him in his mid-twenties, spitting and wiping his mouth, again and again spitting and wiping his mouth, after he's managed to get out from underneath the heavy weight of the other man's half-undressed body, spitting and wiping his mouth, making a face, I can't tell whether he's about to cry or to murder the man and that other who is staring at them with cold inhuman eyes. But then he simply walks away, crying, with his heart blown up like a balloon that will burst at the prick of a pin. And I can still feel my heart burst with despair as he is walking away after looking into the Schindelin's beautiful, cold, dispassionate eyes which tell him that it is over between them and that she is sleeping with someone else; walking away from the Wienbergin in Stralsund who is telling him: 'Don't take it so much to heart, Johann. Perhaps they'll let you out after all. We'll be waiting here, me and Marie. Who knows, they might even give us permission to get married. Man proposes and God disposes.' But he'd long stopped to really trust in God. The despair in his heart was too strong, almost as if he wanted it there.

"But then I can see him come back, he's somehow smaller now, his whole body bunched up with anger and the urge to inflict harm and to kill, kill those he loves most of all, kill himself, kill life itself. He's walking up to the Schindelin and her man on the dance floor, the man draws away silently as he approaches, but the Schindelin faces him, with her hard, dispassionate eyes, her face hardening with pride, as he screams: 'Canaille, you're cheating on me!' and then he hits her right in her beautiful face with the large key he holds in his hand, and he is screaming; screaming again as he is holding the girl in the toolshed by her throat with his scrawny hard hands, and keeping her arms pinned down to the floor with his sharp, pointed knees, when the girl suddenly screams with pain from what's done to her by the other man, then her body shaking up and down, passively, as if it were dead. She's whimpering for mercy, but he has no mercy. He pushes it deep down her mouth, holding her throat with his scrawny fingers, and keeping her

arms pinned down to the ground; he collapses on her, his half-undressed body covering her face; she moans: 'God help me!' But nobody helps her.

"He wants to murder them all. Even those who've done him no harm. Murder the Woostin, the Schindelin, the Wienbergin, even Eric, everyone who either gets in the way, or deserts him. What terror there is in Eric's face, as he sees the man stalking towards him, as if he were measuring every one of his steps. He grips Eric by the throat with inhuman strength, his face distorted and screaming, while the Wienbergin, hitting his head with her weak fists screams: 'Murderer, murderer. Let him go, you are killing him.' Yet, that's what he wants to do: kill them, even if they've done nothing to him, simply because of the bitterness in his heart. And once again I can see him scream, his face a mere mask of rage, and I can see little Marie's face, she was four then, and she is looking at him with her round, wide-open eyes, she flinches, starts to cry and runs to her mother screaming: 'He wants to kill us.' It was the first time she ever used that word 'kill' in my presence. So I stood there, suddenly filled with shame and grief, tears pouring down my face as they do now."

HANS MARTENS' STORY
A Visit to Leipzig

It took me the better part of the night as well as the next day to transcribe the above papers. During all that time I kept as much as I could to my hotel room, only occasionally sauntering forth into the downstairs restaurant for a quick meal, carefully avoiding the *Bierstube*. But my suspicions proved unfounded. Unmolested by either *Staatssicherheits* agents or *Vopos*, I finally managed to return the metal box with the original Woyzeck Papers to Gerda's friend, and to proceed on my journey towards Leipzig.

Before I'd set out from West Germany, I had prepared a detailed tourist itinerary which, on my way from Salzwedel to Leipzig, would take in as many historical sites as possible. Then something strange happened. As I was driving along stretches of original, Nazi-built *Autobahn*, cobble-stone country roads, serpentine tree-lined lanes, through narrow towngates, across market squares, past Romantic mountain-top castles, and villages nestled in sinuous valleys or on forest-clad hills, as I was driving along as I said, I gradually realized something I had not been fully aware of in talking to Gerda and Wilfried. Wherever I went, under the glaring late afternoon sun, I met with life, but had all my thoughts focussed on death.

Here I was overlooking some fields near Auerstedt peacefully being worked by farmers with their horses, tractors, and ploughs. But what I was really looking for were two phantom armies clashing under the roar of the cannons and, by the end of the day, leaving the ground littered with tens of thousands of dead, dying, and mutilated horses and men. Death everywhere, and the imagined screams of the tormented and tormentors. Jena, Auerstedt, Buchenwald. Even in Weimar, whose explosive Renaissance splendour radiates with the spiritual energy of former times, I found myself chasing the ghosts of the past, seeing Schopenhauer, Rochlitz and Dr. Bergk nervously waiting for Goethe to appear through the backdoor of his *salle de reception*.

> *Denn Alles was entsteht,*
> *Ist werth, daß es zu Grunde geht.* *

Standing in that same hall, surrounded by snapshot-taking East German tourists, I thought to myself: how many months, if not years, of my life would I give to be able to hear the old Goethe recite these lines of Mephistophelian wisdom so dear to both Schopenhauer and Adolf Hitler! Stared at by the other visitors who realized that I was from beyond the Iron Curtain, I felt as if I'd become part of that ghostly company.

And finally Leipzig, the city where Woyzeck was born, raised, sentenced and executed! Only for a few moments while checking in at the *Hotel Merkur*, with its international Holiday Inn-like atmosphere, was I jolted out of my deadly reveries. Once outside again, there were reminders everywhere to make me reach back into the various layers of Leipzig's past. Even near the town's inner core, there were huge vacant lots where once there'd been the smoking ruins left by allied bombardment; then the crudely painted, balconied apartment blocks cutting across these desolate spaces in seemingly haphazard fashion.

"Where is the *Marktplatz*?" I asked an old

---

* German, "For everything that has been born / Is worthy of being destroyed." Mephistopheles' words in *Faust* I, line 1339-40.

Leipziger.

"See that row of old houses. Follow that and it will take you right into it."

Seeing the town square for the first time in my life I seemed to be taken back to the time of Woyzeck. On one side only did a building made of steel, glass, and concrete thrust its modern matter-of-factness amidst the square's ornate baroque splendour which, as I heard later, had been restored with the money provided by the DDR's delayed economic miracle of the sixties. There they were: *Auerbachs Keller*, the high-gabled trade houses, and the colonnades, balconies, and the clocktower of the massive town hall—almost exactly as I knew it from the lithograph of Woyzeck's execution.

The archivists of the townhall museum were amused but not surprised to meet this American visitor looking for Woyzeck memorabilia. Many others, especially West German Büchner scholars, had been there before me. The archivists gladly took me around; showed me the old assembly hall hung with judges' portraits where Woyzeck, on that fine autumn day of October 1821, was sentenced to death, or there on the wall, the two-handed gleaming sword with which the executioner had cut off Woyzeck's head.

Could I see the Poor Sinner's Chamber, I wondered? That room, I was told, had fallen victim to pre-Second-World-War renovations. But would I like to inspect one of the dungeons several yards underneath where we stood, a male guard asked me? "That's where Woyzeck lingered during the trial," he told me, as we walked down. I knew he was the victim of a sensationalist error which I would not correct. We finally reached a windowless hole locked by a massive iron door, its Gothic horror only slightly diminished by a heating duct they had recently run through its interior.

Then one last big surprise: would I like to see a replica of Leipzig from the time of Woyzeck? It was found in a separate oval-shaped room and hermetically sealed under a huge wood-framed glass casing. There, down to the minutest detail of chimney stacks, fences, and balconies, were the streets, alleyways, townsquares, and backlanes, where Woyzeck, the Woostin, Bergk, Clarus, Heinroth, and more famous people like Napoleon, Czar Alexander, Schopenhauer and Goethe, had gone about their diverse endeavours and pleasures. Yes, there they were, even the buildings and sites which had disappeared long before World War Two. The old *St. Georgen* where Dr. Heinroth used to torture and shock the sinfully mad back into righteous normalcy in his Punishment Chamber; or the *Anatomie* where they dissected Woyzeck's head and body; *Burgstraße 135*, the ancestral home of the Bergk family; and the *Funkenburg*, notorious amusement park, where Woyzeck had hoped to get drunk one more time in the company of his unfaithful Woostin. Finally, even the *Sandgasse* where he stabbed her to death in her hallway on that fatal day of June 21, 1821.

How strange, I remarked, that this frail paste board replica should have survived while most of the actual city was laid low in the air raids.

It was hidden in one of the dungeons, the guard told me.

PRINCIPLE DRAMATIS PERSONAE

Adelungen, Wolf von: Prussian nobleman (*"Junker"*), army officer, and doctoral student of pagan folk customs surviving in Christian Saxony. Woyzeck reports this ruffian, sadist, and sexual adventurer to have been his employer for several years before 1806; no doubt identical with the "aristocratic Wittenberg student" mentioned by Dr. Clarus's first psychiatric report on Woyzeck. Wolf von Adelungen's associates include Ulrich, improviser of licentious verse, flagitious scoffer à la Thersites, and, like Wolf himself, an early reader of the Marquis de Sade; Helmuth, *Junker*, army officer, and homosexual who, during a drinking bout, rapes the protagonist while Wolf looks on; Leni, Woyzeck's mistress and a prostitute in the hire of Wolf for whom, along with Woyzeck himself, she serves in sexual experiments. Nothing is known about Wolf and his friends except for what Woyzeck's autobiography tells us about them.

Bergk, Johann Adam: born 1769 at Hainichen, died 1834 at Leipzig where he lived as a private scholar with his wife Wilhelmine Auguste Agricola who survived him; author, translator, editor and/or co-editor of some one hundred and fifty volumes including several books on Napoleon, a *Psychology of How to Prolong Life*, his anti-death penalty *Philosophy of Penal Law* as well as the twenty-odd tomes of his notorious journal entitled *Mu-*

seum of the Occult. In his endeavour to save the protagonist from execution, he gradually turned into Woyzeck's pre-Freudian analyst and made him write his own *Life*. This, plus the Bergk-Schopenhauer correspondence, constitute the original Woyzeck Papers rediscovered by Klaus von Bergk's grandfather in the attic of their ancestral home on Leipzig's *Burgstraße* 135 which has since fallen victim to allied bombardment. Adam Bergk, in retaining copies of his own letters, must have thought of bringing these papers out in a volume after first publishing Woyzeck's autobiography separately in F. Nasse's *Journal for Anthropology*. His last letter to Schopenhauer suggests why he desisted from both these plans in the end.

Bergk, Klaus von: born 1915 at Leipzig, missing in action near Trondheim, Norway, in 1940. A poet under the influence of Gottfried Benn (1886-1956), he wrote the novella, *Woyzeck's Head*, reprinted in this volume. Klaus's widow Gerda and her second husband Wilfried S. now live near Salzwedel in the former DDR.

Clarus, Johann Christian August: born 1774 near Coburg, died 1854 at Leipzig where he in turn became professor for anatomy and surgery, head of the *Jacobs Hospital* and town physician; main opponent of Dr. A. Bergk who tried to save Woyzeck from execution by having him declared insane. Dr. Clarus's two psychiatric reports found the delinquent sane and hence fully responsible for his crime; outside the documents in this volume, they are the main source of information about Woyzeck's life. The two reports are easily accessible to readers of German in Lehmann's edition of Büchner's works.

Schopenhauer, Arthur: born 1788 at Danzig, died 1860 at Frankfurt. His major work, *The World as Will and Idea*, appeared when the author was thirty; however, fame came to him late in life, and thanks mainly to the proselytizing by his so-called "Apostles" like Lindner and Frauenstedt. By abruptly breaking off his correspondence with Dr. A. Bergk, he no doubt gave vent to his frustrations over the fact that this first of his "Apostles" had turned apostate after realizing the full implications of his master's nihilism. Schopenhauer, in positing Will (i.e. matter, the life force, instinct, sexuality, the unconscious etc.) over mind, prefigured Darwin and Marx and exerted a powerful influence over later thinkers and ideologues such as Nietzsche, Freud, and Hitler. The latter is known to have carried a set of Schopenhauer's works in his backpack during all four years of his active service in World War One. Schopenhauer was an admirer of Goethe (1749-1832) who alone among his contemporaries recognized his young friend's genius. The affinity between their general outlook on life is revealed by Dr. Bergk's opening letter.

Martens, Hans (1918-1989): the narrator and former friend of Klaus von Bergk, found further corroboration for this affinity in Goethe's grossly indecent *Walpurgissack* poems which were discovered after the poet's death. As a result, he came to dread Goethe, along with Schopenhauer, as the main fountainhead of an unprecedented contempt for humanitarian values which ultimately engendered the anti-Christian gospel of violence preached by Adolf Hitler. As Hans Martens's somewhat reluctant literary executor, I might comment that my former colleague's distinctly humourless temperament completely missed the urbane irony of Goethe's poems which, after all, are meant to reflect the Satanic atmosphere of a witches' sabbath. Even after the interview with his department chairman which he speaks of—an event which happened before my time—Professor Martens was known as somewhat of an oddball amongst his colleagues, and for good reason: as the reader has seen, so much of his lifelong, fateful involvement with the Woyzeck Papers seems explicable strictly in terms of his over-serious addiction to certain ideologies, an addiction which, especially now, after the world-wide collapse of Communism, must seem ever more alien to North Americans. But then who in this volume, whether Dr. Bergk, Hofrath Clarus, Goethe, Schopenhauer, or even Woyzeck himself was not ruled by similar ideational obsessions? Hence the entire book reads much like a document from a far distant time and world.

Printed in Canada